WITCHES' CHILLERS

D0020058

The wind has risen,

and magick is afoot . . .

Bethany peeked out her bedroom window again. The pounding wind screamed, almost like a lamenting woman. Bethany shivered.

Element of air. Element of flow. Who killed Annabelle? Let me know. Bethany shoved open the window, stumbling backward as a gust of wind tore through her bedroom, rattling the bureau mirror, sending papers spinning in the air, pulling in dust and debris from outside.

She stood in front of the open window, the drapes billowing around her, the picture of little Annabelle clutched firmly in her hand. She could feel the power of magick boiling in her blood, urging her onward, pleading to be released into the universe. "It's time," it whispered. "Time."

Other Books by Silver RavenWolf

Nonfiction

To Ride a Silver Broomstick
To Stir a Magick Cauldron
To Light a Sacred Flame
Teen Witch: Wicca for the New Generation
Angels: Companions in Magick
American Magick: Charms, Spells, & Herbals
Halloween: Customs, Recipes, & Spells

Silver's Spells Series

Silver's Spells for Prosperity
Silver's Spells for Protection
Silver's Spells for Love

Fiction

Beneath a Mountain Moon
Murder at Witches' Bluff

Witches' Chillers Young Adult Fiction Series

Witches' Night Out
Witches' Key to Terror (May 2001)

Kits

Rune Oracle (with Nigel Jackson)
Teen Witch Kit

Visit Silver's website at
http://www.silverravenwolf.com

WITCHES' CHILLERS

Witches' Night of Fear

Silver RavenWolf

2001
Llewellyn Publications
St. Paul, MN 55164-0383, USA

Witches' Night of Fear ©2001 by Silver RavenWolf. All rights reserved. Printed in the United States of America. No part of this book may be used or reproduced in any manner whatsoever, including Internet use, without written permission from Llewellyn Publications, except in the case of brief quotations embodied in critical articles and reviews.

This book is a work of fiction. Names, characters, places and incidents are products of the author's imagination or are used fictitiously. Any resemblance to actual events or locales or persons, living or dead, is entirely coincidental.

First Edition
First Printing, 2001

Book design and layout by Rebecca Zins
Cover art by Patrick Faricy/Mason Illustration
Cover design by William Merlin Cannon

Library of Congress Cataloging-in-Publication Data
RavenWolf, Silver, 1956-
   Witches' Night of Fear / Silver RavenWolf—1st ed.
       p.   cm.
   "Witches' Chillers."
   Summary:

   ISBN 1-56718-718-8
   [1. Witchcraft—Fiction.   2. Mystery and detective stories.]
I. Title.
0000000
[Fic]—dc21

Llewellyn Worldwide does not participate in, endorse, or have any authority or responsibility concerning private business transactions between our authors and the public.

All mail addressed to the author is forwarded but the publisher cannot, unless specifically instructed by the author, give out an address or phone number.

Llewellyn Publications
A Division of Llewellyn Worldwide, Ltd.
P.O. Box 64383, Dept. 1-56718-718-8
St. Paul, MN 55164-0383
www.llewellyn.com

Printed in the United States of America

This book is dedicated
to Wilhelmina Keefer—

**Without her gentle instruction,
I would never have survived
my teenage years.**

Chapter 1

Jack of Hearts: Use magick

Leering skeletons, laughing pumpkins, and the loud music began to recede, all swimming together in the weirdest sensation. Bethany Salem blinked and shook her head, thinking that it was too hot in the huge family room of Vanessa Peters' home, or maybe she'd eaten something she shouldn't have. Food poisoning could make you hallucinate. Halloween music boomed from hidden speakers, and a bunch of kids were doing the limbo with a broom held by Wolfman and Little Bo Peep across the room. Her best friend, Tillie Alexander, plopped down beside her on the sofa, prattling about the great decorations, the fantastic catered food, and how much this party must have cost. Her gold costume shimmered and oozed in the dim lighting as she stuffed a worn deck of Tarot cards in a gold-beaded pouch.

Bethany's mouth grew dry and her tongue felt like it was cemented to the roof of her mouth. She breathed in little gasps, her heartbeat quickening. Tillie didn't seem to notice and turned to talk to someone else, waving the gold pouch expressively in the air as she chattered. Bethany's natural vision collapsed to a pinpoint, replaced totally by some sort of psychic vision. Her fingers clawed at the neck of her costume, the orange and black sequins catching briefly under her nails, but no one noticed. It was as if a part of her floated up in the air somewhere, her mind observing a new scene in some sort of weird time lapse. She was no longer at the poshest teen Halloween party in Cedar Crest. Where was she?

She couldn't feel her physical body anymore. The experience was like a bad horror movie, the kind where you yell at the girl on the screen to run. Except she couldn't scream. Her tongue would not obey, and there was nowhere to go. No more party. No more Tillie. She was in a surreal place where she floated freely in the air, and the man below her had a gun.

The man raised his arm. The scene stuck, like a videotape on pause. She saw the dirt around the edges of his mouth, as if he'd just consumed a chocolate bar, but the rest of his face was obscured. A shadow? No, a mask. One of those black masks that only cover the area around the eyes and the bridge of the nose. A garish red-and-white polka dot bandanna covered his hair. He reminded her of a fat, dirty pirate, except the fat was padding, she was sure of it.

Freeze frame.

The woman's shocking blue eyes opened in surprise, devoid of hope.

Paralyzed. The crack of the pistol—a hollow, elongated sound that thrummed through the air, as if the bullet passed within a millimeter of Bethany's ear as it bored straight for the woman's heart.

The yellow wall so bright behind the falling victim; her head snapped back, arms akimbo, then folded like a wilting white poppy with a splashing, crimson center.

Another woman, an older one with dark skin, materialized. The scene began to slip away, the edges growing fuzzy but not completely melting. The wizened figure cocked her head as the long, black tendrils of her hair glowed with white streaks, its ropy length in pieces as if she individually twirled the tresses in boredom moments before. She stared at Bethany with liquid black eyes that carried just a hint of ice blue speckling the iris. Bethany couldn't move. The killer pirate didn't move. And, obviously, the woman on the floor remained frozen in death.

The old woman pointed a gnarled, dark finger at her own forehead, leathery with age and crisscrossed by tiny, intricate wrinkles. Slowly, a third eye appeared beneath her wavering finger. The eye shown with an inner, blue light. "You can see," said the woman. She continued to point to the third eye. "You have the gift. You must use it wisely. This is the awakening. In time your skill will grow. Don't disappoint me."

Bethany's heart pumped an erratic momentum of blood through her veins.

"Hey, snap out of it!" yelled Tillie over the steady cadence of music.

Bethany jerked her head, focusing on the smiling face of her friend. She was back at the party, the murder scene gone. She sighed with relief, not realizing that she'd been holding her breath.

"Have you been sitting here the whole time I was gone?" asked Tillie.

Bethany opened and closed her mouth, then said, "You were gone?"

"For about fifteen minutes, girlfriend." Tillie plopped down beside her on the couch, throwing the gold-beaded bag on the coffee table. "Glad you saved my place. Right beside the food." She smacked glossy lips. "We're supposed to be having a good time, you know," Tillie reminded her, cocking her head and dipping her dark fingers into a bowl of buttery popcorn. "What's with you? You look like you've seen a ghost or something."

"Or something," muttered Bethany, throwing her friend a lopsided grin while trying to ignore the pounding in her temples. She took a jittery breath. Maybe she was just going plain old nuts. She examined her soda can, hoping no one slipped anything in there. Drugs were not her thing, and most of the people here were not her friends.

Tillie pushed the bowl of popcorn toward Bethany. "Want some?"

"Nah, I'm trying to watch my weight."

"Yeah, right," replied Tillie. "Like you're really fat."

Bethany narrowed her eyes. "We can't all eat like you and get away with it. Just think of my abstinence as fat prevention."

Sidney Bluefeather, computer nerd of the century and Native American activist at Cedar Crest High, wandered over and perched on the arm of the sofa. He looked as uncomfortable as Bethany felt. His eyes scanned the crowd but his expression said he was afraid to mingle. Tonight he was dressed in full native regalia, complete with a nasty looking knife that appeared more than real. He'd actually be half-decent looking if he didn't hunch his shoulders and did something better than a ponytail with his hair. He always wore baggy clothes, like he slept in them or something. His eyes were strange, like his gene pool was touched by a Mongolian khan. Too bizarre.

Bethany inclined her head slightly (no need to be a snob) but turned away to deter conversation. It wasn't anything personal, she just didn't feel sociable, which was stupid because that's what you were supposed to do at parties—mix and mingle. Coming here was probably a mistake. She scooted closer to Tillie to further seal the "don't talk to me" message. She wanted to tell Tillie about what just happened, but this wasn't the place to share her vision. Bethany tried to compose herself, running nervous fingers through her heavy, dark hair, then plucking at the black, silky sleeves of her witchy costume. The music was almost deafening and she was glad when, inexplicably, one of the speakers blew out, creating shouts, sparks, and squeals. Still, no one turned off the music.

Kids milled throughout the Halloween-decorated warren of Vanessa Peters' basement family room, spilling soda, laughing, dancing, and trying to scare each other or catch a quick kiss from a willing partner. Minus one speaker, the music played on. Sidney watched the crowd with wistful eyes. Bethany could relate. She wasn't the belle of the ball either. She'd have to remind Ramona that her glamoury spell was lousy. Maybe her housekeeper should brush up on that Hoodoo-bayou stuff of hers.

All the popular kids from Cedar Crest High were here, along with a few other, odd choices. She knew she was the latter. Sidney was another outcast and, of course, Gillian Merriday over there in the corner. All of them were outsiders, but for different reasons.

Sidney said, "I understand that, but—"

Bethany looked to the right. To the left. No one was around Sidney, but he kept talking quietly anyway. Weird. Bethany moved closer to Tillie. Definitely a glitch in the gene pool.

Tillie, it appeared, decked out in gold lamé and topped with a heavy turquoise and gold collar, was the life of the party. Of course, her friend was always the life of anything—outgoing, charismatic, charming. Besides, Tillie spent the last two hours reading her Tarot cards for all the kids, cementing her place as the center of attention, at least for this evening. "How did your Tarot readings go?" asked Bethany.

"Same old, same old. Some of them believe. Some think it's a joke. No biggie," said Tillie, flapping her hand in the air, the gold bands on her forearms gleaming in the low light.

"Anything interesting?" asked Bethany, shifting positions on the couch. She couldn't seem to get the vision out of her head. The murder. The old woman. Maybe she'd been so bored she daydreamed it all.

A loud burst of laughter mixed with the volume of music shrouded Tillie's reply. All Bethany heard was something about Gillian Merriday.

"What about Gillian?" asked Bethany, leaning closer. Gillian Merriday sat in front of her in chemistry class. A big-boned girl with thick, faded brown hair and snapping gray eyes, she walked around with a chip on her shoulder the size of the Titanic. She'd been suspended twice already this year, and it was only the end of October. Other than that, Bethany didn't know much about her, nor did she care to. Look at Gillian wrong and you might find yourself with a black eye, two if she meant business—off school property, of course. Tonight she was dressed like a very large, athletic Cat Woman. The plastic toy whip in her hand was a frightening thought.

Tillie's dark eyes narrowed. "One of those strange ones. She clammed up when I asked her about stuff at home. There were some really negative cards in there, but I wasn't sure what it was about, and there isn't much you can do when people won't open up.

She's kind of snotty, so she fits in with this crowd. Her cards indicate a great talent. I've heard that she paints amazing stuff, but I've never seen it. Hope she gets over whatever it is and puts all that negative energy into her artwork," she added, waving her bangled arm in the air. "You can only go so far in a reading. The cards are tools to the subconscious. Too many people think psychics are some sort of gods that know everything, which is stupid. If that were the case, I wouldn't even need to go to school."

"I wish I didn't have to go to school!" Bethany rolled her eyes. "I've got a calculus test next week that I'd like to avoid. You know, Gillian Merriday doesn't fit anywhere. She's absolutely violent. I was surprised to see her here. No wonder you got a bunch of rotten cards."

Tillie shrugged. "I haven't the vaguest idea how she got invited to this party, unless Vanessa wanted to be safe, rather than sorry. Gillian sure wasn't helpful, and she's in her usual sour mood. Besides, the way she kept flicking that dumb plastic whip sort of messed up my concentration."

"Don't worry about it. This wouldn't be the place to tell your deepest secrets," remarked Bethany, thinking of her strange vision a few moments ago.

Tillie dipped her head. The tight black cornrows of her hair laced with strands of gold made her look like she was a queen herself, apropos since she was dressed like Cleopatra. "Yeah. Right. I see your point." Tillie dug into the bowl of popcorn. "Come on," she said, licking her fingers, "what's up? You're normally not so reserved. Get with it. This is a party!" She stood up and swiveled her gold-clad hips, then flopped back down.

Bethany thought Sidney would tip off the end of the couch. If he could pick his tongue up off the floor she'd be surprised. Worse, he probably heard their conversation. Maybe not. It was pretty loud in here. She was glad she didn't say anything about the Witch thing. Besides, what was he to her? She suppressed a giggle at Tillie's natural exhibitionism, then shoved a torn Halloween spider decoration aside. This wasn't the time to talk about one's insecurities, or the fact that her imagination had just murdered a woman, or what might be lurking in the dark folds of Gillian Merriday's life, especially with Sidney hanging over their shoulders because he didn't have anywhere else to go. She'd save the stuff about the vision for Witches' Night Out next Thursday, when she, Tillie, and Nam got together to learn and work real magick, not that fake garbage Vanessa was trying to do over there in the corner—light as a feather, stiff as a board—geez, what kid stuff! She wanted to think about what the vision meant before she said anything to anyone.

Bethany switched subjects. "What was Vanessa talking to you about when we first got here?" She cast her eyes briefly in the direction of the Peters girl dressed in a Marie Antoinette costume that must have cost a fortune. The girl abandoned her levitation game, engaging herself in a major flirting session with some blonde-haired guy. "She seemed pretty interested in you awhile ago."

"What? You've been sitting here observing everybody?" Tillie shook her head and smiled. "You are your father's daughter, that's for sure! His detective mentality is rubbing off on you. Dangerous. You've got to learn not to be so intense!" She leaned back into the sofa. "There's an open spot on the winter cheer squad," explained Tillie. "Vanessa's the captain. She wanted to know if I'd like to fill the space."

Bethany raised her eyebrows. "What about tryouts?"

"There's only one spot. The coach doesn't want the hassle. I was a cheerleader in middle school, so it's sorta of a been-there-done-that kind of thing."

"Do you want the spot?"

Tillie downed another handful of popcorn. "Dunno. I don't want it to interfere with swim season. Since you've been watching everybody, where's Nam?"

Bethany's eyes swept the ill-lit basement, past the life sized-replicas of the Mummy and Edgar Allen Poe. "Over there," she said, not wanting to point at the petite girl dressed in the leprechaun costume. "By the steps near that Frankenstein poster. Talking to the new kid. I think his name is Michael Raines." Nam's pretty, dark head was bent close to Michael's, their hair almost intertwining. Bethany felt a silly surge of jealousy and then silently reprimanded herself. Why shouldn't Nam find someone she liked?

"Looks like an intense conversation," said Tillie.

"Yeah." *And here I sit,* thought Bethany, *definitely not anyone's major attraction,* discounting the hovering Sidney Bluefeather, of course.

Nam caught her eye and trailed over to the sofa, dragging Michael Raines behind her. He wasn't much taller than Nam, and was a bit on the thin side. Unlike the other guests, he wasn't in costume, as if to say that dressing up wasn't cool. He had those hooded eyes that reminded you of raw wildness. Bethany could see why her friend was so taken, in an odd sort of way, but he seemed too old for her. She'd heard he was a senior. Strange that he would be hanging with a sophomore. His blue jeans were so baggy you could stuff another whole person in there.

"This is Michael," said Nam, her green eyes shining. She brushed a stray, baby-fine black hair from her flushed cheek. Bells around her ankles jingled every time she moved her small feet clad in tiny green elf shoes. "We've been talking most of the evening. We have so much in common!"

Michael gave them a thin smile and shrugged, as if an introduction to the minions was a necessary evil. He squeezed Nam's shoulders, drawing her back slightly from the two girls. The bells whispered.

"He's from New York City," said Nam. "He moved here in late summer. He's living with his aunt." Jingle. Jingle.

"You some kind of Witch?" he asked, his expression bordering on a sneer, his eyes boring into

Bethany's. Not waiting for an answer, he leaned over and whispered something in Nam's ear. Her flush deepened.

"Don't be silly," said Nam hurriedly. "Bethany's not a real Witch."

Tillie's dark eyes widened and Nam jerked her head once, her lips compact.

Bethany opened her mouth to reply but the couple moved away, Nam's jingles swallowed by a rendition of "Monster Mash" blaring from the stereo.

"Correct me if I'm wrong," said Tillie. "But he seems like a turd." She rolled her eyes and flicked her wrist, the gold bands winking in the dim light.

"You know what they say, love is blind but the neighbors ain't."

"I always thought that meant you weren't supposed to kiss in public."

Bethany snorted. "It means that other people can usually see what's going on, even though you're hormones are thinking instead of your brain."

"Oh. Unusual for Nam to do all the chattering. She's not a regular magpie."

Gillian Merriday clomped toward them in black spiked boots, the plastic whip riding over her shoulder reminding Bethany of a shark fin. Her intense eyes focused on Sidney Bluefeather as she brushed past the girls. She positioned her back to Bethany, but her voice was so shrill, Bethany could hear her anyway. "What was that girl doing with Michael Raines?"

Bethany couldn't hear Sidney's answer. She wondered idly if Gillian had a thing for the new kid, too.

If so, she was outclassed. Nam was a sweet girl with a pixie figure and an insatiable desire for feminine clothing. Gillian was built like construction equipment, with a big mouth and a mighty wrecking ball for a fist, though to be truthful, she wasn't fat, just all muscle. If Michael was interested in Nam's type, Gillian wouldn't be in the running. You never knew, though. Ramona was always telling her that appearances could be deceiving. Bethany hoped that, for Nam's sake, Gillian's interest was only in passing.

Bethany kicked a stone and leaned against the hood of her car. The engine ticked slowly as it cooled in the frosty air. Her breath slid in misty plumes from her lips as she hugged herself, trying to ignore the nips of the occasional night breeze. Tomorrow was November first and the claws of winter definitely extended along the river, creeping into Cedar Crest.

Disappointed. She really wanted to go to that party. Couldn't believe it when Vanessa Peters invited the three of them. If you weren't invited to a party thrown by Vanessa, then you just needn't bother to exist. Tillie and Nam seemed to fit in okay, but she still felt out of place. For Bethany, the party turned out to be a major bummer. She and Vanessa hadn't been the best of friends since school started in September. Now Tillie was thinking of joining the winter cheer squad. She'd be around Vanessa all the time. And what about Nam? A budding romance and the denial of WitchCraft rolled into one night. It was obvious Nam didn't want Michael to know about their involvement in the Craft. How would all this affect Witches' Night Out? Or their training with Ramona?

Bethany turned, gazing out over the hood of her red Camaro, the sheen from the heavy wax coating glistening black under the vapor lights. She felt best when she was alone, just herself and the moon, but right now its fullness paled against the lights from the city streets and her heart ached. Yes, change was necessary and a good thing, but did everything have to happen at once? A slight chill raced down her spine. Ramona reminded her before she left that she had to light a candle for her mother when she got home. October 31 was the modern Witches' night to honor the dead, though she and Ramona would follow the ancient ceremony of Samhain when the moon reached fifteen degrees Scorpio, which wasn't until next week. She thought uncomfortably about the strange vision she had at the party. She could still see the victim's stricken expression, as if it were a real memory. Those wide, staring blue eyes . . . and what about the old woman? What was that? Bethany shivered. She'd been working on her meditation exercises, following Ramona's instructions. If this was the result, she wasn't so sure she wanted to continue. Yes, she'd experienced psychic feelings before, a knowing kind of thing. A calmness always came with that experience, but this was different. Definitely scary.

"Hey, Witch girl! You gonna stand there all night, or are you going to actually pump some gas into that fancy car of yours? I gotta git me some lovin' yet tonight. My wife is waiting for me. Get on your broom, girl!"

Startled, Bethany jerked back to reality, long enough to take in the burly guy hanging out of the window of his pickup, scowling at her. A real Ranger Rick, complete with a gun rack that wasn't empty. He edged his truck closer to the bumper of her car. *Impatient jerk,* she thought.

"That's some costume you got there!" he yelled. "Are you a good Witch or a bad Witch?"

Bethany ignored him. She pumped what she needed and headed for the convenience store door, her footsteps hollow on the cold, greasy macadam. She heard Ranger Rick grumbling behind her, something about teenagers and curfews. *How soon you forget,* she contemplated, *that you were once as I am.*

She reached to open the door of the convenience store and caught what she thought was her own reflection.

Until she looked closer.

And saw the transparent visage of the old woman with the third eye staring back at her.

Chapter 2

Three of Spades: Work to overcome challenges

As quickly as her mind registered the old woman, the image was gone. Bethany tapped the side of her head with her fingers, checking to make sure she was still in the real world. Yep. The store was empty of customers and the bright lights hurt her eyes. Bethany squinted as she walked the short aisles. Let's see . . . a bottle of soda, chips. Gotta have chips when you're bummed out. Chocolate. Absolutely! She almost dropped the soda bottle grabbing for the candy bar. The dark liquid sloshed and fizzed briefly. What pump number was that? Bethany turned, her arms laden with her proposed snack binge as she looked out the plate glass windows of the convenience store. Four. Pump four. That redneck Ranger Rick was still there, waiting impatiently behind her car. Why didn't he just go to another pump? Bethany pivoted and stepped up to the counter, her mouth open, ready to spout the pump number before she forgot it again.

She was there. Just like in her vision, but instead of watching the event occur, Bethany stared at the aftermath. Bethany stood motionless, her jaw

16

clenching and releasing methodically, the chip bag against her chest crinkling softly when she finally thought to exhale. She blinked slowly, as if to focus on reality and not the crazy dream in her head, but when Bethany readjusted her eyes the scene remained the same. The convenience store clerk was absolutely dead. No doubt about it.

The sunflower-yellow wall framed the inert woman, her head cocked oddly to the side like a lifeless marionette waiting for an invisible hand to bring reanimation. There was a large swipe of sienna on the wall where the woman's body slid after the impact of the bullet. She sat there—well, slumped there—as if merely stunned, her eyes wide open, her legs oddly bent on the wax-glossed linoleum floor. Definitely, definitely dead.

Outside, Ranger Rick beeped his horn. Bethany remained frozen. Her dad saw stuff like this all the time. *Think, Bethany, think!* Her arms slowly released their burden of snack food, but not in the way she'd planned. The stuff just sort of tumbled from her grip, the soda bottle flipping across the counter, turning in the air, bouncing off the body, then rolling in a lazy arc to bump softly against the wall. A tiny sigh escaped from the cap of the bottle. Bethany flexed stiff fingers, then slowly drew her fear-atrophied digits to her chest. Her fingers were cold, so very, very cold.

She glanced up and noticed that the security monitor was nothing but a jagged maw. Broken bits of glass littered the side counter and the floor by the body. The cash register was closed and undamaged. The phone on the back counter was ripped out of the wall, the cord coiling over the lip of the counter, the receiver dangling dead-still.

The bell over the front door tinkled, the merry notes dropping like ice picks in Bethany's brain. She looked up to see Ranger Rick barreling toward her, a scowl deepening the lines in his forehead. "What's taking you so—" His jaw dropped, eyes widening as his gaze flicked from Bethany to the woman behind the counter.

"The phone's dead. Call 911," said Bethany. It felt like her voice was coming out of a hollow drum in her chest.

"That ain't all that's dead," replied Ranger Rick, his eyes round.

"My dad's a cop. I'll secure the scene until help arrives. Do you have a cell phone?"

He shook his head.

"A CB?"

Ranger Rick stood there and licked his lips, eyes narrowing. He wore a battered jean jacket over a pair of black Levis. His scruffy cheek jerked with a spasmodic tic. Bethany caught a faint whiff of alcohol as he edged closer, then began backing away.

"I said, my father is a cop. Go call 911!"

His big head jerked, eyes fastened on the woman, but his chin pointed at Bethany.

"I left my cell phone on the front seat of my car," barked Bethany. "Use that!"

Ranger Rick stumbled over his own boots, bumped against the door, then turned and ran across the parking lot. Moments later his truck fishtailed onto Interstate 95.

The dead woman, naturally, had not moved.

Bethany hurried to the back of the store, looking for the office. The big metal door was closed. She knew not to touch anything. Scuttling her fingers inside the cuff of her coat sleeve, she tried the knob. Locked. She debated. Should she stay with the woman, or should she go out to her car and get her phone? She didn't want to touch anything in here. Her dad always talked about preserving the crime scene, how investigations got totally screwed because some idiot didn't follow procedure. She didn't want to be that idiot. Her soda bottle already hit the body, for heaven's sake!

Minutes passed. Bethany made her way back to the front of the store. No one came. No sirens. No black and gold Cedar Crest Regional police. Ranger Rick must have put the pedal to the metal and kept on going. Her choice to stay with the body seemed more than stupid.

A pair of headlights swept across the parking lot, followed by the slam of a car door. Bethany rushed out the front door as a slim, dark figure began walking across the macadam toward her. It was Sidney Bluefeather, still dressed in costume, but minus the knife. "Don't come in here," she yelled breathlessly. "Dead woman! She's been shot. Get my cell phone out of my car," she pointed at her Camaro. "Call

911!" Bethany was determined to protect the scene. She aimed her key chain at the Camaro and the vehicle came to life, its headlights slicing through the dim parking lot with an audible beep of the horn. "There. It's open. Hurry! Get the phone!"

Sidney's long, black hair gleamed under the sodium lights of the lot. His dark eyebrows shot up in surprise, then dropped in a heavy frown. He looked at the empty air beside Bethany, staring intently. He continued toward her. He stopped about five feet from her, lifted his chin and gazed at Bethany. "You have a choice," he said, moving closer to her. "If you stay . . . you will face death yourself."

Bethany snorted. "What the heck are you talking about? Did you hear me?" She grabbed the front of his coat and shook the lapels. "There is a dead woman in there! Dead! As in deceased. Not breathing anymore. I'll spell it for you: D-E-A-D. Dead!"

Sidney brushed her hands from his coat, turned and walked slowly to her car. He picked up the cell phone and punched in the numbers.

Bethany didn't budge.

Ramona bustled around the kitchen, her loose white clothing making a comforting swishing sound as she unloaded another stack of pancakes from the griddle, then ferried them back to the table with a beatific smile. "Ramona says it's time to eat. You can't live on nothing, ma cherie!" she said, shoveling a big stack of pancakes on Bethany's plate. The scent of her jasmine perfume filled the kitchen. Ramona definitely reminded Bethany of an exotic species unto itself.

Bethany, chin supported by her hands, elbows on the table, stared at the French-Creole housekeeper. When would that woman stop talking about herself as if she were split in two? It was a habit that drove Bethany crazy. She blinked slowly. Her eyeballs felt like twin, unmovable stones in her head. What little sleep she'd managed to catch cavorted with blood, gore, and an occasional ghoul that looked like Ranger Rick topped by the old woman with the third eye. "I'm not hungry," she said, barely moving her lips.

"Poor cherie," cajoled Ramona. "As if you haven't had enough trouble lately. Eat, and the whole world will seem brighter!"

"I doubt it. It's not every day you walk into a convenience store and find the clerk on the floor with a hole the size of a baseball in her chest."

"You exaggerate," said Ramona flatly. A large platter of bacon followed the pancakes. Bethany's stomach grumbled.

"About the dead clerk or the hole?" She felt something soft winding around her legs. "Hecate!" she said to the cat, reaching down to stroke his ebony fur. "Where have you been?" The cat gave her a superior gaze, as if his whereabouts were none of her business.

Ramona clucked her tongue. "It is a good thing your papa works for the big police, or the little ones would have kept you all night long," said Ramona as she flipped the eggs at the stove.

"I'm sure the Cedar Crest Regional would be impressed that you think they are the little police," remarked Bethany, "and I don't think they view the NYPD as the big police."

Hecate jumped up on the stool beside the stove, leaning far too close to the empty bacon pan, nose twitching. Bacon radar. Ramona waved the spatula in his face until he jumped down and stalked out of the kitchen, tail ramrod straight. "Besides, you've seen dead people before," said Ramona. "Ramona's seen them before. Your father, bless him, sees them all the time. No big deal." She flicked her wrist, twisting the spatula in the air.

Bethany grimaced. Weren't they all just so very lucky. Right. She rubbed her right eyebrow, contemplating the food, debating whether to tell Ramona what she'd left out of her statement to the local police. The housekeeper was fairly trustworthy, as far as secrets went, but she didn't want the woman blabbing to her dad, which she did on occasion if she felt it was in Bethany's best interests. If Carl Salem thought Bethany's studies with Ramona caused her any difficulty, like that precognitive episode at the Halloween party, he would insist that they cease. He was broad-minded, but only to a point, and this would be twice in two months that she'd been witness to a murder. Not exceptionally good odds for a sixteen-year-old who was living over one hundred miles away from New York City because her father felt the Big Apple would be a bad influence, let alone Philadelphia not that far to the ɔuth. She opened her mouth and filled it with a forkful of pancakes. She'd keep quiet. For now.

She finished her food in silence. What was that warning from Sidney Bluefeather for? She didn't get a chance to talk to him after the police got there. Did he know who killed the clerk? Why else would he have given her a warning?

"So much going on," Ramona was saying as she hustled around the kitchen. "Did you remember to light the candle for your mother?"

"With all the excitement, I forgot." Her mother passed away almost five years ago. She'd been an investigative reporter bouncing between Philadelphia and New York City. One commute she didn't make it home. Purveyors of the truth weren't well-liked by the criminal element. Bethany hated the criminal justice system. Because it existed, her mother was dead; and someday, her dad might not make it home either. Why did she keep getting involved in these situations?

Her curiosity, though, was more than aroused. She wondered if her interest was genetic. That made her shiver. Compared to most of the country, Cedar Crest had a history of low crime. A murdered convenience store clerk was absolutely unheard of. Bethany wondered if there was more to the woman's death than what this morning's Sunday newspaper spouted.

"The papers say that it was a robbery," stated Ramona.

Bethany looked at the housekeeper out the corner of her eyes. She hated it when Ramona read her thoughts. It was uncouth invading her privacy like that; however, she rose to the bait. "The cash register wasn't damaged. The door to the office was locked and not a scratch on it. There's a sign over the entrance that says there isn't more than a couple of bucks in the store. It just didn't feel like robbery."

Ramona snorted. "You! The expert?" Yet her eyes held that unusual twinkle. "Maybe they saw you coming in your Witch outfit and knew they'd better skedaddle! People have been known to run from Witches, you know."

"Yeah. And they've been known to burn them, too," replied Bethany sourly. The grandfather clock in the hallway struck nine.

Chapter 3

Two of Hearts reversed: Small present

Bethany hadn't counted on the newspaper reporters.

"Look at them out there," said Tillie, peeking through the break in the heavy, forest-green cotton drapes of Bethany's first-floor bedroom window. Tillie pressed her nose to the glass, her breath temporarily fogging the view.

"Get away from there," grumbled Bethany, snapping the curtains shut around Tillie's nose. "I wonder if Sidney Bluefeather has reporters outside his house, too?"

Tillie flopped down on the bed. Today she was dressed in jeans and a shirt that looked like bands of colorful burlap stitched any which way. Long ribbons of various matching hues trailed from her hair down past her thin shoulders. Hecate, perched on a pillow by the headboard, watched Tillie's head with kitty fascination. "Probably not," said Tillie. "His dad's not a homicide detective. He's just a rich banker type."

"Since when do you know what everybody's parents do?" asked Bethany, trying to keep the sour tone out of her voice.

"It's not like I keep a file or anything," replied Tillie, picking at the quilt on the bed. "Vanessa Peters told me. You don't think she would have invited Sidney to the party unless he had money." The word "money" came out through her nose with a definite nasal sound.

Bethany sat very still. "And . . . like we're rich and ultracool?"

Tillie raised her chin defiantly, but turned her head away from Bethany's penetrating gaze. Finally, her shoulders slumped and she said, "I'm sorry, sometimes I want to forget that I come from an ordinary house with ordinary parents."

"At least you have two parents . . ." muttered Bethany.

Tillie raised her eyebrows and changed the conversation. "He is weird, though."

"Who?"

"Sidney Bluefeather. He talks to himself in study hall."

"You're kidding?"

Tillie shook her head, the ribbons flapping. Hecate's eyes widened, his head cocked. "Seriously. All the time." She touched her temple and flung her hand in the air in a way-out-there gesture. "He gets so engrossed that the study hall monitor has to yell at him to shut up."

"That's funny. He sort of did that last night at the party, and then before he called the police for me. He didn't do a running dialog or anything, but he did talk to the air."

Tillie's dark eyes seemed to glow. "Like what did he say?"

Bethany shook her head. "I can't really remember now. Something about if I stayed, the murderer would get me, too. Creepy. I wonder if he knows who killed the clerk?"

"That's a scary thought. I doubt it. He's the straight type. No booze. No drugs. Perfect grades. President of the Science Club . . ." Tillie jumped up from the bed. Hecate inched to the edge of the bed, trying to catch one of those ribbons with a good swipe. Missed. Tillie walked over to the window, parting the curtains a tiny bit. "They're still out there—those reporters. Oop, there's Ramona swinging her broom. I wondered how long it would take her to unleash that weapon of justice. Now she's swatting some guy over the head. Good thing your dad is a cop or they'd probably get her for assault." They could hear the muffled static of Ramona's rapid French. Tillie backed up from the window, laughing.

"Yeah, good thing," said Bethany dully.

"Hey! Did Ramona bake any cookies recently?"

Bethany groaned. How Tillie could stay thin as a rail and eat so much was beyond Bethany's scope of understanding. All she had to do was look at a cookie and she'd gain a pound. She threw a pillow at Tillie. "You disgust me," she said. "By the way, we've got to talk about Witches' Night Out. Do you think we should look for new members or just let it go?"

Tillie ran her dark fingers over the smooth wood of Bethany's dresser. "Don't know. What do you think? Any candidates?"

"Not that I've seen," answered Bethany. "If we don't find the right ones it could wreck the whole thing. Next thing you know, all the parents in Cedar Crest will be screaming 'cult' if we're not careful. Maybe we should just keep our coven to the three of us."

Tillie continued to roam restlessly around the room. Hecate's golden eyes measured every step. "Nam says she has a couple of candidates, but wouldn't say who. I talked to her this morning. By the way, she's really hot on that Michael Raines guy. Maybe he's one of them?"

Bethany's stomach squirmed, just a little. She noticed Tillie hadn't mentioned the cheerleading squad. If Tillie joined the squad and Nam got herself a boyfriend, where would that leave her? She pushed the selfish thought away. "I don't think she wants him to know she's Wiccan. Did you see how fast she talked and how quickly she dragged him away? As if she was afraid that we might say something. And . . . she's not here today. I called her, but her mother said she wasn't home."

"Nam wanted me to do a reading on him," said Tillie, her dark eyes hooded, wrinkles of concern creasing her normally smooth, caramel forehead. Her fingers traced the delicate webbing of a dream catcher on the wall. She turned and walked back toward the curtained windows.

"And did you?" asked Bethany, getting tired of watching Tillie pace back and forth. Hecate's tail twitched nervously.

"Yeah, I threw the cards. I don't know. I couldn't concentrate. You get that way sometimes, you know?"

Bethany nodded though she really didn't know. Tillie was the expert at the cards. Bethany couldn't seem to get the hang of them, although Ramona tried to pound the meanings into her head. The interpretations just didn't seem to want to stick. In fact, so far, she didn't have a real aptitude for anything magickal, except raising power. She could do that. Big deal. Okay, so she'd done a few tricks or two, but nothing she could really be sure she was responsible for. Tillie, however, flew past her on just about everything. Again, she swatted the jealousy away with mental effort.

Bethany said, "I heard that Michael Raines is fairly popular. He's already dated several seniors, and one or two juniors claim to have gone out with him. He's in the senior class. I wonder why he's interested in Nam? She's only a sophomore."

"What's that got to do with it?" asked Tillie. "If he likes Nam, he likes her."

"Did you hear Gillian asking Sidney about Nam?" asked Bethany. "I hope Gillian doesn't think

Michael is for her. She's a bully and I'd hate to see her turn her talons in Nam's direction."

"Me, too," said Tillie. "Actually, I know more about Sidney Bluefeather than Michael Raines," she remarked.

"You looked at Sidney's cards?"

Tillie smiled, tapping her finger on her teeth. "Vanessa got me to wondering about him. His dad is of German descent, and his mother is full-blooded Cherokee. She does Native American circles in Philly and New York. Travels. Writes. Drums. Activist, I hear. Not home much."

"You didn't get that from the cards."

"Nope, I picked it up from Vanessa's ever-moving mouth, but I did do a fast reading, just for the heck of it. His cards looked good. He might be a great candidate for Witches' Night Out. We really do need that male energy to balance the circle."

For the first time, Bethany seriously thought about Sidney. She kept coming up with mixed emotions. Thinking of him in Witches' Night Out made her uncomfortable. Maybe Tillie was interested in him. No, that didn't feel right. "But if his mother is Native American, how come his last name is Bluefeather?"

"Oh. He had it changed. It used to be Hecklesdorf."

Bethany wrinkled her nose.

"Like I said. His dad has a lot of money and doesn't seem to care what Sidney does as long as he stays on the distinguished honor roll . . . there ya go," said Tillie, looking out the window for the third time. Hecate crouched, his hindquarters wiggling as if preparing for the leap of his life.

"What is your fascination with those reporters out there?" asked Bethany crossly.

"Hey. Black and gold to the rescue. Cedar Crest Regional has arrived. Two squad cars."

"Are they taking Ramona away?"

"Nope. The reporters. I told you it pays to have a daddy who's a homicide detective."

Bethany grimaced. Although she'd come to terms with her father's profession, she still carried a few edges of resentment. His cases often overpowered his life, leaving her on her own, under the watchful eye of Ramona.

Tillie continued her circular pattern around the room, this time picking at the books on Bethany's desk. Finally, she said, "Are we going to do something about it?"

Bethany frowned. "About what?"

"That woman you found last night. Somebody killed her, so we should do something, right? I mean, we've worked on something like this before and succeeded."

Bethany felt a spidery tingle at the back of her neck. She reached up and slapped it away. "Oh, we succeeded, all right. And almost got killed. I get involved in something like that again and my dad's sure to put me in some sort of academy for girls.

He'd spend his whole paycheck if he had to. I don't think your parents would be too keen on the idea, either."

Tillie's dark eyes stared at her intensely. "You're full of it."

Bethany smiled. "Yeah."

"Do we know the lady's name?"

Bethany shook her head. "I heard the police say Mary-something. It wasn't in the newspapers this morning."

"Oh! I almost forgot," said Tillie, rummaging through her purse, her head bending dangerously close to Hecate's reach. "You remember I told you that my mom said my grandma practiced magick—read cards and stuff?"

Bethany nodded.

"Well, my mom found Grandma's old card deck in the cupboard. When I was little I used to sit on her lap while she read for clients. By the time I was five, I knew every meaning. It's a deck of playing cards, and she wrote the meanings on them, so you don't have to learn anything. It's kinda cool because you can't buy them like a prepackaged deck in the mall or at a magickal shop . . . and someone gave them to her . . . so . . . there they are!" She produced a red velvet bag and handed it to Bethany. Hecate looked sullen, as if he'd missed his best chance. He prepared again, hunkering closer. "They're like a mini-divination tool. They don't tell you a whole lot, but they are a good place to start. I wanted you to have them. Then you can share my memories of Grandma with me."

Bethany didn't know what to say. A small "thank you" finally escaped from her lips. She took the red bag and ran her fingers over the soft velvet. She could feel the power in the cards coursing through the material of the bag. Yep. They were legitimate. Tillie flopped down on the bed, her head framed by Bethany's mirror hanging on the wall. Bethany opened her mouth to tell Tillie about the vision, but instead of looking at the reflection of the back of Tillie's head in the mirror, she saw the old woman with the third eye. The image shook her head and held her finger to her lips.

Bethany's throat went dry.

The grandfather clock in the outer hall struck the hour.

Hecate pounced, sucking one ribbon in his mouth and clutching two others in his paws. Tillie squealed and fell off the edge of the bed, the cat tumbling with her, his talons still attached to the ribbons.

Chapter 4

Five of Spades reversed: Watch out for trouble

Bethany plopped down in her chair, easing her books to the corner of her desk while digging in her purse for a pencil. The morning was not going well. First, she pulled a card, reversed, from that deck Tillie gave her. "Five of spades. Trouble on the way," she read out loud. Great. Before she left for school she lit a black votive candle and placed it on top of a small mirror to turn back any negativity. At the last minute she decided to put the mirror and candle in a deep metal cauldron on her dresser. She also locked her bedroom door, just in case Hecate decided to play with the burning candle.

In school for less than twenty minutes, she'd already answered a million questions about the convenience store murder. The last pack of ghoul-hunters almost made her late for class, and Mr. Barrows, the chemistry teacher, stood by the blackboard, his lips puckered and eyes squinting like he'd swallowed a lemon whole because he had to physically remove the crowd around her desk. This was not turning out to be one of her better experiences in life.

It took her awhile to notice that Gillian Merriday wasn't sitting in front of her. Between the Channel One presentation and the babbling of the kids around her, it was hard to concentrate on anything. Sidney Bluefeather bumped her elbow during the "Star Spangled Banner." "I've been trying to get hold of you all weekend, but nobody would give me your phone number," he whispered.

Mr. Barrows was known to give you detention if you talked during the national anthem. He frowned, glaring at Bethany. She shushed Sidney and someone behind her twittered.

Sidney pressed closer, and Bethany shifted uncomfortably. The last thing she needed right now was detention.

"The woman that was killed?" whispered Sidney. "It was Gillian Merriday's mom."

"Mr. Bluefeather!" boomed the chemistry teacher. "If you've got something to share, perhaps you would like to enlighten all of us?"

"I really need to talk to you," Sidney insisted, his dark eyes trying to capture and hold her. He looked over her shoulder and nodded as if someone was talking to him, but no one was there.

"Detention!" cried Barrows, pointing at Sidney. His finger whipped toward Bethany. "You, too!"

Bethany scowled at Sidney. "You jerk," she muttered to Sidney. She thought of the five of spades she drew that morning. Sidney was definitely trouble.

"I don't believe it," said Nam, running her finger, sticky with pink gloss, over her lower lip, her soft voice echoing against the tile walls of the girls' bathroom. "You found Gillian Merriday's mother dead in a convenience store. How awful!" Her mirrored, pale face trembled. Today Nam was going pink. Everything from her shoes to her stockings to the sweater, skirt, and blouse blared various hues of pink, from shocking pink to baby pink.

Bethany ran a brush through her hair, trying to ignore the reflection of all that pink. She hated how the bristles of her brush always stuck. Why couldn't she have that blue-black fine hair like Nam, not this disgusting heavy mess? Bethany slung her blue backpack over her shoulder. The stupid thing weighed a ton. "I didn't know it was her mother at the time. Sidney Bluefeather enlightened me this morning. The idiot got me detention for talking during the national anthem."

Nam's chin rose sharply, her dark, straight hair swinging against her cheek. "Sidney? Detention? That's a switch. He never does anything against the rules. He must have really wanted to talk to you. What a bummer. Of course, that'll give you time to talk to Sidney. What a hottie!"

"You're joking," said Bethany. "The boy is downright weird. Besides, you can't talk in detention. He gives me the willies. He's always whispering to the air."

"I don't think he's so strange. You should have seen his science project this semester. He's just a brainiac, is all. Try talking to him sometime. I think you'd like him. You always go for the jocks. Why not try someone with intelligence this time?"

"I can't see myself liking someone who can run circles around my brain matter."

"In fact," said Nam, plopping the gloss container in her purse and ignoring Bethany's last statement, "I was going to ask you if it was okay to bring him to Witches' Night Out this Thursday. His mom's into Native American stuff. It's not that much of a jump to Wicca. I think he would be a great addition to our coven." Her voice rose as she became more animated. "And he's really smart. Great with a computer . . . that is, if you don't mind."

The bathroom door smacked open and Vanessa Peters, dressed in a green sweater and skirt, strolled in with a few of her sidekick friends, including the redheaded Amanda Nevins. "Someone said you were in here. How come you left my party early?" asked Vanessa, her blue eyes trying to bore a hole in Bethany's skull. "My place just not good enough, or did you have some of that Witch stuff to do? Or maybe you didn't want to be late for a murder." Someone behind her sniggered.

"I had a wonderful time!" twittered Nam.

"I guess so," said Vanessa, turning her icy gaze on Nam's delicate face, her hand on her skirted hip. "You were all over that new kid. What's his name? Michael Raines? You should have just stopped at a motel. Things would have happened faster." Her words withered Nam, who furiously chewed the lip gloss off her lower lip.

Bethany stepped forward. "What put you in such a foul mood?"

"Tillie refused to join the cheer squad," piped up a girl with granny glasses. "Vanessa thinks it's your fault."

"I can speak for myself, thank you!" spat Vanessa, stepping closer to Bethany, her expensive perfume clogging Bethany's sinuses. "So, did you talk her out of it? You and this little geek-slut? I only invited the two of you to my party so I could get Tillie to come, you know. I didn't expect the Chinese Princess to run off with the new guy in town."

Bethany stood her ground, her eyes sliding to Nam's flushed face and back to Vanessa's twisted expression. "What's so special about the new guy?"

"He snubbed her," said the girl with wire glasses.

Vanessa snorted, cocking her chin, her eyes narrowing. "Not hardly likely. The boy's beneath me. Blood's bad, if you ask me, but Amanda likes him." She jerked her well-manicured thumb at the redhead with the furious expression standing by the sink. Nam took a tremulous step backward.

"I haven't talked to Tillie about anything that involves you," Bethany said to Vanessa, trying to put a good chill in her voice. "What Tillie does is her business, not mine. If she wants to join the cheer squad, that's up to her."

Vanessa raised a neatly plucked eyebrow. "So if I convince her to join, you're not going to squawk about it?"

Bethany gave a short laugh, adjusting her backpack to relieve the digging sensation in her shoulder. "Get real, Vanessa. Why should I care?"

Vanessa eyes darted to Amanda, then back. "You won't do anything to stop her?"

Bethany's shoulders tensed. Something was going on here. Some hidden agenda that she wasn't aware of, she was sure. "Look, Vanessa, we're not the best of friends, but I don't have anything against you. I thought we settled our differences and decided to let bygones be just that—gone. Why should I try to keep Tillie from doing something she wants to do?"

Vanessa looked at Amanda again, this time with a hard stare that telegraphed an unpleasant conversation to come.

"Bethany runs that Witch group," said Amanda defensively and taking a step backward, but her eyes remained defiant. "She probably did something to keep Tillie off the squad. Something nasty with black candles and stuff. She does it to people all the time."

"You think you guys are worth doing magick over?" Bethany couldn't help but laugh now. "That's just dumb."

Amanda jerked her squared chin and slit her eyes.

"Come on," said the girl with glasses, grabbing Vanessa's arm. "You got what you wanted. She said she won't talk Tillie out of joining. We're going to be late. You have practice and I want to be on time for the school newspaper meeting. Besides, don't you people know that magick isn't for real?" She looked at Amanda as if she were an insect. "Nobody really believes in that stuff. It's just Bethany's way of feeling like she's better than other people. If she's got low self-esteem, that's her problem."

How do you explain in sixty seconds, thought Bethany, *that magick does work and make someone believe you? You can't.* She also realized that Vanessa wasn't traveling with the other cheerleaders. This was a new group of girls. What was up with that? Maybe there was another reason for wanting Tillie on the squad, other than her obvious athletic abilities. Maybe Vanessa's big mouth and snotty attitude finally got her into trouble. Bethany hoped so.

The other girls started to file out, but Vanessa turned, her crimped blonde hair flipping over her shoulder. "Just stay out of my way, Witch-girl."

"Ooooh. I'm real afraid," replied Bethany, twisting her lips in a sardonic smile.

Amanda Nevins was the last to leave. She stopped beside Nam, pushing her into the sink. Nam's purse fell on the floor, spilling the contents on the gray tile. "Oh, I'm sorry," Amanda snarled, her eyes like snake slits.

Bethany stepped closer to Nam as she bent to pick up her things, catching Amanda's furtive glance at Nam's back. Bethany's father had always told her that you watched the eyes of an opponent. "You can always see a move coming in the eyes." "Don't do it," warned Bethany. "Don't even think about it." She could feel her fingers curling into a fist, knowing that violence wasn't the answer yet reaching to protect Nam.

It happened before she could stop it. That surge. That monster of hatred she always tried so hard to control. She jerked her hand toward the mirror, meaning to motion for Amanda to get out. The mirror cracked . . . a slow-motion succession of pings creeping across the smooth surface. No resounding shatter. No flying bits of glass. Just a simple network of elongated cracks, nothing more. The reflection of the old woman in her dream sprung into a kaleidoscope of pieces, but only Bethany could see her.

Amanda's peaches-and-cream complexion reddened like a Mackintosh apple. She slowly backed toward the bathroom door. Bethany didn't let her gaze waver. She kept looking in that stupid girl's eyes, intensifying her stare. "Ooogie boogie!" whispered Bethany, waving her fingers in the air. Amanda Nevins hurled an obscenity at Nam, then turned and ran.

Nam struggled to her feet. "I don't believe you did that! What are you doing, turning into some horror movie chick?"

Bethany shook her hand, blowing on her reddened knuckles. "Very funny. I smacked it with my fist. Probably just a pressure point or something."

Nam raised her eyebrows and shook her head. "Now the rumors will start again," she said forlornly.

"Hey! I didn't do it on purpose. It was old, like everything else in this part of the building."

"Yeah, right."

A loud banging on the bathroom door rocketed both girls on to the balls of their feet. They relaxed as a wizened janitor rumbled over the threshold, dragging a rolling cart and mop, his head bent as he shoved the protesting wheels into the center of the room, a forlorn whistle wheezing from his lips. He looked up slowly, his eyes registering mild shock, his face the same color as his gray uniform. "I knocked," he said, his voice tinged with petulance. His eyes widened as his glance caught the damaged mirror.

"I broke it," said Bethany. "I'm sorry. I'll go to the office and report it." She wondered how much trouble she would get into for breaking school property.

The janitor only clucked, showing a gap in his mouth where his front teeth should have been. "Don't bother. I've washed that mirror a thousand times. It started to crack two years ago. Only a matter of time."

"Try to get Amanda Nevins to believe that," said Nam.

"Who?" asked the janitor.

Nam sighed. "Never mind."

Chapter 5

Three of Hearts: Possible unhappiness

You shouldn't have done that," said Nam, putting the last of her makeup hurriedly back in her purse and eyeing the janitor, who immediately lost interest in them and puttered around in one of the stalls. "It'll just cause trouble!" she whispered, smoothing out a few pink wrinkles in her skirt with fluttering hands.

Bethany shrugged. "Then . . . I should have let her pound your face in? Over a guy?"

Nam's voice trembled, "No. I used to not be afraid," she said wistfully. "I don't know what's the matter with me. Lately I've been so skittish. Do you know that Gillian Merriday backed me in a corner at the party when Michael went to the bathroom and promised to rearrange my face if I went out with him?"

"I doubt she'll bother you now," said Bethany. "I know it's a terrible thing to say, but with her mother getting murdered, she's got other battles to fight. You know, with Gillian's personality? If I was the murderer, and I found out what Gillian was like, I'd beat it out of here, pronto. She's one mean Gillian machine." Bethany held open the bathroom door and they walked out into the hallway. Only a few students still milled around, some waiting for rides, others rushing to an activity. Nam fidgeted with the strap of her pink purse. "I want to do the right thing, you know? Violence is wrong, but how do you stand up for yourself with people like her?"

"I guess I never really thought about it," said Bethany. "I mean, part of dealing with a bully is realizing that they are the problem, not you, and to keep your courage. Don't let them see you sweat. Hurting people feeds their ego because their self-esteem is so low. If they think they're making a dent in your psychological armor, then they just keep picking at you. Ramona says that a bully is the biggest coward on the planet."

"You lost your temper with Amanda," replied Nam.

Bethany grinned. "Talking about how to deal with a bully and what you actually do can be two different things. She got under my skin, which is exactly what she wanted. Just goes to show you that we all need practice! By the way, did Gillian say why she didn't want you going out with Michael?"

Nam shook her head. "Just that I should keep my Chinese mitts off. It was disgusting."

"Did you tell Michael?"

"And be totally embarrassed? No way. Besides, you're right. She probably won't bother me anymore." She changed the subject. "Don't you have hockey practice?" asked Nam, looking over her shoulder.

Bethany stopped at her locker, relieving her backpack of some of the books and replacing others. "Hockey is over, remember? You went to the championship game."

Nam looked at her vacantly.

Bethany continued speaking. "I was thinking of going out for girl's volleyball. I'm too short for basketball. Unfortunately, I have to serve that stupid detention. Maybe I'll do it in the morning." She didn't want to be in the same room with Sidney Bluefeather.

Nam didn't reply, instead she craned her neck to look past Bethany's shoulder.

Bethany slammed her locker shut. "What's with you? It's like you're living in a dream world lately."

Nam didn't answer.

Bethany snapped her fingers in front of Nam's nose. "Yo, Nam! So, it's true? You have the hots for this Michael Raines guy?" asked Bethany.

Nam blinked and her ivory skin turned bright pink. "I think he's . . . he's . . . okay. He's not quite like high school boys, but I know that's silly, because he's only a senior, not in college or anything." She giggled, looking again down the hall. "What do you think about bringing Sidney into Witches' Night Out?"

"You really think he would fit in?" She groaned internally. What would kids say if they knew she befriended the geek of the school, no less a guy who had a habit of talking to the air. Bethany was not one of the "pretty people." The only thing she could do well was club a ball with a hockey stick and that claim to fame was fading fast. She had the whole rest of the school year to live through. Who cared if Sidney's dad had oodles of money?

Nam walked with her toward the lobby, impatiently tapping the lockers with her delicate fingers. "He's been reading books on magick. I've seen them, and last Friday he was talking about some astrology program he bought for his computer, that expensive one we can only drool over in the magazines."

They stopped at the gym doors. "I don't know . . ." said Bethany. "It would be nice to have someone who knows about astrology, but there's something about him that really bugs me. Does he know who we are?"

This time Nam turned away, looked back where they'd come from, then faced Bethany. "I'm not sure," replied Nam. "I didn't really want to say anything until I spoke to you first."

Bethany resumed walking. "Is something bothering you?"

Nam blushed. "No. No, I'm . . . I just don't want to miss my ride, is all."

"Let's ask Tillie what she thinks. And by the way, you missed your lesson with Ramona yesterday. Sunday afternoon is when we get together with her, or did you forget? Where were you?"

"Out. Just out for awhile. Tell Ramona I apologize. The time got away from me, I guess. I'll catch up on my lessons with Ramona. I had something to do, is all . . ."

Bethany ran her tongue over her teeth. She didn't like that spacey look in Nam's green eyes. "Ramona wasn't particularly happy that you bugged out. If Tillie says it's okay with her about this Sidney character, then go ahead and talk to him." Bethany wasn't happy about Sidney, but she did try to run a diplomatic group. They would vote on Sidney's entrance after they spoke to him.

Nam's pale face brightened. "Okay!" She started to back away, as if she was just waiting for Bethany to reach the lobby so she could run back down the hall. "Tell Ramona I'll be there this Sunday. I promise!" With that, she was off in a blaze of pink, heading for the large front doors.

Bethany sat in Ramona's apartment above the Salem's garage. From her vantage point at the breakfast bar that separated the living room from the kitchen, she could watch Ramona as the housekeeper mixed honey with orange peels. The recessed lighting flattered the housekeeper's cream-coffee skin as she hummed and stirred. Her jasmine perfume encompassed everything from the thick cocoa carpet in the living room to the heavy, brown velvet drapes.

"What are you doing?" asked Bethany.

"I read the shells tonight. To further the prosperity of the family, I must burn five yellow candles and place a mixture of honey and orange peels in a small bowl, and place them on the altar."

Bethany looked at Ramona's altar in the living room, a tremendous clutter of candles, pictures, statues, beads, photographs, and other magickal goodies. Not like a normal Wiccan altar. It took Bethany a while to realize that Ramona was an expert in several magickal systems, and she mixed and matched them at will—a practice, Ramona reminded Bethany, that wasn't particularly wise for a beginning student like Bethany. Studying with Ramona certainly curtailed the spontaneity that Bethany once enjoyed. She wrinkled her nose in response to the thought.

Ramona walked over to a cabinet and withdrew a book. The housekeeper kept all her magickal books on the kitchen shelves. Nothing about this woman could be considered normal.

"Here, read this," said Ramona, slapping the book down on the counter in front of Bethany. "It is an interesting book that explains how Witches view life after death. We call it the Summerland, where we study and learn, and then return to the Earth plane until we have accomplished all of our missions. You read, and Ramona will make us some nice tea."

Hecate meandered around the legs of Bethany's stool, his satisfied purr rumbling in his chest. Bethany believed the cat liked Ramona's apartment better than the main house. She reached down and scratched the top of his head. Bethany straightened, eyeing the cover of the book. It looked boring. "Am I reading this stuff because of Gillian Merriday's mother?"

Ramona shrugged, pouring the hot water into olive-green mugs, a bright yellow tea towel slung across her shoulder. "Murder happens all the time."

"So what are you saying?" asked Bethany.

"The true Samhain this year is Thursday, November sixth. From then until Yule, the time will be for reaping. A time of death. We need to let go of old fears and concentrate on planning for the future. People don't like things to pass away, especially if they have been using their fears as a crutch. What you need to learn is that this is a time of reorganization. A time of challenge. This can be a very intense lesson for those who refuse to learn. You must allow things to die naturally out of your life so that you can make way for the new."

Hecate wandered through the kitchen, his paws soundlessly moving over the smooth, brick-colored tile, sniffing around the bottom of the refrigerator.

"Mrs. Merriday didn't die naturally," replied Bethany.

"Ramona was not talking about Mrs. Merriday. I was talking about you, ma cherie. Things change. We must learn to accept change. Nam has a boyfriend. Tillie is becoming more popular. This is change. How well are you dealing with this change?"

Bethany played with her pencil, rolling the smooth barrel between her palms. She'd been studying under Ramona for a little less than a month and already it was getting tedious. When she first delved into WitchCraft it was a private thing, something the adults knew nothing about. Mysterious. Secret. She could work at her own pace and throw out the things she didn't want to do. Now that her dad knew and she found out that Ramona actually practiced . . . well, it just wasn't the same. Another facet of her life where adult rules intruded. Don't do anything against another's free will. Don't do love magick, it could backfire. Don't threaten anyone with magick, it wasn't civil. Don't. Don't. Don't. Next thing you knew, Ramona would want to participate in Witches' Night Out, just to make sure they were doing it right. She threw the pencil on the breakfast bar and watched it slowly roll to the end and plop onto the brick tile.

Ramona set the hot tea in front of her. "Have you been practicing your meditations like I taught you?"

Bethany sipped her tea, a flowery brew that smelled better than it tasted, but in a few moments she felt the tenseness began to seep out of her shoulders, her breathing becoming a soft, steady cadence of dancing air. "I haven't had much success," she lied, and her shoulders tightened again.

Ramona looked at her curiously but said nothing, slapping the tea towel on the edge of the counter. Hecate growled and grabbed at the edge of the cloth. The towel fell on his head and he immediately went into full attack.

Bethany took a good gulp of tea, then another. She momentarily closed her eyes. The deep-seated chill in her bones that had taken hold since she found Gillian Merriday's mother dead on the convenience store linoleum thawed at such a perceptible rate she almost dropped the mug. She hadn't realized she was so tense. Her eyes snapped open and she set the cup down quickly so as not to drop it.

Ramona settled slowly in her rocking chair beside the counter (another strange addition to the small kitchen), moving the chair gently back and forth. "Humans have a bad habit of allowing things to build within us. If we don't learn to release these energies in a positive way, then the body internalizes the event or emotion, and we become ill. Often, we don't realize that we've been stockpiling negative things." She closed her eyes and continued to rock. "Until it is too late, and we get sick."

"I didn't realize Mrs. Merriday's death bothered me so much," said Bethany, slowly picking up the mug and draining the remainder of the tea. A lovely, warm feeling caressed her insides, from the tips of her toes to the top of her head. She leaned her elbows on the counter and sighed.

Ramona didn't open her eyes. "Even the most hardened people, if they have a soul, are affected by death."

"You're talking about my father, aren't you?" asked Bethany. She hated the way Ramona talked about things but didn't talk about them. Discussing subjects with Ramona was like trying to figure out a locked room puzzle. Right now, she wasn't in the mood for games. "Get to the point."

"Him and others like him." The rocking chair continued to creak at a steady, comforting speed.

"My father's a hunter. A predator," replied Bethany. "Not in a bad way," she said quickly, "but a predator just the same. Sometimes it really bothers me. I'm afraid someone will hurt him like they hurt Mrs. Merriday. I mean, he puts himself in that position on purpose. He really enjoys the chase. Let's face it, he's hardly ever here, always busy with a big case. It's like the dead are his family and not us." Bethany tried to keep the whine out of her voice, but she knew she was doing a lousy job.

"All meat eaters are predators. Why should humans be any different? It is the animal within us. We either use this instinct in a productive or counterproductive way. Your father tries to do good with his fascination. As long as there are people like the individual who killed Mrs. Merriday in the world, the Goddess will make people like your father to find them."

Bethany played with the handle of the mug, tracing her finger along the rim. "I don't know. I don't think we should kill anything."

"I agree."

"But when I saw Mrs. Merriday . . . well, I was hoping someone like Daddy would catch the person who did it and do the same thing to them. It's the same with that little girl."

"The Annabelle Arneau case your father has been working on? Such a terrible tragedy, when bad things happen to the young ones. We should all be more responsible."

"Like you are responsible for me?"

Ramona smiled. "In a way."

"I'm sixteen. I don't need a babysitter."

Ramona laughed. "I will be with you for a little while yet."

Bethany suddenly realized that she didn't want to lose Ramona as much as she didn't want to lose her father. This was not a comfortable feeling. "Ramona, do you think it's wrong to wish the killers dead?"

The rocking chair continued to weave a tapestry of monotonous sound. Finally, Ramona answered. "Some would say yes, and some no. Religion, politics, and personal feelings usually enter into an individual's reply to that question."

"That's not a very good answer," said Bethany. "In fact, it's not an answer at all."

"True."

"You're not going to give me one—an answer, I mean."

"No. Just remember that life is the most precious gift we have."

Bethany closed the book and stacked her homework. She was careful to separate the Witch work from the school work. It would be awful if she turned her spell lessons in to the chemistry teacher. On the other hand, maybe not. It would certainly alleviate some of the boredom. After all, some spell work could be considered alchemy. She wouldn't mind seeing the expression on Mr. Burrows face if he read that three parts alcohol and two parts dragon's blood . . . then she could tell the silly fool that dragon's blood was the name for an herb, not the fluids of a real dragon.

"You're afraid of becoming like your father, aren't you?" The rocking chair stopped, the pause somehow thickening the air. Hecate, tired of wrestling with the nasty tea towel, wandered over to Ramona and unceremoniously jumped in her lap. Twenty pounds of cat immediately set the rocking chair back in motion.

Bethany didn't answer.

"You know," said Ramona, "with the meditations I gave you, your psychism should be improving."

Bethany considered telling Ramona about the old woman and her vision of the murder. Now was the perfect time. Instead, she stood up and stretched, ignoring Ramona's question about her father. "I just remembered, I promised to call Tillie."

Chapter 6

Eight of Spades: A warning!

A high wind whistled outside, pounding against the panes of her bedroom window. Bethany just loved the sound of that wind prowling, screaming, and clawing around out there in the dark, yet she remained inside, safe and secure. During the week Ramona stayed in one of the upstairs bedrooms so that Bethany wouldn't be alone in the house while her father remained in New York. A mystery book tucked securely under her arm and a piece of pumpkin pie in her hand, the housekeeper had retired over an hour ago.

Ramona. The woman certainly knew how to reach right into your mind and touch stuff you really didn't want to share. Bethany sat cross-legged on her bed in her favorite pajamas—the blue ones with clouds and miniature sheep. Hecate snuggled into a pillow beside her. He was a bit miffed that she hadn't allowed him to stay in Ramona's apartment, but since he stole Ramona's lucky crow's foot charm he wasn't permitted there unescorted. At the moment the charm, with its ratted, trailing black ribbon, was underneath the cat's paw. He opened one gold-green eye and stared at her.

"The only way you'll get back in that apartment alone is if Ramona comes up with a mouse infestation." Hecate closed his eye. "You know," said Bethany, looking at the cat, "sometimes I think you're a dog instead of part of the feline persuasion." Hecate didn't move.

Bethany wasn't sure if she wanted to work on her meditation exercises again tonight or not. Yes, she always felt refreshed after she did it, but what about that vision? What about that? Was it a result of the meditation? Ramona talked about the practice of opening up your third eye, and that's what the old woman pointed at, the third eye. If the visions were going to be frightening, she didn't want to go there.

She lit a lavender-scented candle on the night table and sat back against the pillows. The wind howled, slapping something against the side of the house as Bethany closed her eyes and started to count backward from ten to one. A bang this time. Her eyes flew open. She tried again. A crash. She felt just a bit of nervous energy tickling at the back of her neck as she walked over to the closed drapes and peeked out into the night. She couldn't see a thing. Blacker than pitch out there. Bethany let the drapes slap shut and retreated to her bed.

She tried again. This time a tinkling sound, as if a maniacal set of windchimes danced below her window. This was ridiculous. She leaned over and withdrew a picture hidden underneath the night table cover.

Ramona was right. All her life the criminal justice system had taken from her. Killed her mother. Kept her father so busy there was almost no time for her. She hated it. Hated it! Yet the allure was there. Who killed Gillian Merriday's mother? There was nothing in the papers. Supposedly no leads. She knew from her father's conversations that each ticking minute a criminal remained free, the less chance of closure for the case.

Bethany ran her fingers over the picture. Hecate sneezed, blinked, and rolled over, a gentle purr-snore muffling into the pillow.

She'd held her breath yesterday, thinking Tillie would find the picture. That's why Tillie's pacing around the room drove Bethany up a wall. As if Tillie would even think to look for something she'd never seen, and then if she had seen it, what would she have said? "Oh, a picture of a pretty little girl." No big deal.

Bethany turned the picture over and read the neat handwriting on the back. Annabelle Arneau. Age 7. Nonparental abduction September 1. Body discovered September 14. This was the case that was taking her father away from her. It was as if Annabelle owned her dad instead of Bethany. No, that wasn't fair. She was just a little girl who never got the chance to grow up. No parties, no dances, no college. What had Ramona said about taking care of the young ones?

Okay, so this wasn't the only case her father was working on. There was no end to homicide investigations when you worked for the NYPD. It was just that he spent so much time away from home, working extra hours on this case. Bethany fingered the picture for the hundredth time. "What happened to you, Annabelle?" she whispered. Maybe if Bethany could help her father in some way, she could feel like she was more a part his life? Now, there was a thought!

She remembered her father saying something particularly frightening last week. "Too bad people have to die so that I can do what I love," he'd said. "I wish we could have homicide without the dead people." At the time, Bethany found this statement particularly appalling, but now she thought she understood what he meant. It was the chase, after all. The predatory instinct turned in a productive way.

Bethany thought of the speed of the wind, how it moved so quickly through the back yard, dancing along the roof of the garage, whistling under the eaves . . . how fast it traveled.

Wind. The element of air. She felt that familiar sensation. That power that often snuggled dormant within her, waking slowly, making her fingers tingle. A rhyme kept playing in her head, one that her mother had taught her years ago. What was it? "Element of air. Something flow . . . wait. Element of air. Element of flow. Send my message . . . help it go." She snapped her fingers. That was it! She repeated it just to make sure she had it right.

She flapped the picture back and forth. What kind of spell would you do if you wanted to find the killer of a little girl? She stood again by the window. An array of leaves pattered against the panes, carried by the whistling wind. Ramona always said that each spell should be different, that you can't really use the same one repeatedly because the circumstances around each desire are never alike. You could use the same general format, but every spell should be tailored to each individual need, and the more information you had to help you target, the better.

Hecate grumbled and stretched, his cat eyes blinking at her in irritation. He picked up the crow's foot and jumped off the bed. The black ribbon was the last thing to disappear beneath the dust ruffle.

Her fingers clenched around the picture. It was really all she had. If she helped her father catch Annabelle's killer, then he might spend more time at home. A small voice, a calm whisper in her mind, said, "But do you understand the ramifications of what a spell like this might do?" She knew from before that asking for the truth could be dangerous business—and she could find herself in the middle of another very big mess. The last time she and her friends tried to cast a spell to catch a bad guy, she almost got creamed herself. Did she really want to risk it? She thought of the words of Oscar Wilde that they'd read in English class today: "The truth is rarely pure, and never simple." If she went after the truth, how much would this complicate her life? Worse, how convoluted was the truth of Annabelle's murder?

And what about the Merriday woman? This was her town. No one was safe until they found her killer. If they ever found him. No, one spell at a time. She would help her father first.

She peeked out her bedroom window again. The wind pounded around the back yard's flagstone porch. Something white and flat flashed by the window. The wind screamed, almost like a lamenting woman. Bethany shivered, and her hand clutching the edge of the drapes jerked spasmodically.

She vacillated. Why not do something about Mrs. Merriday? She pushed the vision of the bloody, inert body from her mind. She just didn't want to deal with it right now. First, Annabelle. In a way, the little girl wasn't real. Bethany hadn't known her personally. No matter how terrible the murder, Bethany was removed from the heart of the pain. Not like seeing Mrs. Merriday. No, not at all. *This isn't like the last time,* she convinced herself. *I won't come in contact with the killer. I'll just find information that can help my father solve the case. That's all. Yeah, that's good. That's okay.*

Element of air. Element of flow. Who killed Annabelle? Let me know. She flattened her lips, feeling the tenseness around her eyes. Annabelle. Bethany shoved open the window, stumbling backward as a gust of wind tore through her bedroom, rattling the bureau mirror, sending papers spinning in the air, pulling in dust and debris from outside. A forlorn, crumpled paper cup sashayed next to the dust ruffle of her bed. A muffled growl from under the bed informed Bethany that Hecate wanted no part in what she was about to do. "Chicken!" she muttered.

She stood in front of the open window, the drapes billowing around her, the picture of little Annabelle clutched firmly in her hand. She could feel the power of the magick boiling in her blood, urging her onward, pleading to be released into the universe. "It's time," it whispered. "Time."

Bethany gloried in the fresh air, its cloying autumnal flavor slipping down her throat. Her chest heaved in delight and anticipation. She began to chant the rhyme. "Element of air, element of flow, what happened to Annabelle? Let me know!" It took a few times to get the rhythm just right. She spoke softly at first, allowing the words to trail delicately in the wind, to be overcome by the sheer force of the element. With the window open she could see a little better into the back yard, the heavy metal lawn chairs barely discernable, the willow tree bending low, its branches swirling like a maddened banshee in a death-dance of hysteria.

A piece of grit stung at the corner of her eye but she continued to hold her head high, squinting slightly, her eyelashes compressed against her flesh. The chant grew louder in her throat, rising from her belly, bursting from her mouth to match the screams of the wind. She focused on the Divine Mother, asking her to bring them news of the little girl, asking for the Great Mother to release the child from her chains of mystery and to reveal her killer. A picture of Mrs. Merriday's death mask stole into her conscious thought and she pushed it frantically away. Not now! To lose focus would majorly screw up the spell! She must concentrate on one issue at a time.

She held up her arms, beseeching the wind, her cries matching the power of the elements, and she felt the power roil, roll, and spill from her body, joining the fever-pitch vibration of the wind that now howled around her like a maddened animal. The photo tore from her hands and disappeared into the dark maw of the night. One of the drapes ripped free of the rod above her, snapping her in the face, then whipped across the room, landing in a frayed, dark linen puddle by the door.

A shadow darted out from underneath the direction of the willow tree, sending a thrill of fear up her spine. Had someone seen her? Magick done in front of nonbelievers lost some, if not all, of its power. Bethany backed up to slam the window shut, but the wind caught her hair and whipped the ends in her eyes, making her hesitate. In that split second a black, gloved hand reached out from the darkness beyond the window and grabbed her by the throat. She couldn't see the face. It was covered by a nylon black Halloween hood.

Her only thought was, "What the heck did I do wrong this time?"

Chapter 7

Eight of Clubs: Someone makes you unhappy

Bethany tried to scream, but the pain and her own fear constricted her throat. She clawed at the sash of the window. Trying to jerk back, she twisted her neck, the pressure so intense a blackness threatened to explode behind her eyes. The arm now extended through the window but her head was tilted up and back, confining her view of the attacker while her fingers frantically clawed at the window frame. Her knuckles grazed the sharp edges of the catch, drawing blood. Fingers scrabbling, she felt the catch release as the sash plummeted, smashing onto the black sweatshirted arm that held her. Thank the Goddess for old windows, she thought as she broke free. Someone screamed and then the window crashed the final few inches, reflecting her pale, terror-ridden face as it contorted with a spasm of coughs. She clutched her neck, stumbling backward, tripping and falling—but her legs kept moving, propelling her into her bedroom door that vibrated from the force of Ramona's frantic pounding on the other side.

Still hacking, she turned, crawled to her feet, and hit the lock. Ramona came barreling through, arms raised, a berzerker frenzy sending spittle from her lips while she waved her broom in the air as if it were a vicious, double-headed axe. Her presence filled the air with the scent of jasmine.

Of course, the attacker was gone.

Ramona stood there, in the middle of Bethany's bedroom, wearing a fluffy pink bathrobe and huge, pink bunny slippers. Bethany heard the muffled sound of the grandfather clock in the hall chiming midnight, and all she could think to croak was, "Ramona, you're wearing pink!"

Hecate propelled his feline body from underneath the bed, fleeing the room between Ramona's sturdy legs, the crow's foot in his mouth, the rumpled black ribbon dancing merrily along the carpet. Ramona tried to stamp on it. "You thief!" she muttered. "I'll get my crow's foot back from you yet!"

". . . If we tell my dad," ended Bethany, "you'll know he'll want to move. If we call the police, they'll call my dad." Frustrated, she pulled at the ends of her long hair. She'd just sat through a half-hour lecture from Ramona, followed by an equally long dissertation by herself trying to convince the woman to keep her mouth shut.

Ramona remained silent through Bethany's entire diatribe.

Bethany tried to shove her rising panic into a mental place where it wouldn't screw up her thinking. "If Dad moves, you know he won't take you with us. It's more than likely he'll pack me up and take me to his apartment in New York."

Still, Ramona said nothing.

"Even if he does take you along, you know you hate New York."

Absolute silence. Not a peep.

"Or worse, he'll send me away to some girl's school!" cried Bethany, talking with her hands now, waving her fingers in the air. "Oh, please don't let him do that to me! And then he'll send you away!"

The right side of Ramona's mouth twitched.

"I'll lose all my friends!" wailed Bethany, her hands conducting an entire symphony in the air.

The housekeeper rose from the edge of Bethany's bed and picked up the tattered drape, clucking her tongue. A puff of jasmine perfume tickled Bethany's nose. "Ramona thinks that you are being melodramatic." The housekeeper neatly folded the cloth.

"Easy for you to say," snapped Bethany, gathering up the broken curtain rod with a hefty swipe, knocking the darned thing into the wall. A chip of paint fell delicately to the purple carpet. "It's not your whole entire life that will be ruined!" She couldn't help it. She knew she was panicking, but her mouth just kept moving. "I don't want to go to a new school. It's so hard! As soon as they find out I'm Wiccan—and they will, you know they will—it will just be the whole mess all over again, but this time I won't have Tillie or Nam! Please!" She grabbed the front of Ramona's pink bathrobe. "Please let's not tell my dad!"

Ramona tilted her head, her eyes rolling in exasperation. "And how will Ramona explain the marks around Bethany's neck?" Her tone of voice was far from amused.

Bethany ran to the large mirror over the bureau. Yes indeed, there they were, huge, awful bruises on either side of her neck, close to the pulse points beneath her ears. Her fingers rapidly flew to hide the horrible signs of the attack. "I'll . . . I'll wear a turtleneck sweater, I'll use makeup, anything . . . please!" She stared at Ramona's deliriously pink-clad form in the mirror. "Please," she whispered. "Don't let him take me away."

"Get some sleep," said Ramona. The housekeeper sat cross-legged by the window and, to Bethany's knowledge, remained there all night, the broom resting across her lap.

Although the scent of jasmine cloyed in Bethany's sleepy nostrils, Ramona wasn't in her room when she awoke and said little to her as Bethany got ready for school and ate breakfast.

Bethany didn't tell anyone. Not about the magick. Not about the attack. Tuesday morning sped by like a washed-out dream. The news of the murder only three days old, and with Gillian Merriday still out of school, gossip ran high. The whole place buzzed with all sorts of bizarre tales, and it was a good thing Gillian wasn't there to hear any of them. Speculation and rumor insinuated nasty topics. The whole mess made Bethany sick to her stomach. Although she didn't particularly care for Gillian, she felt the evil rumors weren't appropriate. Bethany ran her finger around the collar of her itchy, navy turtleneck. She was hot and sweating. Her neck was sore and she just felt all-around gross.

Nam appeared at Bethany's locker after lunch. Today's fashion theme was yellow, with matching gold belt, scarf, and shoes. Even her eye shadow sparkled gold in the watery hall light. "Where have you been?" asked Bethany. "We missed you at the lunch table."

Nam flushed. "I was in the science room. Michael and I are working on a project."

"Sounds like you're getting pretty serious about this guy," said Bethany, pulling out her books for her afternoon classes. "Is he serious about you?"

Nam only giggled, her delicate fingers touching the gold barrette in her blue-black hair. "Did you ask Tillie about Sidney? And Witches' Night Out?"

"This morning," said Bethany, slamming her locker shut, "after I spent half an hour in detention, thanks to Sidney. Tillie said we can give him a try, but no promises. Anyone that gets me landed in detention is not high on my favorite people list."

Nam clapped her hands, the straight-cut edges of her hair bouncing on her shoulders. "That's great! I'll tell him right away. We have English Lit together. I'm sure he'll be thrilled."

"I'm sure," mumbled Bethany. "Listen, why don't you bring Michael? I'm sure he'd be interested."

Nam's face visibly paled, her small lips forming a golden O. "I don't think so."

"He doesn't know you're Wiccan, does he?"

"Like I'm sure the whole school hasn't told him," replied Nam, not meeting Bethany's eyes.

"Which means you didn't tell him."

"I just don't want to screw it up right now," said Nam. "I'll tell him. Sometime."

Bethany put her hand on her hip. "Right, when pigs fly, huh?"

Nam's small face hardened. "I said I'll tell him. Just not now. Don't push me, Bethany."

"Yeah. Sure," said Bethany, frowning as she watched Nam scoot down the hall, yellow miniskirt and all. Too late she saw Amanda Nevins leaning against the wall. The girl stuck her foot out and Nam went sprawling, her books, papers, and purse flying into the air. Amanda bolted down the hall before Bethany could do anything about it.

Bethany shared her first mod chemistry and her last mod government studies with Sidney Bluefeather, though she never really paid that much attention, which left her a little surprised to find him hovering at her elbow at the beginning of the final class of the day.

"Sidney," she said, trying to keep the get-away-from-me smile off her face. She realized too late there were no assigned seats in this class. Students could sit anywhere they liked, and it was obvious that Sidney was going to park right beside her. She busied herself looking for a mythical pen in her purse, hoping he wouldn't open his mouth and say anything about Witches' Night Out. As if she wanted the world to hear!

Either too excited or too dumb, Sidney began to jabber and the more she ignored him, the louder he got. Some of her classmates started to giggle, others openly stared at her. Bethany inched lower in her seat. Someone made a crack about broken mirrors.

"Why is your neck sore?" asked Sidney, snapping a rubber band around his wrist.

Bethany's fingers flew to the collar of her turtleneck. "What makes you think it's sore, and what's with the rubber band?"

A loud guffaw overrode Sidney's reply. Bethany turned around to see Amanda Nevins whispering to a group of kids in the corner. She pointed at Bethany, and then said, "What are you looking at, Witch-girl. You know, you are really ugly!" The group giggled.

Bethany's blood pressure zoomed.

"Forget ugly! That girl is tramp!" exclaimed one of the senior preps.

A rubber band snapped and Amanda let out a howl of pain. Bethany looked at Sidney's wrist. The rubber band was gone, and Bethany was sure she knew who'd been the recipient of the elastic missile. She stifled a smile.

Mrs. Bixby, the government studies teacher, declared that since the entire class couldn't shut up there would be a pop quiz. Bethany, in unison with the rest of the students, groaned, but part of her was thankful for the intervention. She finished her paper early and took a sidelong glance at Sidney. She'd never really looked at him before, her eyes always skipping over him to focus on someone else. Lanky, dark hair; intense eyes; clear, dusky complexion; an aristocratic nose that didn't quite go with the rest of him, she guessed he wasn't that bad, but still . . . he was a geek. A dork. He did, however, defend her honor with the rubber band attack. She blew air out of her mouth, extending her lower lip in resigned frustration. If he couldn't keep quiet, though, this would never work.

Amanda Nevins snickered behind her. Bethany wished she really did have the power to make Amanda lose her voice. If she had that kind of expertise, she'd be sure to crack Amanda's face and watch the pieces shatter on the floor. Amanda was not one of the pretty people either. She was that other facet of high school society, those who had self-esteem problems that bubbled over into the need to abuse others. Your basic bully. She did anything to please the people she thought were cool, including stealing money from her brother, or so rumor had it. Bethany shook her head as another verbal assault reached her ears. In a way, Bethany felt sorry for Amanda, but the girl's cruelty could hardly be ignored.

Sidney cocked his head and whispered something to the empty space beside his desk, then turned to Bethany. "She went after her brother with a knife," said Sidney.

Bethany started. "What? Who?"

"Amanda Nevins. She's crazy. She's running with the popular crowd because she holds keggers every weekend. That's the only reason they tolerate her."

"How did you know I was thinking about—."

"Miss Salem," came the icy voice of Mrs. Bixby, "can you explain to me why prohibition did not work in the American culture?"

Sidney strikes again, thought Bethany, rising to answer the question.

Chapter 8

Two of Clubs: Sharp words, go slow

"There are four basic rules to practicing Witch-Craft," said Bethany, shaking her finger right under Sidney's nose, the frustration she felt bubbling to the surface. "To know, to dare, to will, and to be silent!" The November wind, not as strong as last night, still carried a bite as it lifted a few leaves and scattered them in a fanned array across the browning grass of the park. Bethany zippered her Cedar Crest High letter coat, the warm fleece lining cutting the sharp slice of air, then leaned against one of the rough poles of the gazebo.

Sidney sat attentively, his dark eyes widening a bit, the ends of his long, dark hair dancing playfully in the chill breeze. He looked sexy, which was more than disconcerting. Nam, sitting beside him, bit her lip, her expression pensive. Tillie shifted uncomfortably, squatting on the wooden steps. Bethany could tell they didn't understand her annoyance with Sidney.

"That means, since I need to spell it out for you," continued Bethany, her hands on her jacketed hips, "that we do not talk about magick or WitchCraft in school or where anyone can hear us."

72

Sidney lowered his head. "Oh. I'm sorry. My mother talks freely of this sort of stuff. I was just so glad to find someone like me ... well ... I guess I got carried away."

A twinge of guilt tugged at Bethany's temples. "*To know* means that we study ... a lot. *To dare* means that we are willing to try new things and we always do our best to keep an open mind. *To will* indicates that we must focus on the matters at hand and continue to set goals for ourselves." She was beginning to feel like Ramona, and wondered if the housekeeper was as irritated with her as Bethany was right now with Sidney. "And finally, *to be silent* means exactly that—shut your trap! If you get me in trouble one more time, I'll happily wring your neck!"

If Sidney could slink any lower on the wooden bench, he would have. Nam patted his shoulder, crooning little it'll-be-okays. Tillie's lips puckered and she smothered an amused grin by turning her head into the upturned collar of her red coat.

Bethany chose Quade Park, a little strip of grass, flagstone walkways, and a few pines, complete with a recessed gazebo, to give Sidney the what-for of Witches' Night Out. Normally, none of the older kids came here because the park was tightly flanked by two businesses—a real estate brokerage on one side and a bank on the other. It was too easy for the adults to check up on what you were doing, which was perfect for what she had in mind. Out in plain sight and, therefore, not worth watching. For some reason she didn't want to bring Sidney to her house just yet. Maybe because she didn't want Ramona to hear, or possibly because she enjoyed controlling the situation. She pushed that second thought away.

"Okay," sighed Bethany. "Lecture over. Has Nam told you about Witches' Night Out? What we do?"

Nam nodded eagerly, her gold lamé coat crinkling as she moved. Sidney did not reply.

"You can talk now," said Tillie, her dark eyes dancing.

Sidney grinned. "Just checking," he said. "I think it's a great idea. Getting together. Learning magick. Doing rituals. It sounds like a lot of fun, though I do know you've got to study. That doesn't bother me at all. I've been looking for something like this for years but didn't know what to call it. Then I started reading some books and it felt like going home, you know?"

The girls nodded. A horn blared somewhere on the street.

"So when Nam talked to me about it this morning, well, I was just so excited. I mean, I'd heard rumors about you guys, but . . ."

The girls exchanged glances.

"I'm just so glad that it's true!" he finished. "I'm glad you're like me . . . or maybe I'm like you!"

Bethany paced the gazebo, the wooden floorboards creaking under her weight. She turned and leaned against one of the posts, her thumb rubbing the opposite palm in a circular motion. "There's just one more thing," said Bethany. "You've got to tell your parents."

All the color drained from Sidney's face.

A tiny "Uh-oh" escaped from Nam's gold-glossed lips. Either the light was bad or Bethany could swear Nam had a bruise under her right eye, but her friend flipped her hair and leaned into a shadow.

Sidney looked over Bethany's shoulder, staring intently. "Not now . . ." he mumbled. "That wouldn't be fair."

"What?" asked Tillie. "Asking your parents?"

"Ah . . . no, I mean yes, I think asking my parents might be a problem. What do I do now?" He stretched his long, blue-jean clad legs out before him, the heels of his boots scuffing loudly across the wooden floorboards.

The four of them sat around Bethany's kitchen table. The aroma of fresh-baked chocolate chip cookies, laced with the smell of recently halved onions and garlic, assaulted Bethany's nose. Oh, and add the tinge of Ramona's jasmine perfume. Unfortunately, the atmosphere was far from comfortable. Even Hecate refused to enter the kitchen, preferring to zip up the stairs with his tail puffed bigger than a feather duster as soon as they trooped in the house.

Ramona, back to her usual white attire, was not a happy housekeeper. One hand on her hip, the other shaking a long finger under Bethany's nose, she hovered at the table, her soft clothing swishing gently as she rocked back and forth on the balls of her white slippers. "You are telling me," said Ramona, her voice booming off the kitchen walls, "that this boy's parents will not be happy that he wants to study WitchCraft."

"Just my dad, my mom probably wouldn't mind," muttered Sidney. "I didn't realize I had to have anyone's permission." Ramona glared at him, then turned to lock Bethany with a dark gaze. "And that you want me to teach him anyway! It's bad enough that I'm already lying to your father about last night."

Tillie munched on a cookie, eyes wide. All of them zeroed in on Bethany. She winced.

"And now . . . now you want me to lie to some kid's parents. Well! Ramona won't do it. She simply will not do it! Every time you get into trouble, Ramona has to twist her words. No!"

Tillie leaned forward. "What about last night? What did you do?" she asked, grabbing another cookie off a platter piled high with cooling goodies.

Bethany splayed her hands. "Nothing. I didn't do anything."

Ramona made a demonstrative gesture in the air. "Nothing? Ma cherie! You don't call a man reaching through the window and trying to strangle the stuffings out of you nothing! This is why Ramona spends all afternoon halving onions and crushing garlic, and placing these protections about the house!" Her speech denigrated into rapid, unintelligible French.

Nam's green eyes seemed to empty of cognizant

thought. Sidney looked at the table. Tillie's jaw dropped. No one said anything for a moment.

"Who would want to hurt you?" asked Nam, her voice soft and fearful.

Bethany shrugged. "Beats me." She swallowed, feeling the dull ache of the bruises on her neck.

"Ooh. Poor choice of words," said Tillie. "You sure do get into a lot of weird jams."

Bethany slit her eyes, wrinkled her nose, and shook her head slightly.

"And you didn't tell your dad?" asked Nam, terror lurking along the edge of her voice. She grew paler than usual. In fact, she looked thinner, if that was possible.

Bethany did not like Ramona telling her private business in front of her friends, especially Sidney, who wasn't a friend at all. "He'd make me go away," she said angrily, looking at Ramona. "You know what almost happened the last time," she added, grinding her teeth.

"Last time?" asked Sidney, finally looking up from the table, his heavy, dark brows lifting in gentle arcs.

"Old news," replied Tillie, giving Bethany an I-understand-you look and waving her hand in the air.

"None of this solves Sidney's problem," said Bethany, trying desperately to draw the conversation back to the original point of reference.

Ramona turned her back and tapped her foot.

"What if Sidney at least told his mother?" asked Nam. "Then one parent would know, as long as she didn't yap to your dad." She looked at Sidney questioningly.

He shook his head slowly. "My parents don't especially get along . . ."

The housekeeper turned around. "Ramona doesn't think that is such a good idea. It could cause many difficulties in your home. You'd better think before you make such a request of your mother. There is nothing I can say about your desire to socialize with the girls on Thursday nights, if your mother approves, but I cannot teach you until you get permission from both of your parents. Ramona will not budge on this issue. A Witch is as good as their word. We do not lie."

"What is she saying?" asked Sidney, looking at Nam.

"She's trying to be nice. She means that you can join in Witches' Night Out if your mother says it's okay, because that's our group and Ramona doesn't participate, but she can't teach you like she does us unless both of your parents agree."

Sidney lips turned down at the corners, his cheeks deflating, but he said, "I understand. I'll at least ask my mom."

"Ramona wants to read a book now," said the housekeeper, looking at Bethany. "Dinner is at six." She swirled out of the room leaving the strong scent of jasmine in her wake.

Tillie passed the plate of cookies around and Nam refused, saying, "Who would want to hurt you, Bethany? Do you think it's because you found Mrs. Merriday's body?"

Bethany shrugged her shoulders, wincing as her bruises sent a sharp pain tingling down her neck. "I don't know why that would scare anyone. I didn't see the crime in progress, just the horrible aftermath. Has anyone bothered you, Sidney?"

He silently shook his head, an uncomfortable expression on his face.

Nam shuddered. "They're still looking for who killed her. I saw it last night on the evening news."

Bethany eased back in her chair, crossing her arms over her chest, observing her silent compatriots. The weak lighting in the kitchen cast soft shadows on the usually merry-yellow walls. A loon screamed somewhere from the back yard, drawing her attention to the window, and the dusky sky beyond the sparkling pane of glass offered little light. Piled onion halves obscured part of Bethany's view, each half positioned precisely in the center of its own little saucer. It looked like an onion garden up there. The sun slipped slowly toward the horizon, bathing the windowsill with orange-gold light. For a moment she thought she saw the reflection of the old woman with the third eye, but she blinked, and nothing remained but clear glass and vibrant sky. Bethany returned her gaze to the kids at the table, straining to make out anything unusual in Nam's face, but her cheeks just looked pale and drawn. "Nam, are you feeling okay?"

"I'm perfectly fine!" said Nam, looking up at the clock on the kitchen wall, then standing quickly. "I've got to go. I'm going to be late." She slung her purse over her shoulder, madly trying to put on her coat afterward, the gold lamé material rustling and getting stuck on the belt buckle of her designer purse. There was a fearful tinge to her voice, something you pick up with your inner self rather than anything plainly vocal. She finally extricated herself from the coat, took off the purse, and put the coat back on.

"What is with you?" asked Bethany.

"Nothing-nothing," Nam repeated rapidly. "Just got to go." She looked again with anxiety-filled eyes at the clock. "I'm late, that's all. Late."

Bethany looked at Tillie, but she was lost in the delight of another cookie. Sidney, however, noticed it, too. Bethany could tell by the way his eyes focused, unwavering, on Nam's trembling chin.

Sidney's eyes flicked past Nam's shoulder. He shook his head and said, "I can't."

"What?" asked Nam.

Sidney said, "Can't see the clock because you're standing in front of it."

"Oh. Well. See ya," she said, and rushed out the door.

Tillie finished her cookie. "Where did she have to go in such a hurry?"

Bethany and Sidney exchanged glances, but neither said anything. How do you put into words something you don't quite understand? Bethany eyed Sidney. He could see that clock perfectly. Nam wasn't obstructing his vision. What was that all about? Nam rushed out the back door in a gold blur.

"There's something funny going on," said Tillie. "I don't like it. Nam has been acting too weird. She looks awful, like she's not healthy."

"Sometimes," remarked Sidney, "love is not love at all, but something truly dark and twisted."

Tillie reached for another cookie, then withdrew her hand. "Hey, you're scaring me. Do you know something we don't know?"

Sidney looked at the empty back door. "Call it a hunch. I think we should pay attention, though. You're right, something is very wrong in Nam's life."

Tillie contemplated her cookie. "I think we should all light a candle, asking Nam's guardian angel to help her."

"Good idea," said Bethany. "I've got extra candles in my magickal trunk in the family room. I'll go get them."

"I don't know how to do that," said Sidney.

"No sweat," Tillie said. "We'll show you how. It's easy. If you're going to be a part of Witches' Night Out, you might as well start now."

CHAPTER 9

Two of Spades: Lies, gossip

Bethany's father telephoned after dinner. "How's my little pumpkin?"

Bethany held the receiver to her ear, listening to the warm cadence of her father's voice, though she wished he wouldn't call her pumpkin. She was too old for that kind of stuff. "Just fine," she said, peering across the living room at Ramona, who was still engrossed in her book. She knew, however, that the housekeeper's fox-ears were tuned in her direction. Bethany turned her back to the housekeeper, facing the wall of the hall stairs. She could almost feel Ramona's ears rotating in her direction. "Everything okay there?" she asked, fingering the edge of the framed portrait of her mother that hung over the telephone stand. Hecate was daintily descending the steps above her. The cat stopped at crown level, displayed an evil kitty grin, and tried to bat at her head. She ducked.

"I have a couple of promising leads," her father replied.

Bethany carried the remote receiver into the living room and plopped in the chair across from Ramona. If the woman was going to eavesdrop, she might as well have a front seat. Hecate padded across the carpeted floor and tried to claw the chestnut-colored corduroy of the easy chair. Bethany good-naturedly swatted the cat away. He nipped at her fingers, but didn't bite. It was an old, comfortable game between them. "On Annabelle, the little girl?" asked Bethany, trying to concentrate on the thread of conversation. She couldn't keep the hope out of her voice, which was perfectly all right. Her father had no idea about the magick she did last night. He would merely believe, like anyone, that she was looking forward to a good turn in the case due to his excellent police work, not that he wasn't a bad homicide detective. If rumors were true, he was one of the best.

"Yes," he replied. "That's sort of why I called you, but I have to ask you something else. Henry Hecklesdorf's wife, the woman married to the investment banker fellow that lives in those manor estates across town? Her son is Sidney Bluefeather? She called me this evening."

Bethany made a sour face that Ramona didn't miss. "What did she want?"

"Don't play coy with me, pumpkin. I sat on the phone with her for over an hour explaining Witch-Craft, which I don't know much about in the first place, and which I really wasn't comfortable discussing with an outsider, especially a woman married to the richest man in the tri-county area. Get my drift? Luckily she has a fairly good idea of what Wicca is, and was more interested in knowing if I provided a safe environment in my home for her son. She was very adamant that she didn't want her son to be exposed to anything dangerous."

"I am not dangerous," huffed Bethany.

"I didn't say that you were, but you could have warned me."

"It's not my fault," replied Bethany. "Nam's the one who wanted to bring him in."

"That's not the point," said Carl Salem, his tone taking on that authoritative edge Bethany hated so much. "I thought we agreed that it would just be the three of you. No one ever said anything about extending this little group of yours, especially after the fiasco you had last month. It's not that I don't support what you're doing, but what you do does affect both of us. Wouldn't you agree?"

Bethany grimaced, but kept her mouth shut. Hecate chased his tail in the center of the room, hoping to gain her attention. She ignored him.

The drone of her father's voice continued. "I realize it is a perfectly legitimate religion. God knows we've been through all that, and I know you would never harm anyone because you are my daughter and I've taught you what's right and what's wrong, but it's very hard to explain something like that to the rest of the world. Many people still live in the Dark Ages, Bethany! I ought to know."

Bethany gripped the telephone, anger prowling along her shoulders, making her tense. The bruises on her neck ached. Ramona clucked and Bethany threw her a dirty look. It wasn't fair. If she was Christian, or Jewish, or even Buddhist, no one would make a stink about it. Say the word "Witch-Craft" and everyone slid at breakneck speed into Hollywood melodrama. Her hatred for the common stupidity of the human race flared.

"Pumpkin?"

"So what's your point?" she said sarcastically.

Carl Salem cleared his throat. "She isn't happy about her son's interest in your group. She's afraid that you'll somehow invite another catastrophe."

"I can't control Sidney."

"No, and we discussed that issue as well."

Bethany shifted in the easy chair, throwing her leg up over the padded arm. Ramona looked at her disapprovingly. Bethany didn't care. "So, Sidney isn't allowed to come over here?"

There was a pause, and Bethany could hear ghost whispers on the line. The grandfather clock in the hall ticked noisily. "Although hesitant, his mother has agreed that he can visit with you girls on Thursday evenings, but that's all. Working with Ramona is out of the question. For now."

Bethany didn't know whether to be delighted or disappointed. Sidney wasn't shaping up to be her favorite person. He made her uncomfortable and had a habit of getting her into trouble, but for Nam's sake she was willing to deal with him. Bethany kept her tone neutral. "Okay. What else did you want to talk to me about?"

"I'm staying here this weekend . . ."

Now she was disappointed. "Annabelle?"

"Yes, but I wondered if you'd like to come and spend the weekend here at the apartment. You could either catch the Amtrack train right after school from Philly, or you could take one of the commuter lines over the border in Jersey. Jersey would probably be a shorter car ride. I'll meet you at the station, but I need to know whether to pick you up at Grand Central or Penn Station. Then I'll take you out to your favorite restaurant and maybe a show."

Bethany brightened. "Can I bring Nam and Tillie?"

"I suppose so," said her father. "Of course, while I'm working on Saturday, and if I get called away Friday night or Sunday, you'll have to deal with Sergeant Laslow."

"Aw, come on Dad," complained Bethany. "We're big girls. There are lots of sixteen-year-old kids living in the city. They don't have a cop escort them around!" Bethany vaguely remembered Sergeant Laslow, an attractive but tough woman. Just what they needed, a drill instructor type. Then something else struck her. "Dad . . . you're not dating Sergeant Laslow, are you?"

The silence on the other end of the line gave her the answer she dreaded. "What happened to Beatrice, the psychologist lady?"

Carl Salem cleared his throat. "I had to arrest one of her patients. Ah, we didn't get along too well after that."

Bethany signed. Her father had the worst luck with women. They ended the conversation with additional arrangements for her w_ekend stay in the city. Her father promised to call the other girls' parents to get the all clear so they could go with her. Bethany punched the disconnect button, throwing the telephone in her lap.

Ramona set her book down. "Going to the city this weekend?"

Bethany nodded. Hecate, tired of inattention, jumped into her lap, kneading her upper legs vigorously. He finally circled and plopped down.

"Ramona will give you a list. I want you to stop at the botanical on 57th Street. I'm low on a few ingredients."

Frowning, Bethany said, "We may have Daddy's new girlfriend with us, Sergeant Laslow. She's a real piece of work. I don't know how she'll feel about going into a botanical. I wanted to go to that new shop on 10th Street. Even if the botanical doesn't bother her, she might have a dim view on a store that sells supplies to Witches." Bethany stroked the cat. His purr vibrated her legs.

Ramona laughed. "Isn't that the one you were telling me about that is right across from the precinct building your father works in?"

Bethany nodded, swinging her other leg over the arm of the chair. Hecate grumbled in protest.

Ramona closed her book. "If the policewoman works right there, then she'll be familiar with the shop already. There are all sorts of stores in New York. I highly doubt that one will raise her eyebrow."

Bethany wasn't so sure about that, and the more she thought about the conversation with her father, she wasn't overjoyed that Mrs. Hecklesdorf had given her uneasy blessing for Sidney to join Witches' Night Out. The last thing she needed was some dorky guy ruining what little social life she'd managed to create. She hoped he wouldn't start following her around. She touched her neck tenderly. Crap. She would need to be extra careful this weekend. If Sergeant Laslow or her father saw the bruises on her neck, there would be a lot of explaining to do.

Ramona put her book down and folded her hands over the paper cover. "Sidney will be coming on Thursday nights?"

"Looks that way," replied Bethany, picking at a loose thread on the arm of the easychair.

"You don't like him?"

Bethany removed her leg from the arm of the chair and leaned back, allowing the chair to unfold beneath her, raising her legs to a relaxing position. Hecate complained with a slight yowl. The grandfather clock in the hall struck the hour. "There's something not right about him." She shrugged. "He's strange. He talks to the air."

Ramona leaned back in her own chair and looked at the ceiling. "He's very gifted."

Bethany cocked her head. "In what way?"

"He hasn't told you? Then we must wait and see."

She hated it when the housekeeper answered a question with a question, coated with a statement of pseudo-wisdom. *Great,* thought Bethany, *someone else who had some sort of great Witchy talent, and here I sit, normal as day-old butter.* Just what she needed. A Witch whiz kid. At least she'd be going to New York this weekend. Maybe she'd find something terrific at that shop.

"Are you unhappy that your father is dating a police officer?"

Bethany looked at Ramona in surprise. "I don't really know. I want him to be happy. I know he needs a companion, but sometimes I'm jealous that I can't fill more of his life. I mean, I understand that I'm his daughter and he'll always love me, but I'm afraid that the person he finally picks won't like me, and then he won't love me as much. Sergeant Laslow is awfully stern. I'm sure she's a nice lady, but—"

"You don't want your life changed any more than it has already."

"Exactly."

"Sounds to me that this harvest season you will learn all about change."

Bethany couldn't keep that sinking feeling out of her heart. "Whether I like it or not."

"Precisely."

Chapter 10

Queen of Spades: Jealous woman

Thursday evening, Nam lounged on the couch in the family room of Bethany's house while they waited for Tillie to show up. Tonight she wore various hues of blue. "I told Sidney," she said, "that we normally use our weekly Witches' Night Out meetings for study, meditation, spellcasting, and the occasional Sabbat. What are we doing this evening?"

Bethany's brow wrinkled in confusion. "We were going to have our Samhain ritual tonight. You were going to write it. Did you forget?"

Nam adjusted the cuff of her blue sweater, then said, "I'm sorry. I guess I forgot. Couldn't we just make something up?" Hecate jumped on the couch beside Nam and sniffed her carefully. Satisfied, he plunged into her lap.

"You're kidding."

Nam hesitated. "No, I really did forget."

"How could you forget Samhain? It's your favorite holiday!"

"Not anymore."

"What's that supposed to mean?"

"Oh, nothing."

Bethany tried not to stare at her. Nam seemed to have gotten so much thinner in the past few days. How was that possible? Maybe blue just wasn't her color, but no one normally lost that much weight in a little less than a week. Or had she been growing increasingly thinner over time? And how could she forget Samhain? A red flag flapped madly in Bethany's mind. What was going on here? Bethany bit her lip lightly. Maybe it was just her imagination. She decided to change the subject until Tillie arrived. "So, you think Sidney's going to be okay?" asked Bethany, for now pushing Nam's appearance to another part of her brain.

"I think so. He seems awfully nice once you get to know him." She stroked the cat under his chin. "He's so lonely. His parents don't pay too much attention to him, though it seems like he's closer to his mother." Hecate tilted his head, a cat smile on his black lips.

Bethany noticed that Nam's normally shining hair looked listless, dirty.

Nam misread the expression on Bethany's face, quickly saying, "Just give him some time. I know you'll like him." Hecate slipped off her lap, kneaded the sofa pillow, then curled into a particularly cute cat pose.

"Are you sure you're feeling okay?" asked Bethany. "Ramona made ham and cheese sandwiches for us. Do you want one?"

Nam's unnaturally dull eyes rolled. "I'm just fine! But, no, I'm trying to watch my weight." She patted her nonexistent stomach, so nonexistent it was concave. No wonder the cat didn't want to sit in her lap. It was all bones.

"What weight?" blurted Bethany. "You're already no bigger than a toothpick. If I stand beside you I feel like a giant. Stop insulting me."

"Oh, I didn't mean you were heavy," said Nam hurriedly. "It's just me. I'm into the eating right thing." She stretched out her tiny legs clad in blue tights.

"Since when does eating right make you almost transparent? And how come you haven't brought Michael to the lunch table?"

Nam's fingers crawled over each other like they were live snakes and she refused to look Bethany in the eye. "We've been busy in the science room."

"Too busy to eat? Did you tell him yet? That you're Wiccan?"

Nam jerked, anger flashing in her eyes. "Michael doesn't believe that a woman should—." A bang and a loud laugh floated into the family room from the hallway. "I think Tillie's here."

Tillie blew in, her arms filled with snack foods. "You want this stuff here, or in the kitchen?" she asked Bethany.

"In the kitchen, I guess. Is Ramona gone yet?" asked Bethany, taking the bags from Tillie and heading for the kitchen. "She was in the living room last I looked."

Tillie trailed after her and the cat followed, nose in the air. Nam didn't budge from the sofa. "She's still there," said Tillie. "What's she waiting for? She's usually gone by now."

Bethany dumped the potato chips into a large, green ceramic bowl. "She wants to make sure Sidney understands the house rules. You know, no long-distance phone calls, no drinking alcohol, yada, yada, yada. And then she'll finish with the lecture of 'Ramona is right next door in the apartment over the garage.'"

"Oh, great," muttered Tillie.

"I know. It bites. Can't do anything these days without an adult hovering around." Bethany put the soda in the refrigerator and lowered her voice. "Have you seen how thin Nam is getting lately?" she whispered. "It's not normal!" Bethany looked over her shoulder, just in case Nam decided to follow them.

"Yeah," Tillie answered. "She looks like a starvation candidate to me. What's going on?"

"I tried to talk to her about it a moment ago, but she just got mad."

"Pretty weird," whispered Tillie.

"Do you think it has something to do with that new boyfriend of hers? She mentioned his name right before you came in. I'm really beginning to wonder about that guy."

Tillie munched on a potato chip. "I'm thinking the same thing. I've been asking around. Vanessa Peters meant more than what we thought when she mentioned him to you. Remember? In the rest-room?"

Bethany nodded. She'd filled Tillie in on that lit-tle fiasco.

"Seems he's some kind of control freak . . . and a sex fiend. Rumor has it he was suspended from his last school because he was caught messing around with some girl on a school trip. The cops came and everything. He tells all his girlfriends he wants to be famous someday. He even brags about the cops picking him up."

"Famous for what?" said Bethany archly.

"Beats me. Being a crazy, maybe." Tillie dumped the pretzels into another bowl. "Like I said, though, it's just rumor. Nobody seems to have any specifics and the girls he's gone out with aren't saying any-thing. Anyway, I can't wait to do the ceremony tonight. Nam always writes such cool stuff."

"She forgot."

Tillie's eyes widened. "You're kidding!"

"She also says that Samhain isn't her favorite hol-iday anymore."

"Nam not like Samhain? That's ridiculous!"

Several voices raised in tandem drifted from the living room, and the sound level seemed to be vi-brating against the wall of the kitchen. "That's aw-fully loud if it's just Sidney," said Bethany.

"Sounds like too many voices. Maybe Nam is in there, too," said Tillie, trying to look around the frosted glass of the French doors that led to the liv-ing room.

Bethany and Tillie walked into the living room, then stopped in shock. Ramona stood between a girl and a boy, and the expression on the housekeeper's face was not a happy one.

"Isn't that Gillian Merriday?" whispered Tillie.

Bethany nodded.

"Oh, man!" said Tillie, her hand raising quickly to her mouth. "Why would he bring her here? Tonight?"

Gillian looked like a prizefighter, her hands trembling by her sides as Ramona questioned Sidney. Her washed-out, limp brown hair hid most of her face. She looked bad, like she'd lost twenty pounds in two days, and those unusually tense eyes looked more like smoky holes in her head.

"This is not good," replied Bethany, advancing into the room. Tillie trailed behind.

"Sidney," said Bethany. "Why is Gillian here?" She didn't mean to talk about the girl while she stood right here, but Ramona stood firmer than the Empire State building. There was nothing she could do.

Sidney faltered. "I told her about Witches' Night Out." He looked over Bethany's shoulder. "Not now!" he said sharply.

Tillie rolled her eyes and Nam, looking like a tattered blue nymph, drifted into the living room, uttering, "Oh, no!"

"I didn't mean to! I mean, I told her before you gave me that stuff on 'to be silent.' I thought that we could . . . I thought . . ."

Tillie stepped forward, her eyes blazing.

Sidney's shoulders drooped.

"You could have told us in school today," said Tillie, disapproval thickening her voice. "It isn't fair to bring her here. You'll get Bethany in trouble. Besides, you know Gillian doesn't like Nam. We overheard her at Vanessa's party. Why would you bring her here? We never bring dissension into the circle, it simply isn't done. Bethany's dad has house rules, and one of them is no guests at Witches' Night Out. We were suspended at the beginning of the school year for allowing someone to come who didn't have permission from their parents. I know it isn't logical, but that's what happened. All of our parents," she looked over to include Nam, "asked us not to invite new members unless we get the parents' permission first. We agreed. Now you're making us liars, let alone the fact that we have enough trouble controlling the rumors at school."

"But I won't tell anyone!" wailed Gillian. Everyone turned to look at her. "And I don't have anything against Nam!"

"I didn't know . . ." repeated Sidney.

Tillie's dark eyebrows arched. Gillian trembled with anger, eyes large and liquid. She looked at Sidney. "You didn't tell me you had to have permission to come here," she said gruffly.

"Yes, I did," insisted Sidney, "and you said that it wouldn't matter. I tried to tell you, but you said . . ."

"That's not true," breathed Gillian.

"Someone's sure lying," said Tillie, looking squarely at Sidney.

Nam finally spoke up, her tiny voice competing with the chimes of the grandfather clock in the hall. "Maybe it was just a breakdown in communication."

Ramona grumped. "Doesn't matter what it is. The girl has to have permission to be here. She doesn't. She goes." Ramona folded her arms across her chest. "Ramona is not budging until the girl leaves. She can come another time. Just not tonight. Those are the rules."

"Please don't let them make me leave! I know they can help me find my mother's killer." Gillian grabbed at Sidney's arm, and he winced.

"What's the matter with your arm?" asked Tillie, leveling her gaze at Sidney.

He rubbed his sweatshirt sleeve. "Nothing. My dad and I were putting a new computer in my room and the monitor slipped out of his hands. I banged my arm."

The little hairs on the back of Bethany's neck stood up. "I think you should both go," she said quietly.

Sidney looked as if his heart would break.

"No!" exclaimed Nam. "I'm sure we can work this out. Please. Why couldn't we let them be here just this one time?"

"Maybe they can come over another time," said Tillie gently, "after Gillian has gotten permission from her parents . . . er . . . father."

Gillian's lower lip trembled, a tear escaping the corner of her eye. The expression of sorrow changed to anger and Bethany feared the girl would become violent, but instead she turned on her heel and walked out of the house, slamming the door.

"Fine!" shouted Nam, nearly hysterical, her thin frame shaking violently. "I thought we were sisters. I thought our main reason for existing was to help people, not shove them away!"

Bethany smiled at Nam. "Yes, you're right, but we also promised our parents, and we should keep our word."

"A Witch is as good as her word!" announced Ramona.

Nam's small mouth puckered in defiance. "You're supposed to know things! But you don't! You don't know anything. None of you! You're just playing at being Witches. You haven't got any power. You're just like everyone else, ordinary. Horribly, horribly ordinary!"

Tillie's mouth dropped open.

Bethany stepped forward. "Nam! How can you say that?"

Sidney stood between Nam and Bethany, shuffling his booted feet, his eyes darting back and forth. Nam marched to the front door, her face contorted with rage. "Come on, Sidney. They're just frauds. I've known it all along. There's no such thing as real Witches. If they were so darned psychic, they'd know right away about your gift. Oh, don't worry . . . I haven't told them," she sneered, throwing a nasty look at Bethany and Tillie. Sidney's face held a stricken expression. Or was it fear?

"I said, let's go!" She pulled on his arm.

Sidney stood still, as if in a trance. Slowly, he turned and looked at Ramona. "I'm sorry," he said, "but I can't stay." He sluggishly walked to the door, finally drifting out into the cold air. "Too soon," he muttered.

"Oh dear," said Tillie as Ramona firmly closed the door. "Now look at the mess we're in. Nam's gone!"

"Sidney should never have presumed," Ramona stated flatly. "Obviously his ancestors have never met me!"

"What's that supposed to mean?" asked Tillie.

When Ramona didn't offer any explanation, Bethany said, "Maybe we should have let them stay." She walked to the bay window and watched Nam's lime-green Tracker squeal away from the curb. A nondescript compact with a dent in the side followed after. That must be Gillian's car.

Tillie said, "I just can't believe Sidney brought her here! My God! You found her mother dead, for pity's sake."

"You can't blame her for wanting us to help," remarked Bethany. "Maybe we should have offered to do magick to find out who murdered her mother."

"The last time we got involved in something like that," said Tillie, "we were almost killed. I've had enough sleuthing, thank you very much. I just want to finish high school and get into college all in one piece. I mean, I was thinking about it on Sunday, about finding the murderer, but when Ramona said someone tried to grab you through your own bedroom window the other night? Nope. Not for me. I'm done with that stuff. My parents moved here to keep me from big city crime. If I go looking for it, they won't be happy."

"But Nam is right," said Bethany. "Witches are supposed to help people. We all took an oath of service at our dedications. We should do something."

"People grab at straws when bad things happen," said Ramona, settling herself into her favorite living room chair. "Your father will be very upset if you get involved any more than you are now, upset enough to sell this house out right from under you. Or have you forgotten what you told me the other morning? You can't risk it. It is one thing to help a person heal, it is quite another to do anything else. Ramona thinks you should keep your big nose out of it. If you ask me, you've done too much already." She looked pointedly at Bethany and wiggled her fingers. "Ramona smells a no-no."

"I thought you were going to your apartment for the night?" growled Bethany.

Ramona picked up her book. "I was right at the good part. I think I'll just hang around for awhile. You and Tillie go ahead and do whatever it is you had planned. I promise Ramona won't interfere."

"As if you haven't already," mumbled Bethany. "And what was that stupid, special gift Nam was babbling about?"

"I haven't a clue," replied Tillie, "and at this point, I don't think I want to know. Sidney has already brought enough trouble into our little group. If you ask me, he's not worth our worrying about."

Bethany sighed. "Maybe he's not worth it, but Nam is."

Chapter 11

Four of Spades: Journey possible

You know, tonight's the new moon," remarked Tillie as she flopped down on the couch, almost up-ending the ham and cheese sandwich on her plate. "It would have been a great time to do that ceremony and some magick." She shook her head and slapped a nubby, cream-colored pillow. "I can't believe what just happened."

Bethany sat down beside her. "Me neither."

"No sandwich?"

"Not hungry."

Tillie took a big mouthful. "Ramona makes the best food in the world."

"It's only a ham and cheese sandwich," replied Bethany, trying to keep the caustic edge out of her voice. Yesterday, Witches' Night Out had a firm base with three close friends. Today it was in tatters. Well, almost. She watched Tillie guzzle her soda.

Tillie took another bite of her sandwich, swallowed, and said, "Did you notice how Sidney said he hurt his arm?"

"Sounded strange to me."

"Wonder if it was him at your window?"

Bethany turned, scooting one leg underneath her and leaning on the arm of the couch. "I know it sounds stupid, but for a moment there, I thought the same thing."

"Nah," said Tillie. "Why would he want to hurt you? Doesn't make any sense. Besides, his old man has so much money, if there was a reason to harm you, he'd have someone else do it." She rubbed her fingers together and said, "Money talks and gets dirty things done so the rich can keep their hands clean."

"Maybe he's involved in the murder of Gillian's mother and is afraid I saw something. I mean, he did pull into the convenience store parking lot that night. Maybe he was there before me, killed Mrs. Merriday, and then left. They say that criminals often come back to the scene of the crime to see everything play out."

Tillie made a face. "Sidney is weird, but I don't think he's a killer. Besides, what's his motive?"

Bethany rubbed her fingers over her eyes. "I have no idea. Do you think Nam's really quitting the group?"

Tillie tilted her chin. "This sandwich would be even better with a dill pickle. Got any?"

"No. Answer my question," said Bethany.

"I don't know. She's been pretty strange lately. She looks sickly. I hardly ever see her in school. She doesn't sit at our lunch table anymore. It's like she's glued to that Michael guy."

"Don't you think it's strange that she hasn't brought him around us?" asked Bethany, playing absent-mindedly with the ends of her hair, winding it around her head, then letting it fall. "I thought she might try to bring him into Witches' Night Out, not this Sidney guy."

"Maybe she hasn't told him," said Tillie thoughtfully.

Bethany took the ends of her hair and crushed them repeatedly in the open palm of her hand. "Or maybe she has told him."

"Why do you say that?" Tillie took another bite out of her sandwich, her eyelids fluttering with enjoyment.

"I don't know . . . just . . . something. Like maybe he's been talking against us. Trying to separate her from us. The whole school knows we're friends. The place isn't that big. You know who runs with who. Maybe the rumors are true."

"He's not bad looking," said Tillie, swallowing. "Maybe the rumors aren't true. He's new. People make things up all the time. And you know how Vanessa is . . . such a snob. If he ignored her, it isn't beneath her to invent awful stuff. Who are we to judge?" asked Tillie. "Lots of people don't like me because I'm African-American. Let's face it, there aren't too many of us at our school. Just how many black people do you find hanging around Cedar Crest, may I ask you? He probably feels really out of place, but strong enough not to change what he likes just because everyone else does something different. I can respect that. And look at Nam. Her parents are straight out of China. Everybody in town knows that, and she gets crap for it sometimes, though she's been here since grade school. She probably befriended this guy so he wouldn't feel out of place."

"Gee, you're African-American? I never noticed. Wow!"

Tillie threw the pillow at her. "Put a lid on it."

Bethany laughed, then grew serious. "I don't know, Tillie. It's true that rumors can get out of hand, but look at the way she's been acting, like she's being abused or something. It really bothers me. I bet she won't go with us to New York."

"Why? She's been mad at us before. She'll get over it."

Bethany shook her head. "Not this time."

"So what are we going to do tonight? I don't want to do a Samhain ritual without Nam, even if we have to wait until the holiday is long gone," said Tillie, biting into the second half of her sandwich.

"We could do some meditation, but you just majorly grounded yourself eating all that ham and cheese."

Tillie put the plate down. "Oh. Sorry."

"Feels weird without Nam here."

"Yeah."

"I thought we agreed that we'd always be there for each other," said Bethany, trying to keep the sadness out of her voice.

"Yeah."

They both stared at nothing.

"What do we really know about Sidney?" asked Tillie. "I mean, he's with that Gillian girl, he hurt his arm, he's done everything the opposite of what we ask him to, and he's gotten you into trouble more than once. I don't know," she said, picking at the last potato chip on her plate. "He never talked to any of us before Gillian's mother was murdered, and he seems to talk to Nam a lot when we're not around."

The grandfather clock in the hallway struck the hour.

"I don't trust him," said Bethany. "I think we should find out where Nam has gone."

Tillie grabbed her purse. "Let's go!"

"What about Ramona?" asked Bethany, hurrying after her.

"We'll think of something."

Ramona was nowhere to be seen. The light was out by her reading chair and her book was gone. Past nine and dark, Bethany and Tillie drove by Nam's house. Although the light in the windows cast cheery panes of yellow on the front lawn, Bethany shivered as they peered through the dark, trying to discern if Nam's car was in the driveway or anywhere on the street. They couldn't find it, nor did they see the car that Gillian and Sidney drove.

"Now what do we do?" asked Tillie, drifting her car slowly down the street.

"Where could she have gone?" muttered Bethany.

"I wish I knew." Tillie turned right. "I can circle the block."

"She wouldn't have gone to Sidney's house," mused Bethany, "because most likely his parents would be home, and he doesn't want his dad to know he's taken up with the big, bad Witches, or have his mother find out that we didn't want him."

"So," said Tillie, making another right. "They might have gone to Gillian's."

"Nam? At Gillian's? That doesn't feel right—besides, I don't know where she lives," said Bethany. "The most I ever talked to her was to borrow a pencil in chemistry class and she almost bit my fingers off."

Tillie took another right. "What do you want me to do?"

"Let's check Nam's house again, just in case. I feel pretty bad about the way we treated Gillian. I mean, we all stood around her and talked like she wasn't even there. Her mother was just murdered, and then we made her feel unwanted and invisible."

Tillie tapped the steering wheel. "Rules are rules, and Sidney should not have put us in that position. We can't have just anybody in Witches' Night Out."

"That sounds so snobbish," replied Bethany, turning up the heat in Tillie's car. The warm air was comforting. She was in such a hurry to find Nam she'd forgotten to grab her coat.

"It doesn't matter what it sounds like," said Tillie, braking slowly as they pulled up to a traffic light.

"You know that some kids would try to get in for the wrong reasons. We're not well liked. We're not the preps. Some kids would tell terrible things about us, like the last time. That's why we made the rules in the first place. The only reason that we're not totally denigrated is because we're both in sports. If we didn't have that, you know some of the popular kids like Vanessa Peters would do their best to make our lives miserable."

Bethany nodded. "As if they don't already."

As Tillie eased her car onto Nam's block, she said, "Hey, isn't that girl getting out of that Mustang one of Vanessa's minions? The chunky girl with the red hair? The one that's always so nasty to everybody. What's her name?" She snapped her fingers.

"You mean Amanda Nevins?"

"Yeah, that's her. What's she doing sneaking into Nam's front yard?" Tillie parked several doors down from the front of Nam's split-level, quickly dousing the headlights, but she kept the engine running.

Bethany craned her neck, trying to make out the pudgy silhouette dressed in black that slipped warily along the opposite hedge. The only thing she could really see clearly were the girl's white sneakers. Why would you dress all in black and then wear white shoes? "She's carrying something," whispered Bethany. "She hasn't seen us yet."

"She's leaving something at the front door. Looks like a shoebox," observed Tillie. "You don't have to whisper, you know. We're in the car. She can't hear us."

Bethany stifled a giggle. "You can see all th... the dark?" asked Bethany, glancing at Tillie. "Geez, you must eat a lot of carrots."

"Ha, ha. Wait! What's she doing now?"

"I can't see! You don't think it's a bomb, do you?" asked Bethany fearfully.

Tillie snorted. "A bomb? Why should she do that? Besides, the girl's no rocket scientist. She failed algebra last year and had to go to summer school. Geez, Bethany, sometimes having a cop for a father makes you too weird."

They watched Amanda run back down the walkway, her white sneakers slipping into one of the flower beds that lined the flagstone, almost pitching her into a blanket of dying mums. On the street she dropped her keys and looked around fearfully, as if catching the sound of their idling car. She quickly snatched the keys off the macadam and jumped into her vehicle. Moments later she was nothing more than an uneasy memory and a set of taillights.

"Now what do we do?" asked Bethany.

"Amanda hates Nam," said Tillie, tapping her finger on her cheek.

"Amanda hates everyone," replied Bethany.

Tillie toyed with one of the exquisitely braided bands of hair at her temple. "It can't be anything good. Let's take it!"

Bethany drew back in surprise. "Steal the box? But what if it was something Amanda promised to give Nam? Like homework or a class project? What if we get caught? How would we explain that?"

"If this was kosher," said Tillie confidently, "then Amanda would have rung the doorbell and handed the package to Nam's family."

Bethany shifted uncomfortably in her seat. "I don't want anyone hurting Nam . . . which one of us is going to go up there and get it?"

"Doesn't matter to me," answered Tillie, a gleam in her eye.

Bethany opened the car door. "I'll do it. Just keep the engine running. I might as well add theft to my checkered past."

Chapter 12

*Queen of Clubs: Good advice
but watch for mischief*

Bethany clutched the box, panic seizing her tongue.

"Oh, shit!" swore Tillie as she parked the car in Bethany's driveway. "They caught us. I was sure no one saw you take that box!"

Bethany looked at the empty black and gold squad car sitting in front of the house. With effort she shook her tongue free from the roof of her mouth. "We'll say . . . we'll say that . . . oh, man! We'll just tell the truth, that's all. That we know Amanda hates Nam and we wanted to check out the box first, just in case."

"That sounds limp," muttered Tillie, "and that box smells. I think Amanda filled it with dog-do."

"If that's so, I'm not opening it in here!" declared Bethany. "The interior will smell for months." She tucked the box under her arm as they got out of the car. Tillie was right. The undeniable aroma of excrement drifted up to her nostrils. Yuck! Right before they entered the house she shoved the box under the wooden porch step. They'd check it out later.

They found Ramona and two Cedar Crest Regional police officers in the kitchen, laughing and drinking tea, one of Ramona's more famous brews. The cracked pig cookie jar sat open on the table. Tea and cookies? The smell of jasmine permeated the kitchen.

Both police officers stood up. The housekeeper wrinkled her nose. "Ramona smells something distasteful. Where have you young ladies been?"

"Just out driving," said Tillie quickly. "We've only been gone about a half hour."

"I think I stepped in something," added Bethany. She made a show of checking the bottoms of both her shoes.

"The officers are here to ask you some questions," said Ramona. "They have already spoken to your father."

Bethany felt her guts shaking. If they asked her about the box she would just tell them right out and go get the darned thing. That's all there was to it.

The first officer, the taller, younger one, looked at Bethany sternly, but the other fellow, a heavyset little guy with flushed cheeks, asked them to sit down and relax. "We have some pictures we want to show you," he said.

Tillie and Bethany exchanged relieved glances and sat down at the table. Pictures? Then this couldn't be about the box. Ramona poured them some tea and refilled the cookie jar. Bethany hated the leering face of that cracked pig's head. Tillie eagerly buried her hand inside his head.

"You're on the hockey team, aren't you?" asked the older officer, pulling a few snapshots out of his breast pocket and looking at Bethany.

Bethany nodded.

"Whupped Dark Spring?"

Relaxing, Bethany said, "Yes. We took the championship this year."

He nodded. "I have two pictures here, and I want to know if you can identify this man." He put the two color pictures on the kitchen table and slid them over in front of Bethany.

"That's Ranger Rick!" she exclaimed, looking from one picture to the other.

"Who?" barked Officer No Smile.

"The guy who came into the store after me," said Bethany, trying to contain her excitement. "The man with the pickup truck. I kept thinking of him as Ranger Rick because he drove a Ford Ranger. He's the man who refused to call the police for me when I found Mrs. Merriday."

"You're sure?" asked No Smile sharply.

She nodded vigorously. "That's him. How did you find him?"

The older officer coughed. "He was in a traffic accident two nights ago."

"Then he's told you all this," said Bethany. "You didn't need me to look at the pictures."

No Smile stood up. "He was a fatality, Miss Salem."

"We think he may have been involved in the attempted robbery and subsequent murder of Mrs. Merriday," said the older officer.

Bethany's mind reeled. "But that's not possible!" she said. "He pulled up behind my car after I was parked at the pump for several minutes."

"He could have circled around. Some criminals like to see the crime scene play out," said Officer No Smile.

"Where have I heard that before?" mumbled Tillie.

Officer No Smile glared at them. Bethany didn't like him. He reminded her too much of her father when he was in cop-mode: eyes focused, watching every muscle twitch, every facial expression, even the rise and fall of your chest while you struggled to breathe. She was glad they didn't linger over the tea and cookies. She knew the good cop, bad cop scenario as well as anyone.

Bethany let her head fall back on the seat, turning to look out the train window as the scenery sped by. The steady clackity-clack of the wheels on the track and the swaying movement of the car lulled her into a relaxed mental envelope. Dusk slowly overtook the skies in an amazing display of soft pink-purple light, the same color as the smooth underbelly of a pearly seashell. She was right. Nam's mother called and said that Nam wouldn't be going with them to New York. The woman's voice sounded strained. Nam didn't make an appearance in school today, either. Bethany looked over at Tillie, whose eyes were already closed. A gentle snore escaped from her friend's lips. Bethany smiled.

The box that Amanda left on Nam's front stoop contained precisely what it smelled like—dog excrement. Bethany wrinkled her nose at the thought of it. No note. Amanda Nevins was sure some sick puppy. The girl looked pleased with herself today in chemistry class when she heard that Nam wasn't there. Bethany almost said something to her, wanting that nasty girl to know that she didn't have a chance to hurt Nam, but then she thought better of it. They would be gone all weekend and if Amanda thought her plans were thwarted, she might try something else. Something worse. Bethany sighed. She just couldn't believe that someone would be so petty.

Ramona got them out of school early and hustled them over into New Jersey. Bethany had an idea that Ramona had plans of her own for the weekend and was eager to see them off. Who could blame her? After all, she was stuck looking out for someone else's kid almost 24/7. Although Bethany's dad paid her well, it probably wasn't very fair. Bethany never really thought too much about it. She'd been through so many nannys and housekeepers since her mother's death five years ago, she'd lost count of them. Only Ramona rose above the others, and that was because she had a personal stake in Bethany.

She couldn't believe Ranger Rick was dead. Before they left, Officer No Smile told her that Ranger-Rick had been out on bail for burglary, and that there was speculation that he killed Mrs. Merriday in an armed robbery attempt. Bethany didn't think so. She remembered her dad telling her that burglars rarely switched to armed robbery. Ranger Rick's specialty was houses, never convenience stores. She sighed. No pattern was ever perfect and there wasn't any other reason not to believe Ranger Rick hadn't moved up the criminal scale.

Still . . .

He'd looked scared. Really scared. Like he'd never seen a dead body before. Bethany knew what that facial expression was like. It was in the eyes, a kind of startled, frozen horror. No, she didn't think Ranger-Rick killed Mrs. Merriday, but then, who did?

Maybe Sidney? Oh, that was ridiculous! The kid had enough money to buy the town three times over and then invest in the stock market on the riskiest venture. He was probably just a friend of Gillian's and that was all. She'd known stranger couples. What a silly thought. Tillie was right, she was starting to think weird stuff.

The monotonous clanking of the train wheels as they sped along the track brought on welcomed drowsiness. She hadn't slept well since the murder. The pastel dusk turned into deep purple, a star or two twinkling in the panorama of the heavens. Wish upon a star . . .

Slowly, her eyes drifted shut, the gentle rocking motion of the car lulling her away from her churning speculations. Who had reached through her bedroom window? The muscles in her neck relaxed. Why would they do that? Her breathing began to deepen. Was it Ranger Rick? If it was, he was gone now and she didn't have to worry about anything. She sighed deeply.

No worries.

Chapter 13

Three of Hearts: Someone new

A dream world. Pretty colors. Soft sounds. Delightful, earthy smells, as if a rain storm just swept her moisture skirt on the emerald grasses. Bethany's mother, Annabelle Arneau, and Ranger Rick sat on a park bench, feeding pigeons, their coos dancing on the warm air. The sky above them had an odd greenish-blue cast. "There are fifty-nine stars," said her mother, holding a jabbering Annabelle and pointing heavenward, her slender white arm lowering in a delicate, graceful gesture. Her hand trailed over Annabelle's blonde curls. "She can't stay here," said Bethany's mother. "She has to go on."

Ranger Rick's eyes darted back and forth as he sat hunched on the other end of the park bench. "Gotta get me some," he said plaintively to no one in particular. "Gotta get me some."

Bethany tried to speak to her mother, but when she opened her mouth, nothing came out. Her mom looked just like she did on the day before her death: healthy, slender, beautiful. Bethany's heart constricted. A tiny croak tumbled from her quivering lips.

Bethany's mother smiled sadly, looking at Ranger Rick. "He hasn't quite gotten used to everything, but he'll be okay. He needs your prayers to help him."

"Gotta get me some," mumbled Ranger Rick, fingering the edge of the bench, absorbed in the wooden texture beneath his fingers.

Clearing her throat, Bethany looked at her mother and asked, "Are you okay?"

Her mother smiled, that sweet crooked way she would hold her lips when she found something secretly amusing. "Of course! The only things I really miss are you, your father, and the food, but I check in on you from time to time. Your father, too." Annabelle snuggled in her arms, a solemn look on her tiny face. Bethany's mother continued to stroke the child's hair.

Bethany nodded and tried to walk toward them, but found she was frozen, like a small snowflake caught on a frosty, metal post.

"Gotta get me some," announced Ranger Rick as he rocked back and forth. A few pigeons crooned, then flapped their wings, soaring into the air, alighting a few feet further from Ranger Rick. One bird stood quietly, cocking its head, observing poor Ranger Rick. "Gotta get me some!" the man repeated.

Bethany couldn't help it. She laughed. "What does he want?"

Her mother shook her head sadly. "Life."

The old woman with the third eye materialized as the scene with her mother faded away. An array of golden light coursed around her. Slowly, the old woman changed into a tall, regal African female holding a small babe in her arms. "You have the gift of second sight," she said, leveling her glowing dark eyes at Bethany. "Use it wisely. Don't assume that what you see with your normal vision is reality. It is nothing but your perception. Learn to depend on your intuition."

"Next stop, Grand Central Station!" announced the conductor.

Eyes gritty, Bethany blinked several times. Tillie roused and fumbled in her purse. "Wow! Here already! Soon as we pulled away from the station, I was out like a light."

Bethany tried to catch the tendrils of her dream. Something about her mother and Annabelle Arneau . . .

"Gotta get me some," said Tillie, blinking sleepily, tossing her mountain of intricate braids laced with red ribbons over her shoulder.

"What?" Bethany jerked, her mind flashing on Ranger Rick. "What did you say?"

"I'm out of lipstick. I'd like to pick a tube up while we're in the city. There's this great little store where—."

"Never mind," said Bethany, gathering her coat around her as the train laboriously slowed. The train windows looked like rectangles of pitch black dotted by the stars of city lights. "Dad said he'd meet us on the main concourse, by the marble staircase."

Friday evening rush hour and Grand Central was packed. Commuters anxious to get home scurried beetle-fashion on just about every square inch of the platform. Bethany almost lost Tillie twice. Nylon-soft overnight bags slung over their shoulders, they made their way to the main concourse, the luscious aromas from many of the balcony restaurants enticing their growling stomachs. The vaulted ceilings above threw back a thrumming echo. Bethany had to shout twice for Tillie to hear her.

Bethany's father wasn't waiting for them at the staircase.

"Now what?" asked Tillie as some guy in a fancy business suit carrying a black leather laptop computer case jostled past her, almost ripping her bag off her shoulder.

"Bethany?" came a clipped voice behind them.

Groaning internally, Bethany looked over her shoulder. "Sergeant Laslow?"

"Every time you visit you seem to grow more beautiful," said the woman, taking both Tillie and Bethany by the arm and walking purposefully toward the exit. "Your father got caught up with a case, so I said I'd be happy to come and get you."

Bethany tried to hide her disappointment. Sergeant Laslow was nice enough. She was trim, efficient, with short blonde hair and expressive eyes. Her dad could do worse. Correction—*had* done worse.

Laslow surveyed Bethany. "Don't worry. He's not abandoning you to my clutches. I'm to take you to the precinct. He'll meet us outside."

As they listened to the babbling of a celebrity on a recording inside the cab, the driver slid the vehicle up to the entrance of the Manhattan precinct building. Bethany could see her father waiting at the curb. He gave the cabby directions to her favorite restaurant. She guessed that Sergeant Laslow would be joining them for dinner after all, especially since her dad gave her one of his mushy smiles that he usually reserved for his girlfriends. To give him credit, he waited until after he'd asked the obligatory father questions of "how was Bethany doing" and "any problem with the commute?" Tillie said nothing, which was unusual for her. She seemed fascinated with looking out the windows of the cab.

Bethany truly enjoyed the dinner, despite Laslow's presence. In fact, it was kind of interesting, as Laslow was part of the runaway squad. She and her partner scoured the streets of the Village for underage runaway teens. Once they found them, they bundled them up and sent them home, usually to a little town in another state that no one ever heard of before. Some of her stories were funny and others were horribly sad, but they were real life, just the same, and Bethany appreciated that. It almost reminded her of the conversations between her mom and dad over the dinner table when she was a little girl. They rarely held anything back, believing that she should know the world she'd entered. Thinking of her mother tugged at the dream memory, but she just couldn't put her finger on it. Something about stars.

" . . . shopping tomorrow," finished Tillie. "Bethany?"

"Right," mumbled Bethany. "Whatever you said."

Carl Salem looked at his daughter closely. "Gathering wool?"

Bethany didn't like the sallow pouches under her father's eyes. The bland lighting in the restaurant made him look so old. So tired. A thrill of fear ran up her spine. What if she lost him? Then what?

Laslow picked up the conversation. "I'd love to take both the girls on a shopping excursion tomorrow. It's been awhile since I've managed to get out and spend some hard cash!"

Bethany's stomach gurgled and it wasn't from too much dinner. Her eyes slid over to her father. "I thought you were taking us." She tried to keep her voice noncommittal.

His eyes raked the table, his discomfort obvious, but Bethany could not will herself to let him side-step the issue. "Annabelle Arneau, isn't it?" For a split second she hated that dead little girl, hated her with all her being. Yes, it was unfair. Yes, it was selfish.

"Who is Annabelle Arneau?" asked Tillie.

"A dead little girl," Bethany replied evenly, glad she could keep her unpleasant feelings out of her voice.

Carl Salem continued to look at the white tablecloth. "I may have another lead. I have to pursue it."

Do I hear the word "obsession"? squeaked a little voice inside Bethany's head, but instead she answered, "It's okay, Dad," although it really wasn't.

Sergeant Laslow was oddly silent, but Bethany assumed that the woman didn't want to get involved in her relationship with her father. That was a good sign. Maybe this girlfriend wouldn't turn out to be a jerk.

There was always hope.

Chapter 14

King of Spades: Beware, stern critic

Bethany loved the apartment in the Village. Her grandparents purchased the building in the twenties, then willed it to her mother. In the heart of Greenwich Village, the area boasted its own charm, historically a place for all sorts of nonconformists, artists, writers, students, poets, and other motley humans who dared to be different. She loved the endless variety of shops, restaurants, cafes, and off-Broadway theaters. Although most traces of her mother were gone from the apartment (Dad said he just couldn't take all the reminders), it still felt like home. Bethany's old bedroom, however, remained the same.

Tillie threw her overnight bag in the corner and flopped down on the canopy bed. "I just love New York!" she said, running her hands back and forth over the white satin spread. "It's too bad your dad makes you live in Cedar Crest. Everything here is so exciting!"

Bethany circled a few ends of her hair around her finger. "The city has its drawbacks, like high crime and the private school I was forced to go to.

My parents didn't trust the public schools. I actually didn't get to see all that much of ye olde city, though I heard plenty about it. When I was eight they bought a house on the Jersey shore and he and my mother drove in every day. I wasn't allowed to come into the city unless they were with me. They kept the apartment building, and my mom had an office here. Sometimes we would do weekends in the city, but that usually happened when Dad was on a tough case and couldn't go home."

Tillie rolled over on her stomach. "You never told me your mom had a job. What did she do?"

Bethany unzipped her overnight bag. "She was an investigative reporter. One of the best."

"Then why did your dad move you all the way to Cedar Crest? Why didn't you live in the house in New Jersey?"

"I'm really tired, but I'd like to take a shower. Would you like one first?"

Tillie sat up. "Look, if you don't want to talk about it, just say so. You don't have to switch the subject."

Bethany tried to control her tremulous smile. "Maybe some other time?"

Tillie stroked one of her dangling braids. "Sure." Her dark eyes focused on Bethany's face. "Is that what's been bothering you lately? Memories of your mother?"

Bethany began unpacking her overnight bag, slowly putting things in bureau drawers. "Not really. Maybe."

"Come on," said Tillie, with a reassuring smile. "You can tell me. I *am* your best friend, you know."

Are you? thought Bethany. Could anyone understand how she felt? Slowly, she shut a dresser drawer. "I saw what happened to Gillian's mother. I mean, sure, I saw her after she was killed . . . but, I mean that I actually *saw* the murder take place." There. She'd said it. It was out. Bethany expelled a deep breath.

Tillie's eyes grew wide and her shoulders tensed. "For real?"

"No, in a vision. Before it actually happened." Gently, she sat down on the bed. "It's so hard to explain."

"Do you know who the murderer is?" asked Tillie, her chest lurching as if she was hyperventilating.

Bethany shook her head. "No, it wasn't like that. And then I had this dream on the train . . . ," she said, and proceeded to tell Tillie about the vision and the dream.

Tillie moved her head back and forth, her braids whispering against the material of her red blouse. "Wow!" was all she could say for several moments. Finally, her brow furrowed, she said, "I wonder who the old woman is. You should tell Ramona. I bet she knows."

"I don't want her to know," said Bethany quickly.

"Girl? Why not?" asked Tillie, a sharp edge to her voice. "She could help you!"

"I just want to work through this on my own," replied Bethany.

Tillie made a "mmm" sound through her nostrils.

"Okay," finished Bethany. "I told you my saga. Why were you so quiet in the cab on the way to the restaurant? You hardly said anything other than order from the menu. What was up with that?"

Tillie stood up and rummaged through her overnight bag. "You're not going to believe this," she said, her back to Bethany. "But I was sure that I saw Michael Raines, with his arm around Nam, standing behind your dad when we picked him up at the precinct."

Bethany made a face as Tillie turned around. "That can't be right. There are millions of people in New York City, and I'm sure half of them look like somebody. You must've been mistaken. Why would they be here, and behind my dad no less?"

Tillie bundled her pajamas under her arm. "Yeah, you're probably right. It's too late now, but I'm going to call Nam in the morning. Just in case. If you don't mind," she said, grabbing her toothbrush, "I'm going to head for the shower."

Bethany padded into her father's haven, the office that once upon a time belonged to her mother. She was pleased to see that he'd re-hung the awards her mother won throughout her career. That was a good sign. He didn't hear her come in, his head bent over the large oak desk, the crown of his silver hair illuminated by the soft yellow glow of the desk lamp. The rest of the room held pockets of sooty shadows that fluttered like bird's wings as she sat quietly behind him. She mentally kicked herself for not knocking at the doorway. Oh well, when he was in this deep concentrating on a case, a bomb could go off and he wouldn't hear it. He probably wouldn't have heard her knock anyway.

He tapped his pencil several times on the edge of a manila file folder.

"If you can talk," said Bethany, "I can listen. Really got you stumped, huh?"

Maybe it was the close proximity of her voice, or perhaps the sound of the screeching pipes as Tillie turned on the water in the bathroom, but her father jerked and then slowly turned around. "Your mother used to say that to me," he said kindly. "When I had an especially bad one."

Bethany nodded, leaning over the back of his chair and patting the top of his head. "I think I can remember that." The smell of his Old Spice aftershave brought back pleasant memories of childhood.

"I'm sorry I wasn't very attentive to you this evening," he said, turning his chair around to face her. "I just can't help but think this little girl could have been you when you were that age. I know it's silly. . . ." He stood, stretched, and walked over to the window, hands clasped behind his back. His gaze traveled out over the sparkling city. "Somewhere out there she met a monster."

"Then I guess it's up to you to catch the beast," said Bethany, holding onto the back of the empty chair. This time she meant it.

"Your mother would have said that, too."

Bethany didn't answer.

"What do you think of Sergeant Laslow?"

That took her by surprise. Segue from mother to new girlfriend. It was inevitable, she supposed. "I like her well enough. She's better than some." Bethany traced a finger down the arm of the wooden chair.

Her father continued to stare out the window. "And worse than others?"

"I didn't say that. She's a little . . . younger than you."

"A few years. She holds her age well."

Bethany spun the chair slowly. "Should I be worried?"

"Not yet. Much, much too soon."

Bethany sat down in the padded chair beside the desk, easing her head back, trying to work out a kink that suddenly tightened the muscles in her neck. Since her mother died, Carl Salem's luck with women was abysmal. Sometimes, although she didn't get to see him much lately, Bethany felt more like his mother than his daughter. Disconcerting. *He's supposed to be raising me*, she thought grimly, *not the other way around.*

He walked back to the desk, sat down, and swiveled his chair to face her. "How are you doing?"

Bethany shrugged. "Fine."

"No. Really. It wasn't pleasant finding Mrs. Merriday, was it?"

She felt tears push at the corners of her eyes, but fought them back. "She looked so—."

"Dead."

Bethany nodded and bit her lip.

"Haven't solved the case, have they?"

"No." She took a deep breath. "I did talk to those police officers."

Carl Salem ran his blunt finger over the crease at his trouser knee. "They treat you okay?"

Bethany laughed, a hollow, shaky sound. "I didn't like Officer No Smile but the other guy was okay."

"No Smile?"

Easing back in the chair, she answered, "The tall guy that refused to crack anything. He reminded me of you."

"That's not so good."

Bethany laughed. "No, like when you're hot on a lead. Real intense. Watching everything. It's unnerving, even if you haven't done anything wrong."

The swivel chair creaked as he shifted. "Oh."

"I think the police believe Ranger Rick killed Mrs. Merriday."

It was his turn to laugh. "You remind me so much of your mother sometimes. She used to make up amusing names for people. Who is Ranger Rick?"

"The guy who wouldn't call the police for me."

"The man that died in the traffic accident?"

Bethany ran her fingers through the hair at her temples. "That's the one. They think he killed Mrs. Merriday, but that's just not right."

Carl Salem leaned forward, his eyes glittering in the low light. "Why do you think that?"

Once a cop, always a cop thought Bethany, recognizing her father's interest. "Because of the way he looked at Mrs. Merriday all messed up on the floor. He was scared. Really and truly scared. I know that feeling. I've been there. You can't fake that expression."

"Did you say anything to the men that interviewed you?"

Bethany shook her head. "They wouldn't have believed me. I'm sixteen, remember? Nobody listens to a teenager's hunch."

Carl Salem frowned. "Anything else unusual?"

She rubbed her neck and yawned. "Well . . . the cash register wasn't disturbed, and the room to the convenience store office was locked, and there were no marks on the door. If it was robbery, they didn't get anything. At least, not that I know of. You know the police," she smiled crookedly, "they don't tell the newspapers everything. They may be holding information I don't know anything about."

He nodded, then looked at her intently. "Nothing else happening?"

Bethany shifted uncomfortably. She didn't want to lie, but she couldn't bring herself to say any more. She wasn't about to tell him about the strangling incident at her bedroom window. A terrible thought struck her—what if Ranger Rick's accident wasn't a roll of the dice on the highway after all? What if it was murder?

"Bethany?" Her father's voice sounded worried. "Are you sure you're okay?"

She avoided his gaze and nodded. He didn't look convinced.

"Why didn't Nam come with you this weekend?" he asked. "I okayed it with her parents. Everything all right?"

"We had a fight. Sort of. It's not important. I'm sure we'll patch it up." She turned to look out the windows of her dad's office, the city lights winking to their own symphony of life. A lone cloud danced close to one of the buildings, tumbled, curled, and turned into the face of the old woman. Bethany blinked and the apparition was gone. She silently wished she didn't have such a vivid imagination.

Before she went to bed, she pulled one of Tillie's divination cards. "Jack of Spades," it read. "Do not flirt with darkness. Beware of two-faced person."

Chapter 15

Two of Hearts: New friendship

They ate breakfast at Cowgirl Hula's, a strange little restaurant on 10th Street that combined the great cooking of the Old West with a Hawaiian motif. As with everything else in New York City, the odd was commonplace. Slate-hued clouds hung low on the skyline and, like most city residents, they walked from the apartment to the restaurant. No one with any brains drove through streets infested with delivery trucks, maniacal foreign-speaking cab drivers, frightened out-of-state drivers, and various herds of pedestrians, bicyclists, and the very brave on rollerblades. Bethany and Tillie loved it.

Sergeant Laslow met them in the restaurant as they were about to leave. "Sorry," she said breathlessly, adjusting a turquoise and gold scarf that had blown free from the collar of her navy coat. "We shipped one out this morning. Back to Kansas. We've been trying to get her to leave for weeks. I managed to hook her up with her favorite uncle on the phone. I think she'll stay put when she gets there," she said, pulling on black leather gloves. "It's nippy out there."

Carl Salem smiled, brushed her arm in welcome, and left them to pay the bill. The intimacy of his touch did not escape Bethany, and she wondered just how involved her father was with this woman. Her breakfast churned in her stomach.

"As much as I like the city," remarked Tillie, zipping up her red jacket, "I wouldn't want to be here alone without friends or family."

"They look at New York like it's a mecca of freedom," said Laslow, herding them toward the door. "Things are bad at home, or they feel stifled by adult rules. Sometimes they're just bored. They watch movies and television shows about the city and they think that it will be all better here. That the bad things in life will go away." She shook her head. "The sad thing is," she continued, opening the restaurant door and stepping outside, "the predators are waiting for them. And if by some great chance of luck the bad guys don't get them in the first few weeks, poverty will. This is a scary place to be cold and hungry."

Bethany ran her hand over her full stomach and shivered.

The precinct building squatted in the middle of the block, its gothic gray-stoned entrance reminding her of a medieval castle, complete with sculpted cherubic cornices. She wondered idly if the building once had a moat rather than the present set of formidable concrete steps. Her father walked up a step or two, turned, kissed her on the top of the head, then hurriedly made his way to the entrance, his dark coattails flapping in the slicing autumn air.

"So, where to?" asked Sergeant Laslow, turning up her collar to combat a particularly nasty gust of wind. The colorful scarf tendriled out, snicking Tillie on the cheek. She grinned, batting the silk away.

"Ramona wants us to stop at the botanical on Hudson. Tillie wants to look at some vintage clothing."

Sergeant Laslow raised a delicate blonde eyebrow.

"My mother collects it," Tillie said. "Go figure."

"And there's a new shop down the block," Bethany pointed to her left, "called the Witches' Attic." She held her breath, wondering about Sergeant Laslow's reaction to that one, but Laslow turned her face in the opposite direction and Bethany didn't catch it.

Laslow walked to the curb and hailed a cab, saying, "Let's start with the vintage clothing. There's a great shop in Soho."

Most of the buying accomplished, they ate lunch at one of those movie-star hangouts, but both girls were disappointed that none of the pretty people seemed to want to brave the chilly gusts pumping across the Hudson River. Sergeant Laslow just laughed at their disgruntled mutterings.

Actually, it was fun having Sergeant Laslow along. She knew all sorts of historical tidbits and although Bethany was familiar with the city, she didn't resent the woman's presence. She was sure, though, her luck was about to change as they stood in front of the Witches' Attic. Laslow definitely did not want to go in.

"Oh, come on!" urged Tillie, pulling at the woman's arm. "They don't bite in there, I promise!"

Still, Sergeant Laslow hung back, and Bethany's stomach started to sour. If she was afraid of a place like this, or worse, hated it, then her views would definitely mess up Bethany's life. After all, her dad was dating this woman. This morning Bethany found some of Sergeant Laslow's cosmetics in the medicine cabinet at the apartment. Not a good sign, though there wasn't enough there to signal ultimate takeover.

"It's too cold to stand out here," declared Tillie, the wind tossing her braids crazily around her head in Medusa fashion. "If it's that big a deal to you, we won't go in." It was obvious that Tillie had fallen in love with Sergeant Laslow. This was really not good, not good at all. *Some best friend,* thought Bethany caustically.

Bethany threw Tillie a dirty look. "I've been counting on going to this store since I heard it opened," she said firmly. "I'm not about to bypass it because Sergeant Laslow is afraid to go in."

To her surprise, Laslow laughed, but refused to budge from the windy pavement. Tillie's dark eyes radiated distress.

"Tell you what," said Sergeant Laslow, fighting with the turquoise and gold scarf. "I'll go down to the corner and get a cup of coffee if you two promise me," she looked at them sternly, "*promise me* that you'll go in this store and not come out until I get back. I gave your father my word that I'd stick with you all day, and I don't want to break my promise."

"If Dad thinks the city is so bad, I can't understand why he still works here," said Bethany.

Laslow's smile was a little sad. "Thanks to bad movies, politics, and journalistic sensationalism, too many people from out of town think that all sorts of lurid creatures lurk in the doorways just waiting to pounce on the unsuspecting."

"And you're telling us that we really don't have to be concerned about it?" asked Tillie. "If that's the case, why are you worried about leaving us for a few minutes?"

Laslow shifted her weight. "Let's put it this way. New York City is number fifteen on the nationwide city crime list. Your father is right to be protective. We do have the occasional monster," replied Laslow. "And I'm the occasional monster eater, when it comes to you two." She smiled.

The girls laughed.

"So, promise me."

Both girls nodded eagerly.

Sergeant Laslow squared her shoulders. "All right then." She shook a black-gloved finger at them. "I've heard a Witch is as good as her word." With that, she turned on her black-booted heel and strode off down the street.

"How would she know that?" mumbled Tillie.

"My dad probably told her. I found some of her stuff in the bathroom this morning. There probably isn't anything he hasn't told her by now." She rolled her eyes.

A little bell over the shop door tinkled merrily as they entered and passed a sign that said "Shoplifters Will Reap Ten Years Negative Karma" in black calligraphy. A musky, floral incense pleasantly tickled Bethany's nostrils.

"Ten years!" screeched a voice that didn't belong to anyone they could see. "Ten years!"

Both girls craned their necks, scanning the glass counters and packed walls of the shop. "What was that?" whispered Bethany.

"Customers! Screech!"

Tillie pointed to a big golden cage hanging over the cash register near a curtained area. A large black bird preened his glistening feathers. "Cute," whispered Tillie. "Remind me not to touch anything. He might screech 'thief' or something."

A small woman, hair jet-black, bright eyes matching the color of the amber beads she wore around her neck, appeared from behind a blue curtain patterned with neon yellow stars. Bethany's first impression was that of a merry elf.

"My name is Linnex," she said, her delicate voice matching her tiny features. "Welcome to the Witches' Attic. May I help you find something in particular?"

"Screech! Witches' Attic. Best Hoodoo place in town!"

"Hush, Rapunzel!" Linnex chided.

"We heard about your shop," said Bethany, trying to act as if she came to a Witches' shop everyday, "and we decided to investigate."

"Help yourselves," replied Linnex, sitting down on a high stool behind the counter and opening a book.

The girls began perusing the shop. There was so much to see! Books, candles, jewelry, oils, clothing, incenses . . . oh, and the place smelled heavenly and felt so safe . . . secure. The curtain rustled once, but Linnex didn't pay the movement any attention, and neither did the bird. While they shopped, soft drumming music filtered from an unseen sound system. More than once Bethany looked closely at Linnex. Her face seemed so familiar . . . but she couldn't place the resemblance with anyone she knew.

Slowly, Linnex pulled out of them who they were and where they lived. She smiled slightly when Bethany told her of her father's profession but said nothing, passing on to the far more interesting topic of Ramona. The girls finished paying for their purchases and Bethany asked if she could use the rest room.

"I don't normally let customers go back there," said Linnex, inclining her small head at the curtain, "but I guess it would be okay. The bathroom is behind the curtain, first door to your right. Just don't touch the candles burning in the shower."

Bethany frowned.

Linnex laughed. "I use seven-day candles for a lot of my spellwork, and I don't want to burn the place down, so I put them in the shower stall. It's solid tile so if they do fall down, no big deal. Just don't touch anything."

Bethany parted the curtain. The back portion of the store was cluttered with full and empty boxes, stacks of black tissue paper edged with gold stars, and piles of odd or damaged merchandise. There was a statue of the goddess Diana on the floor, and a large, clay rendition of a scowling gargoyle in the corner. A card table with a bent leg leaned in the back corner. An assortment of cracked coffee mugs dried on a wooden drain board beside a deep porcelain sink, stained and chipped from years of use. In all that mess, it took Bethany a moment to find the bathroom door.

A slight tingle of anticipation curled around her temples. She wanted to see what sort of spellwork a New York City Witch actually did, but when she stepped into the restroom door she found the shower stall came complete with a set of frosted glass doors.

Bethany stared at the soft glow of what she thought might be several candle flames wavering behind the glass. What did a New York Witch's spellwork look like? She hadn't actually promised she wouldn't touch the candles. Besides, she didn't want to move anything, she just wanted to see. . . . Did she dare?

Chapter 16

Jack of Spades: Do not flirt with the darkness

Cautiously, Bethany reached out and touched the glass doors, the bumpy surface cool on her fingers. Her hand slid around the chrome, then touched the handle. She pulled gently but, as all shower doors are wont to do, the magnetic catch stuck. Bethany tugged harder and the door opened with a clang and a rattle of glass. She looked fearfully over her shoulder, holding her breath, but didn't hear anyone beyond the restroom door. *Don't be silly,* she thought, *it's not like you're planning to wreck it or anything. I just want to take a quick peek . . .* but she reached over and snicked the lock of the bathroom door anyway.

Slowly, her heart beating wildly, she eased open the glass door of the shower, aware of the rush of blood in her veins, the quickness of her pulse.

And almost pitched forward as her shocked eyes focused on the scene before her.

The floor of the shower contained an exquisite sand painting pentacle done in blue, black, and gold granules. At each point burned a black seven-day

142

candle, five candles in all. The edges of a photograph peeked out from under a pile of black sand in the center. The candles must have been going for several days, the flames dancing deep within their once-clear glass casings that now looked like miniature chimneys coated with soot.

What sort of spell was this? She held her hands over the center, but couldn't detect any vibrations. Her mind raced through Ramona's teachings and the books she'd read, trying to remember the odd sand symbols surrounding the pentacle. There was the astrological sign for Mars, the planet of action and war, but the rest of the meanings for the remaining symbols escaped her. Why couldn't she feel the magick here? Her eyes drifted over the once-white tile walls, now blackened from the burning candles. From the condition of the tile, Linnex must have cast more than one spell in this postage stamp-sized bathroom. Eyes wide, she gazed at the flickering candles, trying to sense the motion of the unseen. Nothing. Did this woman not have any power? She tried again, holding her trembling palms as close to the drawings as possible, the flames of the candles nearly singeing her palms. A void. A vacuum.

Her shoulder muscles tingled uneasily. There must be something here . . .

Whose photograph was hidden under the mound of black sand? She couldn't stop herself. With trembling fingers she reached out and brushed the sand away. The focus of the work sent horrific chills up her spine, almost stopping the heart within her that a moment ago beat so furiously.

A little girl's face smiled up at her. Burnished curls. Eyes as blue as cornflowers in a sun-gold field. It was a picture of Annabelle Arneau, the little girl that, in death, captured her father's total attention.

This was an identical picture to the one contained in her father's file. What was this Linnex woman into? Child snatching? Worse—murder? Was this a trophy? Some serial killers took trophies, she thought as she checked the scattered mound of sand with gritty fingers. Nothing. Her eyes swept the shower stall for body parts or jewelry, but found none. This couldn't be right! Harming a child was against all the laws that governed the Wicca, even Bethany knew that, and Ramona certainly pounded the ordains of her religion into Bethany's head at every opportunity.

Bethany bent closer to the sand drawings. There. What was that? Something white under the candle set at the top of the pentacle, or at least, it was once white. She carefully moved the candle and poked a piece of dirty cloth with her finger. What . . . she drew it closer and picked it up. A small sock, caked with dried blood and black sand. Bile rose in her throat.

Bethany's fear changed to anger. How dare this woman do such a terrible thing! She thought about the spell that she, herself, had cast. The spell asking for information about Annabelle. Here it was! But what should she do now? Leave it? Destroy it? She rubbed moist palms on her blue-jeaned thighs. What to do? How long had she been in here? A few minutes? Longer? She had to do something!

But what if she was wrong? What did her intuition tell her? Goddess, she couldn't think straight. Usually insight came to her in a calm, peaceful feeling, not overridden by emotion. She was upset. She couldn't think. She thought she heard someone calling her name. Her chance to stop this horrible mess would be lost. What to do? A tiny part of her believed that the spell was okay, but fear and hatred of the monster that killed Annabelle rose within her.

She clenched her jaw, took a deep breath, and blew out the candles, whispering, "I snuff you out. I release the energy. I send it back. I call reverse to this evil curse!" as each flame sputtered and died. Then she sat on her haunches and said the words so many times her mouth dried out and her tongue grew thick. She snatched the picture and brushed it off, finally sticking it in the pocket of her jeans. Quickly she knocked over the candles and destroyed the sand painting, obliterating the design. With her finger she drew an equal-armed cross in the sand, sealing her own work. "Take that!" she muttered, brushing off her hands.

It wasn't until she made her way quickly to the front of the store that she realized exactly what she'd done. Ruining another Witch's work, breaking her word of honor that she wouldn't touch it . . . well . . .

she didn't exactly say she wouldn't . . . and if the woman was doing something evil, no, not if—she was doing something evil. Why else would that child's picture be there, covered with black sand, surrounded by black candles? Why else would there be a piece of bloody clothing? She should have taken that and given it to her father. But it was too late! She couldn't go back, she'd already been gone long enough. Bethany wasn't really stupid enough to think she could take on Linnex. Her chest constricted. Wasn't that exactly what she'd just done? Declared war on one of her own kind? She snorted. Linnex wasn't a real Witch. There was no power in that drawing. She was just a sick, perverted woman playing a dangerous game.

Tillie stood in front of a bulletin board, looking at all the ads. "Hey! They have classes here on the weekends. All sorts of neat stuff. I wouldn't mind taking the meditation class."

Bethany smiled sweetly at Linnex and gathered up her packages. She intended to burn everything she'd paid for when she got back to the apartment. And she would tell her father. If this wasn't a good lead, she didn't know what was! "We'll have to check into that. We gotta go," she said to Tillie, trying to keep her voice light.

"In such a hurry?" asked Linnex. She seemed genuinely disappointed. "Tillie was telling me about your vision."

Bethany looked frantically at Tillie. What if her friend mentioned about the dream? About Annabelle? Oh my stars! They had to get out of here. "We've got to go," she said firmly, trying to grab Tillie's arm. "I think I see Laslow . . ." she looked over her shoulder toward the front of the store.

Tillie clutched her large bag of purchases. "There's someone waiting outside for us, and I bet she's frozen solid," said Tillie, following the fast-paced Bethany to the front door.

"I see her," lied Bethany.

"Where?" asked Tillie. "She's not out there," she said, pressing her face close to the glass. "Maybe she went back for another cup of coffee."

They had to get out of there before Linnex checked the bathroom. Bethany's stomach cramped. "Maybe we should go out and look for her," she said nervously, her hand on the door.

"Screech! Karma!" screamed Rapunzel.

Bethany's entire nervous system trembled. They'd practically told this stranger their life history, where they lived, where they went to school, who their parents were—the impact of their combined loose lips tore through her brain. Tillie must not have told Linnex about the dream, because the woman jabbered on about the empowerment of visions. How many times had her parents instructed her not to tell strangers about her life history? How many times had they cautioned her about the dangers of the city? The impact of her stupidity rocked her to the very core. She tried to drag Tillie out the door.

"No, she made us promise to stay here," insisted Tillie. "We gave our word."

Bethany elbowed her. "We've got to go!"

"Ow!" growled Tillie. "What did you do that for? That hurt!" She dropped one of her packages, spilling an assortment of incense and oil vials on the floor. Bethany lost her grip on the door and it slammed shut with a resounding bang. "Now look what you made me do!" whined Tillie. "I hope nothing's broken. I spent all of my allowance!"

Bethany bent down quickly, shoving Tillie out of the way and jamming the stuff back in the bag.

"Bethany!" complained Tillie, "you're going to break the oil bottles!" She grabbed the bag and finished picking up her purchases, giving Bethany a nasty look in the process.

As Bethany yanked opened the door a cold gust of wind slapped her in the face, momentarily taking her breath away. The little bell tinkled crazily and the bird screeched and screamed, "Karma!" Maybe Linnex already knew Bethany destroyed the spell. That stupid bird was ratting on her! Maybe he should change species. They had to get out of there! She grabbed Tillie's arm again and tried to push her struggling friend through the door, but Tillie just wasn't having any of that. She resisted like an angry bull.

"What has gotten into you?" she snapped, jerking away from Bethany. "I'm not breaking my promise!"

The bird screeched. "Laslow! Laslow!"

Tillie and Bethany turned, eyes wide. The wind whipped through the store, shoving papers off the counter and sending ads on the bulletin board fluttering madly. Sergeant Laslow leaned her elbows on the counter, cheeks apple-red, eyes glittering.

How had she gotten in the store without anyone seeing?

Chapter 17

Three of Clubs: Study the situation

You two look like I materialized out of thin air. There is a back door, you know," said Sergeant Laslow, unbuttoning her coat.

This is a conspiracy, thought Bethany, *and my father is dating one of the criminals.* She reeled from the thought.

Tillie, clueless of the danger, rushed further into the store. "Laslow!" She cocked her head, looking at the two women closely, her heavy braids decorated with red ribbons seeming to quiver on their own.

Bethany hung by the door. The precinct was only a block or two up the street. If anything happened, anything, she would rush right out of there and barrel straight for the place.

"Hey! Are you two related?" asked Tillie, furthering the difficulty of their escape by putting her packages and her purse back on the counter.

"We're friends," said Linnex.

"Not evil twins?" asked Bethany, trying to keep the disgust out of her voice.

Linnex frowned, while Sergeant Laslow cocked her head inquiringly.

Tillie turned to Bethany. "What has gotten into you?" She moved closer to the two women, and now stood right between them.

Bethany could not believe the stupidity of her friend. Now what was she going to do? "I think we should go and see if my father is ready to take us home," she answered stiffly.

"Relax," said Laslow. "I know you haven't seen your dad much this weekend, but he isn't in any hurry to leave. I just checked with him on my cell phone. He's out doing an interview. We're to go back to the apartment whenever we want. He doesn't think he'll be done until around eight. We'll all go out and have dinner then. I think he bought tickets for an off-Broadway show. It's only four now, so we have plenty of time. We could even go grab a snack, if you like."

Anything to get us out of this store, thought Bethany quickly. "Okay. Sure. I am a little hungry." She couldn't eat now even if she'd been starving for a week!

With the word "food" Tillie's dark eyes sparkled. "All right! I just love the food in this town!" She scooped up her packages and purse, and headed toward Bethany, a big smile plastered across her face. Why couldn't Tillie sense that something was wrong?

We could run for it, thought Bethany, but then considered carefully. No, if they ran away from Sergeant Laslow and went to the precinct, her father wouldn't be there, and no one would believe them.

Laslow was a favorite with all the cops. Bethany's father talked about the woman's popularity long before his interest in her. She was quick, smart, and pretty. Bethany was only a teenager. No one would buy her story. At least they could get away from this place. Give her time to think.

Laslow adjusted her scarf and buttoned her coat. "Why don't you come with us, Linnex?"

"She can't," said Bethany quickly. "There'd be no one to watch the store."

"Karma!" screeched the bird, cocking its head and peering through the bars of the cage.

Bethany tried not to tremble.

Laslow looked at Linnex, and grinned. "I'm sure you girls bought enough merchandise to keep her going for a bit."

"Saturdays are usually good days," said Linnex, "but other than my two new friends, I haven't had many customers this afternoon. I don't know why I couldn't leave a little early. Just a moment and I'll get my coat."

She started for the back of the store and Bethany held her breath.

"Does anyone have to use the restroom?" she called from behind the curtain.

Bethany's eyelids fluttered. When no one answered, Linnex appeared from behind the curtain, tugging on a sheepskin coat with a black and white zebra-striped poncho on top. "I can't abide the cold," she said, her little voice fluting merrily.

The air released from Bethany's lungs with an audible whoosh. Linnex must not have checked the spell in the bathroom. She would've said something, screamed out in alarm to alert Laslow. Maybe it was good that Linnex was going with them. If they left her, as soon as she discovered the mess in the bathroom she would alert Laslow by cell phone. This way, even when they parted company, it appeared that Linnex was going home. She wouldn't know about the broken spell until morning, and by then Bethany would have told her father, and he would be looking into it. Relief washed over her. Her guardian angel must be working overtime. Besides, Linnex must not have any real power, or she would be able to feel something wrong with her work.

Linnex stopped suddenly and shivered.

"What's the matter?" asked Laslow.

Linnex turned and looked at the curtain.

Bethany's heart nearly stopped beating. The woman did know something wasn't right. If she walked back there . . . but Linnex turned to face them and continued to button her wild outer wrap. "Just a goose walking over my grave," she said, digging in her pockets. "I was sure I had my gloves . . ." she turned to walk behind the curtain, stooped, and said, "Here they are!" She scooped her gloves off the floor. "Must have dropped out of my pocket when I put on my coat."

Bethany glanced briefly around the store as they left. How could she have been fooled, thinking this place was safe and secure? She shivered. She had to get Tillie alone somewhere before she said anything about Bethany's dream. Telling Linnex about her vision was bad enough. Anger surged through her. She'd told Tillie that information in confidence. Why would she blow it like that?

They stood around the outside of the store, braving the wind while Linnex pulled down the double metal gates and secured them with a set of padlocks bigger than Bethany's hand.

"So where to?" asked Linnex.

Bethany was more than frustrated. She'd tried to lure Tillie into the ladies' rest room and Tillie wouldn't go. Then she tried to talk to her while they were waiting for a table, asking her to walk across the lobby of the restaurant to look at some pictures, but Tillie brushed Bethany away. She stayed glued to Laslow's side as if she were physically attached. When Laslow paid the check, Bethany tried to lead the way outside. Tillie hung back with Laslow, sticking Bethany with Linnex.

"You've been awfully quiet," Linnex remarked, brushing her short hair with pixie fingers and looking intently at Bethany. "Does it bother you for some reason that Laslow is my friend?" She put on her coat, then swept the zebra-striped cloak over the top as she walked to the wide, double doors of the restaurant. A few customers stared at Linnex's cloak.

Bethany felt like she was following a miniature zebra. Add a bush hat and a safari guide and they'd be all set to go big game hunting in the Big Apple. "I don't care who your friends are," said Bethany, trying to keep the harshness out of her voice. Only a few more minutes and they would be rid of Linnex. She didn't like the way the woman stared at her with those strange amber eyes.

Linnex shrugged, putting her hand on the brass doorknob. "I know she's dating your father. Is that the problem?"

Bethany straightened her shoulders. "He dates lots of women."

"I see."

No, you don't, thought Bethany. *Not by a long shot.* Bethany paused, staring right into Linnex's tawny eyes. "There is something you could help me with, though."

Linnex smiled. "Certainly! I'd love to help."

"I'm trying to catch a murderer. Do you have any idea how to do that?"

The woman's little face remained transfixed between a smile and an expression of horror. Finally, she fluttered her free hand. "Why ever would you want to do that?"

Bethany didn't answer. Instead she knocked Linnex's hand off the door and opened it herself.

They did not get rid of Linnex. Instead, Laslow dragged her along to the apartment. Laslow breezed through the door as if she lived there, throwing her coat on the couch. Resentment flooded Bethany's overloaded senses. She excused herself and went into her bedroom, shutting the door. Tillie refused to follow.

She watched the digital clock on her dresser click the minutes away, her anger, fear, and frustration mounting. Withdrawing the picture of Annabelle from her pocket, she whispered, "We're going to find out what happened to you and we're going to put them away, Annabelle. I promise!"

Finally, she heard her father come home. She'd have to be careful when she told him. Laslow, like most cops, carried a gun somewhere on her person. If she knew they'd been discovered, she might try to do something drastic . . . maybe Bethany should wait until they were rid of the women? But what if they escaped? She didn't know how much longer she could be publicly civil. If she let her guard down . . . Linnex was already curious, trying to dig in her mind.

A knock sounded on her bedroom door, followed by the muffled voice of her father asking to come in. Carl Salem entered the room, shutting the door behind him. He still wore his dark overcoat.

"I hear you've had a rough day," he said, worry lines creasing his forehead. "Have I done something?" He sat on the edge of the bed, startled eyes raking across the picture clutched in her hand.

"Oh, Daddy!" sobbed Bethany, burying her head in his shoulder. Once she calmed down, she told him everything, but her relief was only momentary. What would they do now?

Chapter 18

Queen of Hearts: Burn a candle for success

How many human expressions are there, thought Bethany, *to convey the emotion of stunned?* Her father's face seemed to be going through all of them. He bowed his head, closed his eyes, and splayed his fingers across his forehead.

When he finally lifted his brow, he steepled his fingers in front of his mouth, moved them to a prayer position, and then clasped them to support his chin. Bethany had never seen her father at a loss for words. He put his hands down and ran his tongue over his teeth behind a closed mouth. His chin jutted, then relaxed. His Old Spice after-shave permeated the room, but the normal comfort she usually felt from the smell escaped her. Something was wrong. Very, very wrong.

"Should we call for backup?" she asked tentatively.

He cocked his head, his face devoid of expression. "I don't believe that will be necessary."

"But Tillie is out there with them!"

"You remind me so much of your mother," he said softly. "Always a sucker for the weak, the under-privileged, the downtrodden, to the point where—."

"I don't understand," she said, holding Annabelle's picture tightly, the edges crinkling under the pressure of her fingers.

"Bethany, I'm touched that you love me so much that you would try to employ your magickal skills to help me catch a criminal, but a part of police work includes common sense."

"Have I done something wrong?"

"This case. This little girl. I've spent entirely too much of my time on this one, to the point where you felt that, to be a part of my life, you had to involve yourself. A father couldn't ask for a better daughter. I'm ashamed of myself, Bethany. I should have paid more attention to you." Her father rose slowly from the bed and took off his coat. His shoulder holster moved slightly. She looked at the heavy, latticed grip of the gun.

Bethany could feel her eyes widen. "Are you getting your gun out?"

He sighed, shoulders slumping. "You stay in here."

"You can't go out there alone!"

He looked at her sternly, holding his splayed fingers out toward her. "Let me handle it. Please, Bethany."

Okay, she thought. *He is dating the woman. He can do this. They're only friends, she and Linnex. Laslow probably doesn't even know. Or maybe Laslow was a plant. Undercover, sort of.* Maybe her father and Laslow already knew. By the time Bethany walked out there, Linnex would be under arrest and all would be well.

Her father left, shutting her bedroom door behind him. Bethany grabbed the remote receiver of her phone and rushed to the door, smashing her ear against the cold wood, her heart pounding. She held the receiver tightly. Any funny business and she'd dial 911 in a heartbeat.

Again she found herself watching the digital clock on her dresser, the lime-green numerals flicking away the minutes. Five minutes. Why hadn't her father sent Tillie in here? She should be protected, too. Maybe he couldn't disengage her from Laslow. After all, she couldn't get Tillie to leave her either, and she was Tillie's best friend. Bethany heard a slight screech and she punched in 9, 1, . . . and waited. A gentle rumbling of voices. Nothing threatening. The receiver started to beep in her hands. She disconnected. The minutes seemed to crawl slowly by.

The knock on her door gave her such a start, she yelped. Her father asked her to come out.

"Is it clear? I didn't hear the police come," she said, walking out into the hallway, following his broad back into the living room. Her first thought as he moved from blocking her sight was that her father didn't believe her. Everyone was as she left them, and there were no other police in the room. A crushing weight squeezed her chest. Linnex and Sergeant Laslow were sitting on the sofa and they didn't look afraid. Laslow's face was a stony white.

Linnex dabbed her eyes with a tissue. Tillie sat on the arm of the couch. It was the first time Tillie wore no expression at all. Perhaps Linnex had confessed and no one saw her as a threat?

"Why haven't the police taken you away?" she blurted to Linnex.

Carl Salem cleared his throat. A bad sign.

Tillie shifted uncomfortably on the edge of the couch.

Her father took her by the arm and led her gently over to a chair opposite the sofa. She raised her head. Even if they talked their way around all of it, she knew the truth. Bethany sealed her lips tightly and glared at them.

"Bethany," said her father in a quiet voice, "I'd like to introduce you to Annabelle Arneau's mother —Linnex Arneau."

Die. Die of embarrassment a hundred times over. Bethany sat across from them with her head in her hands, her heavy hair shielding her face from the awful sight of their staring eyes. The mortification. The shame. The disgrace.

"I'm sure we'll all laugh about this . . . later," said Tillie, patting her shoulder.

Bethany slunk deeper in the chair.

"Actually, I'm quite flattered," said Linnex, her voice carrying a husky edge. "That you would do so much for my daughter."

"It's my fault," said Carl Salem, "I've been so tied

up in the case. This was the first one I've ever shared with Bethany."

That made her feel even more miserable—as if he would never tell her anything again. Bethany tried to hand the picture back to Linnex, but the tiny woman shook her head sadly. "You keep it," she said. "Anyone that was willing to put herself on the line to save my little girl deserves, at least, to keep her picture." Linnex turned her head and burst into tears, sobbing into Sergeant Laslow's shoulder. Bethany wanted to melt into the thick Persian rug beneath her feet.

Naturally, they missed the theater. Linnex took a cab home while her father and Laslow walked down to a corner deli and brought back meatball subs, giant salads, and liters of soda. They played rummy until after midnight, though the game was less than animated and Bethany couldn't eat a thing. Tillie ate part of Bethany's sub as well as her own. Laslow left around midnight.

The digital clock in her room glowed a green 2:00 A.M., and Bethany moved her head uncomfortably on her tear-soaked pillow.

Tillie flicked on the bedside lamp. "Can't sleep?"

Bethany turned her back. She didn't want Tillie to see she'd been crying.

"You did what you thought was right," said Tillie softly.

"Some Witch I am," answered Bethany bitterly. "I couldn't tell evil from good. I didn't pick up that

Linnex and Laslow were friends. I reversed the spell Linnex cast. If I actually did it right, which I doubt, I might have ruined the chances of anyone ever finding that little girl's killer. Nam was right. I'm a fraud. A fake. I might just as well have killed that little girl myself!" Her voice wavered and the tears threatened to spill again.

"The only person responsible for that girl's death is the person who kidnapped her and took her life away," said Tillie in a matter-of-fact tone. "You know that."

Bethany sat up and clutched her pillow to her chest. "I just wanted to help."

"So who says you haven't?" said Tillie. "Okay, so you were off on your assumptions, but at least you tried. A lot of people wouldn't even care. Don't be so hard on yourself."

"I'm sorry I made you miss the show. I know you've never seen one."

Tillie smiled. "I'll catch one next time around. No big deal. You still want to help that little girl, don't you?"

Bethany nodded, a thought slowly forming in her mind. "I made a mistake because I didn't do what I've watched both my parents do for years. I didn't research. I didn't look into the background. I never realized how important it is to always get the facts."

"So?"

Bethany's confidence grew. "I'm going to tell my dad tomorrow morning that we need to do some homework. We brought our books along. I have some chemistry questions to finish. I'll tell him that I need to use his computer . . . and you keep him busy . . ."

Tillie held up her hands, warding off Bethany's idea. "Oh, no . . . reality check."

"I'll attach his case file on Annabelle to an e-mail and send it to my account, then I'll open the e-mail on my computer at home."

Tillie shook her head. "You can't do that!"

"Why not?"

"It's illegal for one thing, let alone how much trouble you'll get into with your dad. I mean, he might even lose his job if anyone at the department found out you got into his stuff and then sent it over the Internet. The World Wide Web isn't secure. Anybody can read anything."

Bethany waved her off. "That'll never happen. The e-mail accounts we have allow us to encrypt the messages."

"If you're so worried about it all, why don't you just ask Ramona when we get home to help you do another spell?" asked Tillie.

Bethany pounded her pillow. "Because real Witches don't just do spells—they're proactive! Ramona even says so. Besides, you know her opinion on not getting involved."

"Maybe she feels that way because she's been doing magick a lot longer than us. Experience does have its benefits, you know," remarked Tillie, curling a braid around one of her fingers.

"If people didn't take chances, then nothing would ever happen," said Bethany.

"Just don't send it over the Internet," cautioned Tillie. "Download it on a disk instead."

Bethany chewed on the inside of her cheek. "Yeah. You're right. But you'll have to keep him busy. I have a feeling he's going to try to get rid of us early tomorrow."

Tillie groaned and flopped back on the bed. "Did you save anything from dinner? I'm starving."

"I think they put the leftovers in the refrigerator."

Tillie pulled on her robe and stuck her feet in bright green frog slippers. "Want anything?"

"Nah."

Tillie quietly left the bedroom. Bethany could hear the slap of her slippers as her friend crossed the living room toward the kitchen. She thought about tonight's fiasco, and the painful feelings of shame and embarrassment surged around her heart. The old woman in her psychic experiences told her to trust her intuition—that things weren't always as they seemed. She made a wry face. Tonight's experience was certainly a testament to that! Why hadn't she listened to that quiet spot in her mind when she first looked at Linnex' spellwork? Why did she allow her emotions, followed by faulty logic, to override what she knew in the calmness of her mind? Because she wasn't used to flagging that feeling, that's why, and truthfully, most people were the same way. With the fast pace of modern life, it was hard to pinpoint true intuition, because everyone was taught to think instead of feel.

She vowed to learn to recognize that sensation the next time it surfaced, and to use it responsibly. Bethany withdrew the playing card divination deck from her purse and tried to shuffle. The Queen of Hearts flipped from the deck and landed squarely on her pillow. "Burn a candle for success," muttered Bethany. "Guess I have my work cut out for me."

Chapter 19

Six of Clubs reversed: Confusion

Sergeant Laslow hustled them into Grand Central Station, checking her watch. "I've got less than twenty minutes to get you girls on that train," she announced, guiding them through a small knot of tourists. It wasn't as crowded today, and patches of sunlight streamed through the high windows. The vaulted ceiling was a brilliant greenish-blue speckled with tiny lights.

"It took them more than two years and 175 million dollars to renovate this place," remarked Sergeant Laslow as she led them across the main concourse. "Pretty snazzy, isn't it? Those constellations up there are made out of little lights, each surrounded by 24-karat gold. They light up through fiber-optic cables with different intensity so that they look like the real stars in a winter sky above the city. Impressive, if you ask me."

"How do you know so much about this place?" asked Tillie as Laslow propelled them toward their destination.

"I'm psychic."

Bethany looked at the bustling woman out of the corner of her eye. Laslow hadn't mentioned the embarrassment of last night, acting like it never happened, but there were circles under her eyes and her skin appeared sallow. Linnex never mentioned if Laslow was a practicing Wiccan, too. Just because they were friends didn't mean they shared the same faith.

They rounded a corner, and Laslow said, "Just kidding. I used to date one of the electricians that installed the lights. I always thought it was funny because his last name was Starr. You know, he installed the stars and he had the same name. Crazy, I know." She giggled, leading them forward.

"So what happened to the boyfriend?" asked Bethany.

She shrugged. "Just didn't work out. Annabelle was murdered. I spent a lot of time with Linnex or trying to dredge up leads of my own on the case while I was off duty. Besides, he was the controlling type. He thought his woman should stay at home. My career is important to me. I like feeling that I'm helping other people. You should always plan your career on what you like to do, not what you have to do. When I work even though I'm off duty, I do it because I love it."

"You're not supposed to do that," said Bethany, "do police work on your own time. You could get into trouble."

Laslow paused. "If it happened to a close friend, what would you do?"

Bethany looked right at her. "Anything I had to."

"Smart girl," replied Laslow.

As they hustled to board the train, Laslow pulled Bethany aside. *Here it comes,* she thought. *The condemnation. The threats.*

"Listen," said Laslow. "It took courage to do what you did yesterday. Yeah, I know, you blew it—but who doesn't? Listen, kid, if you ever need any help, just let me know." She handed Bethany her beeper number on a business card.

"So what did you find?" asked Tillie, leaning over Bethany's shoulder as she sat in front of her computer. "I thought that your dad would catch you. He walked toward his den more than once. I almost had heart failure each time."

Bethany leaned back in her chair. "Annabelle Arneau disappeared approximately one month ago. She was in the park with her mother feeding pigeons. Linnex turned and claims when she looked back, Annabelle was gone. No ransom note, which figures because according to this, Linnex is deeply in debt. She rents an apartment and the shop space. Dad's note here says that Linnex is part of 'New York City counterculture.' If that's how they define Wiccans these days, I'm not impressed."

"Anything else?" Tillie bit into a cookie, scattering crumbs on Bethany's shoulder.

Bethany brushed them off irritably. "Annabelle's father is dead. Run over by a cab four years ago.

Only other close surviving relative is in California and estranged. Never even met Annabelle." Bethany lifted her head and looked at the ceiling. "I wonder if Laslow is dating Dad to make sure he stays hot on the case."

"That's really cold," remarked Tillie.

Bethany shrugged. "About a month ago he was dating a psychologist. Dad doesn't date a bunch of different women at the same time. He's too old-fashioned, plus he doesn't have the time. He can't remember to get his suits cleaned, let alone keep up with a busy social life," she said, trying not to giggle.

"But . . . he's a homicide detective," said Tillie. "And you said he was a good one."

"He is, but his whole life revolves around it. He's a cop 24/7 but, like everyone else, he isn't perfect. He can work through a case and find the minutest detail, yet he leaves eight cartons of milk in his refrigerator because he refuses to look at the dates and just buys new ones. Every time I visit I usually clean out his kitchen."

"Yuck."

"Life."

"I didn't see any milk cartons this weekend," remarked Tillie.

"That's how I know Laslow's been spending time in the apartment," answered Bethany. "That and some of her junk in the bathroom. The relationship must not have gone too far, though, because I found only a few things in the apartment, and it was all little stuff."

"You were snooping."

"It is my father. I have a right to know what he's up to."

"So you say." Tillie ate another cookie. "So much for research. We really don't know any more now than we did before."

Bethany scrolled down through the file. "He has a lot of interviews here. I'm sure if I keep looking, I'll find something."

Bethany practically tripped over Nam in her hurry to get to the parking lot. Nam, dressed in black jeans, a black silk blouse, and black boots sat shivering and crying on the front steps of the school. Most of the other kids were gone. Bethany decided to linger so she could be sure to sign up for volleyball. The weather warmed up a little, but it was getting dark, and the icy tendrils of a November breeze mixed with bits of fog slipped across the parking lot.

"Nam?" asked Bethany, bending over the frail, hunched figure. "What's the matter?"

Nam slowly raised her tear-streaked face, black lines of mascara painting her cheeks in zebra fashion, reminding Bethany of Linnex and her strange cloak. Long black-beaded earrings seemed to drip from the sides of Nam's head. "My project . . ." she moaned.

"What? Your science project? Did it explode?"

"No!"

Bethany sat down beside her, laying her purple gym bag across her knees. "Then what?"

Nam hiccuped. "Somebody . . . smashed it!"

Bethany's chest constricted. "Why would someone do that?"

"I don't know!" wailed Nam, smearing more of her makeup across her face with a trembling hand. "It was fine in fifth mod. I almost had it finished. All the kids said it was sure to win, or at least get something . . . and now it's ruined. I just can't believe it. All those hours of work. All that time . . ."

"Did you report it?"

"Mr. Hendricks, my science teacher, said that it probably fell off the table. Can you believe that? How can a twenty-five-pound project just fall off the table!" Her slender hands moved in an expressive downward motion. "He says I have to start all over again. I only have three weeks left in the semester and then it's the science fair. There's no way I can re-create all that work in so short amount of time. Mr. Hendricks says that if I don't do it over, he'll fail me for the semester!"

"What an idiot!" said Bethany. "Don't you worry. Tillie and I will help you put it back together. If the three of us work on it, I know you can do it. You should tell your parents. Maybe they can speak to Mr. Hendricks. He's a major dork to the kids, but if your parents say something, I'm sure he'll listen. Have them come into school tomorrow morning."

"They left for Japan this afternoon," mumbled Nam. "Something about my Dad's business. They don't care about me or my silly project." Nam buried her head in her hands and wept. "My notes are gone, too."

"Didn't you have them at home?"

Nam shook her head. "Mr. Hendricks asked us to bring in what we had so far so that he could check on our work. I laid mine on his desk. Michael put his there at the same time. Both notebooks are gone and Mr. Hendricks claimed he never saw them, and therefore they never existed."

"Didn't you keep a copy on your computer?"

Nam sniffled. "I did it all by hand. I was going to type it out when I was finished with the project."

"Did you tell anyone that?"

"I don't know. I can't remember," she said sadly, brushing more black makeup down her pale cheeks.

Who would hate Nam so much to ruin her project and steal her notes? Bethany thought she knew. "Is Amanda Nevins in your science class?" asked Bethany, her suspicions rising.

"Who?"

"That Amanda Nevins girl. The one that was so nasty to you in the bathroom last week. You know, the one that tripped you in the hall."

Nam shook her head, her fine, dark hair catching on her wet cheek. "No, I don't have any classes with her. In fact, other than in the bathroom last week, she's never spoken to me. Why?"

"Just wondered," said Bethany, helping her friend to her feet. "Look, we'll go get Tillie and then try to put your project back together. I know we can do it."

Nam looked at her miserably. Her face was so thin the bones looked like they would pop out of her skin. "I'm sorry about what I said on Thursday. I've got . . . problems lately. Thanks for offering to help me."

Bethany patted her gently on the back. "You think you've got problems, wait until you hear about our weekend! By the way, Tillie tried to call you on Sunday, but your mother said you spent the weekend with a relative. Where were you? We called because we thought we saw you in the city. Of course, that's ridiculous. I told Tillie it was foolish."

Nam physically withdrew from Bethany's touch. "I was visiting an aunt. In Philly."

Something about Nam's tone of voice didn't ring true. Somehow, Bethany knew she was lying, but didn't know how to tell her. Did Nam really think she was that stupid? That a friend wouldn't know something was wrong? Maybe while they worked on her project she could get it out of her.

" . . . gotta get me some," Nam finished.

Bethany stared at her. Twice now. That was twice. No, three times. The dream, then Tillie, now Nam. "You've got to get what?"

"I didn't say anything," replied Nam.

"But—."

Tillie wasn't at home. Her mother said she'd stayed after school for cheerleading practice. *So*, thought Bethany, *Tillie decided to join the squad after all. Nice if she would have told me about it.* Bethany stared listlessly into space. She promised Nam that they would begin working on her project tomorrow after school, then dropped her off at her car in the school parking lot. Why did life have to be so complicated?

Chapter 20

Seven of Clubs reversed: Deep talk

"Ramona wants to know why you are sitting in the dark on the basement stairs?" The wooden steps wiggled and groaned under the housekeeper's weight as she maneuvered herself beside Bethany.

Bethany answered, "I'm thinking."

"Strange place to contemplate life's twists and turns, mon ami." Her white clothing picked up the minimal light seeping through the high casement windows.

"I screwed up."

Ramona nodded. "We all do that from time to time." She straightened her legs, smoothing out the fabric of her skirt with slow, languid hands. "Want to tell Ramona about it?"

"No."

Ramona stretched her neck. "I see."

"Someone at school is messing with Nam."

Ramona's eyes flashed in the dim light, her shoulders drawing back in a challenging position. "Someone is trying to hurt my little Nam?"

Bethany told her about the box, and the project. "Do you think Amanda Nevins did both things?"

"I know how to find out, but I don't know how long it will take. That is the only thing with magick. It's not like on the television. The universe takes its own good time. One of the hardest things for a Witch to learn is patience. Sometimes it takes months to find the truth of the matter, other times it takes only a few hours."

"That stinks."

Ramona rose slowly from her seat on the cellar stairs. "So does terrorism."

The bright motif of Ramona's apartment gave a lift to the dull day. Bethany loved the wild rugs splashed with yellow, red, and turquoise threads hanging on the living room walls, the odd knick knacks, and the plush pillows . . . she wandered into the kitchen.

Ramona opened a cabinet and pulled out a black notebook, licking her thumb as she turned each page slowly. "Ramona has a recipe in here somewhere . . . ah, here it is. In the pantry is a large, wooden box," she said. "Would you get it for me?"

Bethany opened the door and pulled the chain to the overhead bulb, her eyes assaulted with bright light and shelves packed with candles, incense, herb jars, and a few things she couldn't name and didn't know if she wanted to. A large, intricately carved box sat on the floor in the corner. "You mean this one? The one with all the animals on it?"

"That's the one," called Ramona.

"It's not a box, it's a chest!"

"Whatever!" floated into the pantry.

Bethany grabbed the leather handle and began pulling the chest along the floor and into the kitchen. The surface of the box glowed with an amber cast. "What kind of wood is this?" She stood up and took a deep breath.

"Teak."

"That thing is heavy! What do you have in there, a dead body?"

Ramona chuckled. "Not yet."

"Very funny. It's beautiful," remarked Bethany, running her hands over sculpted lions, tigers, and tropical birds. There was even a giraffe and an elephant, and of course the scene would not be complete without a zebra. "Where did you get it?"

"It belonged to Ramona's mother," replied the housekeeper, taking a battered, spiral-bound book out of the kitchen drawer. "Almanac," she said, waving the tattered pages in the air. "Always check the almanac before you do magick. We need to see what sign the moon is in and what phase she's currently wearing."

She set the book down on the counter. "You look, I'll get my things together."

Bethany picked up the book, leafing through the pages, trying to find today's date. She noticed that Ramona used it like a personal journal, but it was hard to read the housekeeper's tiny writing. Most of it looked like it was in French. So much for snooping. "Okay, I found today's date. Now what?"

"Read Ramona what it says."

"Ah . . . just a bunch of symbols . . ."

"Ramona thought you've been studying the information she gave you!"

Bethany flushed. "I fell behind?"

"How many times have I told you? Witchcraft is fun and empowering, but it is much work. This is no game!"

"Don't I know it," grumbled Bethany. She hadn't told Ramona about wrecking Linnex's spell. She didn't want to admit she'd been so stupid. The embarrassment still stung.

As if thoughts could move through the air and enter Ramona's brain, the woman said, "So you had trouble in New York City this weekend?"

Bethany raised her head and looked out the kitchen window—anything to keep from answering Ramona's question. The sun had already dipped behind the horizon, casting long purple shadows across the browning lawn.

Ramona said, "When one asks a question, one expects an answer."

"Dad called you?"

"Sunday morning."

Bethany said, "Why didn't you say something when I got home?" Heat fired through her cheeks, warming them as if she'd stood in front of an overworked furnace.

Ramona cleared her throat. "Everyone makes mistakes, ma cherie. You thought you were doing the right thing." She brought the last of the supplies she wanted out of the box and closed the lid softly. "Perhaps we should get to work, eh?"

Bethany whirled. "I put my hands over Linnex's spellwork before I did anything. Honest I did! I didn't feel anything! Not a single bit of energy. I think I'm not cut out for this. I think I may not really have any power at all. There's so much book work! I thought that either you had it, or you didn't, all the fictional books say so. All the movies say so. It isn't fair! I didn't realize that it could get so complicated."

Ramona cocked a dark eyebrow. "Odd words from your mouth. You've raised the power. You've cast successful spells. Self-doubt isn't going to solve the problem. To be proficient in anything takes practice and study. If you are going to be in medicine, you must study biology. If you want to be a lawyer, then you must immerse yourself in the law of the land. Why should this be any different?"

Bethany puckered her lips.

Ramona said, "You thought that it would all come naturally."

Bethany didn't answer.

"Even athletes with natural talent must exercise, train, and enhance their skills. Besides, nothing is worth anything unless you work for it. Just like hockey, understand?"

Bethany nodded.

"Hand me the book and I will explain the symbols to you . . . again. The moon is in Gemini. This is good. We want to get information, to find out who is trying to hurt Nam. We want things to surface. Actually, Virgo or Scorpio would be better, but we must use what we have."

"Would we do the same thing to find Annabelle's killer?"

"You mean the person that killed the little girl? Yes, but that would be a far more complicated working."

Bethany thought about the spell she'd cast to find information about Annabelle Arneau. It wasn't so complicated . . . but, then, she hadn't gotten the information she wanted, although she did discover Linnex. On the other hand, she would have met the woman anyway, because she'd been planning for a while to go to that store. Logic ate at her swimming thoughts like an octopus after small fish.

"Let's just stick to Nam's problem at the moment," said Ramona, arranging several black candles on the kitchen counter. "Besides, Annabelle's mother has not asked us to help her. We need her permission to do that type of work. Nam, on the other hand, accepted your offer of assistance this afternoon. Big difference." She looked at Bethany sternly as if she knew that Bethany had already done work without Linnex's permission.

Bethany's shoulders drooped, and she mumbled, "You don't ask the police to investigate a murder. It's their job."

"Yes . . . well . . . the last Ramona checked, hiring a Witch to cast a spell for you is still considered a little on the wild side. You won't find us listed in the telephone directory under Investigative Services." She snorted. "Let's see . . . today is Monday, the moon's natural day."

"Who made up that rule?"

Ramona rolled her eyes. "What rule?"

"The one about asking permission. Who made that up?" asked Bethany, hands on her hips.

The housekeeper frowned. "How would Ramona know who made the rules?"

"Somebody had to. It isn't really a rule, is it? Asking for permission?"

"Let's just say it's a common courtesy," she turned and rummaged through a cabinet. "Now where did I put that allspice?"

"So you don't have to follow the rule all the time," Bethany stated bluntly.

Ramona threw up her hands and turned around. "Times change. New rules are made. Old ones are discarded. The Craft moves with the times. If a religion changes, it does not die. We no longer live in the old days. Eventually, you will have to use your best judgement. That is all I can tell you; however, if you interfere with another person's life, then you may be ruining their spiritual plan. We learn from our mistakes and our successes. If life had no challenge, then we would not strive to become better people, n'est-ce pas? And if there were no rules, chaos would ensue. So, we always ask permission."

Bethany would have to consider that one; however, she wasn't done. "But I am involved. I wrecked the spell Linnex cast."

"I think," said Ramona "—ah, here it is! The all-spicc!—I think that you've already done too much." She shook a brown finger under Bethany's nose. "I thought you said that you can't do anything? If that is so, no damage was done."

Bethany didn't like the housekeeper's superior tone. "You're cruel, you know that, Ramona? So which is it? Either I did or I didn't mess it up."

Ramona chewed on her lip. "You will have to call Linnex and ask her if you may right your wrong, but personally, I think you should stay out of the whole mess."

Bethany swallowed hard. That wouldn't be easy to do—calling Linnex. Maybe she should just leave the whole situation alone. She'd already done enough damage.

Ramona tilted her white-scarf-clad head and looked at Bethany with intense eyes. "We must own up to our mistakes. It is necessary to live a balanced life. If you feel bad about it, and you know what you did was wrong, then you must correct it. I think an apology is in order. Beyond that . . ." she waved her hands in the air, "you must decide."

"I was afraid you'd say that," muttered Bethany.

Ramona continued. "Back to our work. The moon on Monday covers things like children and family, so this is a very good day to do our spell. Nam is still considered a child."

Bethany frowned.

"And she is part of your magickal family. We want to choose the planetary hour of Mercury, Gemini's ruling planet, so we need to look in the back of the book to determine which hour on this day belongs to Gemini. Do you remember how to do that?"

Bethany was confused. Should she call Linnex and just apologize, or should she call and ask permission to fix what she ruined? Ramona wasn't being helpful. This whole conversation was one big riddle.

"Bethany?"

Bethany nodded. "I heard you. You want me to figure out which hour today belongs to Gemini. There'll be two, normally. One for during the day, which has probably already passed, and one for this evening."

Ramona smiled. "Then you figure that out. I'm going to mix the incense. We need a special blend." She began sprinkling various herbs into a heavy porcelain bowl on the kitchen counter.

"What did we need out of the box?" asked Bethany, handing Ramona her math. She couldn't believe she had to do a math problem to practice Witchcraft!

"We need a tiger-eye stone, that big one there, the pretty one with the amber and brown stripes. Then get out a black candle and a silver one. Once you finish that, carve a pentacle on the black candle and the symbol of Gemini on the silver one, then write

Nam's full name on both candles. Coat the black candle on the counter with protection oil and the silver candle with the Gemini oil. Concentrate on banishing negativity from Nam when dressing the black candle, and bringing information about Nam's enemy when working with the silver candle."

Ramona finished adding the herbs to the bowl, then sat on a stool in the corner, working the pestle in a circular motion, humming to herself. The harmony of her voice with the singing motion of the pestle stirring through the herbs brought a soothing energy into the room.

Bethany finished her tasks and wandered over to the window. It was so dark her own reflection stared back at her through the glass. She stepped forward to look past herself into the blackness of the yard, playing with the smooth tiger-eye stone, passing it from palm to palm.

"I need some fresh mint," said Ramona. "There is a little left in the garden. The frost hasn't completely done it in. Turn the yard lights on and I will watch from the window," she said.

"I thought you were worried about me getting attacked again," muttered Bethany, looking down into the blackness of the back yard.

"Not tonight," said Ramona, a slight smile on her face. "Your intuition is correct, but nothing bad awaits you down there."

Bethany didn't like the sound of that.

Chapter 21

Six of Diamonds: Clear path ahead

Bethany flipped on the floodlights, pulled on her coat, and descended the outside steps from Ramona's apartment over the garage to the back yard. A loon screamed and she jumped, her sneakered foot slipping slightly on the lower step. In her hand she held a bolline, the white-handled knife that Witches traditionally used to harvest herbs.

Autumn mist hung like torn gray gauze along the ground, shifting silently through the deadened foliage. The willow tree's stripped branches hung listlessly in the still night. Bethany glanced up at the apartment. Ramona stood in the window.

Bethany pushed through the ground fog, trying to discern the cinderblock rim of the raised-bed gardens that Ramona so meticulously cared for. One bed was reserved specifically for magickal herbs. The other held the table vegetables—or rather, what was left of them. Ramona pulled out most of the summer crop of beans, peppers, and onions around the first of October, but a few turnips and carrots remained. She found the mint separated in a patch by itself. If you didn't watch the stuff, it would overtake everything. A few healthy runners remained.

Bethany weighed the knife in her hand. She should have brought a flashlight. Even with the floodlights it was hard to tell the healthy shoots from the dead stalks. She bent forward, nearly sticking her nose in the plant. Something behind her snapped, and she pitched forward, her sneakered foot stumbling against the cinderblock wall of the bed. Before she could pitch forward, a strong hand caught her.

"I was only trying to attract your attention," blurted Sidney, shivering in a nylon windbreaker. "I didn't mean to scare you."

Bethany straightened her body and pushed Sidney away, brushing off her hands caked with wet dirt. "What are you doing, sneaking around my back yard?" she said nastily.

A chilly breeze rose from the direction of the Delaware river, carrying the musky scent of late autumn. The branches of the willow trees sighed. A brown leaf or two scuffed across the driveway. The November air was sort of like ice cream—chilly but sweet.

Ramona tapped her knuckles angrily on the window above the garage. A moment later she was pounding down the steps, a white shawl clutched tightly around her shoulders. "Ramona is calling the police!" she announced.

Bethany threw her a dirty look. She'd seen enough police to last her forever.

"Oh, please don't do that," begged Sidney. "I didn't mean to scare you. Honest!"

The housekeeper cocked an eyebrow, glaring at both of them. She crossed her arms over her chest. "Why are you here?"

Sidney bent his head, pushing his dark hair away from his worried forehead. "I wanted to apologize for breaking the rules last week. For bringing Gillian. I thought about it all weekend. I tried to call Nam, but her parents said she wasn't home. Did she tell you what happened last Thursday night? I feel so bad about it."

"I haven't really talked to Nam about much of anything," said Bethany, "except for the fact that someone destroyed her school project, which really isn't any of your business anyway."

Sidney looked genuinely surprised. "Why would anyone want to do that?"

"You tell me," said Bethany.

That darned loon squealed again. Did Sidney look scared? What was this all about?

Bethany said, "I don't really care what happened with you. It's Nam's business. If she wants to talk to me about it, then fine. Besides, she has other things on her mind right now. I'm sure whatever happened with Gillian wasn't important enough for her to share. I don't mean to be rude, but I don't trust you."

Sidney tried to reach out to her, but Bethany took a step backward, almost pitching herself into the garden. "Honestly," said Sidney, "Gillian insisted that I bring her that night. I never would have done it if

I'd known you would all get so mad. I tried to talk to you in school today, but you ignored me."

"Gillian said it was your idea," replied Bethany, waving the bolline in the air. This time it was Sidney that took a step backward, his head cocked, his eyes startled. Bethany ignored his fear. In a way, she almost relished it. "Look, Sidney, a Wiccan circle is based on trust. If we can't rely on one another, then it isn't worth doing. Right, Ramona?" The housekeeper didn't answer. Bethany turned. Ramona had disappeared. Bethany hated when she did that. "Just go, Sidney. I don't really have anything to discuss with you." She flicked the tip of the bolline in the air for added emphasis.

Sidney looked at his brown boots. "You don't understand. Something's wrong."

Bethany backed up toward the stairs leading to Ramona's apartment. "Something is wrong with Gillian, I don't deny that. She wasn't a nice person to begin with, and now she is dealing with the grief over the death of her mother, which to me just seems to make her nastier. You'll have to talk to someone else about it. Whatever it is, you can figure it out for yourself. I've got enough on my plate at the moment. I don't need you—or that Gillian girl in my life."

She turned on her heel and mounted the stairs to Ramona's apartment. She didn't look back, although she could swear that he was still standing in her yard, carrying on a hushed conversation with someone. Maybe someone was with him, hiding while he talked to her. She shivered and hurried up the steps. Forget the darned mint. If Ramona wanted it so bad, she could get it herself.

Bethany actually never worked magick before with an adult, let alone Ramona, who could be scary just being herself. They waited until nine (Ramona wanted to catch the right hour).

"Ramona prefers working alone," said the housekeeper, "but the only way you will learn is to work with me for awhile."

Thank you for the kind favor, thought Bethany sarcastically. Up until Ramona came along she was doing just fine by herself, but she kept her mouth shut. This past weekend had shown her there was still a lot she didn't know. She was sick of vacillating between thinking she knew things and worrying that she might not know anything.

"You missed Samhain on Saturday night."

Bethany groaned internally. "It's just been so crazy."

Ramona ignored her excuse. "The spell is very simple," said Ramona. "We light both candles, then you kneel or stand on one side of the coffee table, and I on the other."

Bethany got down on her knees and faced the candles while Ramona lit a charcoal incense brick, then slowly began to feed the herbs in the bowl to the glowing cube set safely on a clay dish. Puffs of flowery smoke filled the room. Smiling, Ramona lit the candles, muttering in French. She held the tiger-eye stone over the incense, and then the candle flames.

"What are you doing?" asked Bethany.

"Asking for the blessings of the Mother upon our task and purifying the stone so that it can clearly do its work," Ramona answered. She turned out the living room lights, then took her place opposite Bethany, kneeling as well. Her voice spiraled softly in the candlelit room. "I will cross my arms and you will cross yours, then we will clasp each other's hands, making the design of a figure eight in the air. Our arms will become the symbol of infinity, and the candles will be in the center, the stone at the base of the candles."

"Won't we burn our arms?" asked Bethany.

"No, we will be careful. Just put your hair back so it doesn't catch a flame."

Bethany did as instructed, feeling a jolt of energy spring from Ramona's firm grasp.

"No matter what," said Ramona, "do not let go of my hands. It will spoil the spell. Take a deep breath, and we shall begin."

Bethany did as instructed, concentrating on pushing any negativity out of her body.

Ramona began to chant quietly, "We are the old ones, we are the new ones, we are the Witches stronger than before." Bethany followed suit. Her hands tingled as her breathing fell into unison with Ramona's.

"I call forth my ancestors," said Ramona, listing off a variety of French and Spanish surnames, ending with her mother. She looked pointedly at Bethany, who at this moment could remember only the names of her grandparents and her mother. Bethany intoned their names and Ramona nodded with a look that said "Good enough for now."

The temperature in the room dropped several degrees, and Bethany shivered. The candle flames flickered, then flared.

Closing her eyes, Ramona made her petition, asking for information and protection for Nam. She rocked slightly back and forth. Bethany kept her own eyes open for fear Ramona would move too much and burn their arms. The temperature in the room continued to drop. One of the rugs on the wall billowed slightly. Bethany stared nervously at the candle flames. It wasn't as if she hadn't raised power before on her own, but this was different, and she wasn't in control. She didn't realize how much she needed to be the leader. This self-observation was unsettling and, lost in her own thoughts, she started when Ramona whispered harshly, "You're not concentrating!" It was true, her mind was everywhere but where it should be . . . on Nam.

She closed her eyes, but all she could see in her mind's eye was Sidney's face—saddened, tears, feelings of . . . love? Bethany shook her head and opened her eyes. The room seemed so very dark. She closed her eyes and tried again, willing herself to think only of Nam. She pictured Nam's small face and her almond-shaped green eyes. The girl's fine, blue-black hair. The slight body. Her penchant for crazy clothing. Bethany smiled. Yes, that was Nam. A cool breeze fluttered across her eyelashes and she shivered. Ramona gripped her hands tighter. Was something wrong?

She opened her eyes but the room seemed much dimmer than before. How was that possible? It was as if a sooty fog hung above their heads, growing heavier, taking shape. Nothing like this had ever happened when she worked alone. What the heck had Ramona called? Something in French that she missed? Ramona continued to hold tightly to Bethany's hands, almost cutting off the circulation.

"Element of air, element of flow, find the enemy, let us know!" chanted Ramona.

Bethany fell into verbal step, repeating the chant, allowing the positive energy to flow from Ramona to herself, and back. As their voices grew stronger, the fog shimmered, as if they were poking it with their fingers. It was so cold in the room that Bethany could see the misty plumes of Ramona's breath. Something crashed off an end table. A glass tumbled from darkness beyond, perhaps from the kitchen counter, exploding onto the tile floor. Still, Ramona held on and the chant continued, their voices growing louder as the rugs on the walls trembled, the candle flames danced hysterically, and Bethany nearly stopped breathing from fright.

A blue-white light emerged from the design created by their linked arms, spreading, growing, and encompassing them in a warm embrace. The temperature began to rise. Ramona changed the chant, calling upon a goddess name that Bethany never heard before: Mere Noir, for protection. The circle of light expanded. Bethany followed suit, this time closing her eyes and concentrating as hard as she could on the goddess. Human monsters she could handle, but whatever was in this room she definitely didn't want to see!

"Mere Noir, come to us, come to us. Be here, be with us, be with us," sang Ramona. Bethany peeked one eye open, feeling the power surge between herself and Ramona. It felt wonderful! Magnificent! She opened the other eye, the energy filling her. Let that big bad whatever just bring it on! She was ready. She could handle anything. The energy built in her throat and she sang with Ramona, louder. Louder! Her entire body shook with glowing energy. She felt as if she was one with the universe.

The blue-white circle exploded into thousands of tiny sparkling bits of light with a boom that shook the foundations of the garage.

And the room was filled with tranquil peace.

Ramona said, "So mote it be," letting go of Bethany's hands.

"So mote it be," Bethany replied, rubbing the circulation back into her arms and hands. They sat quietly staring at each other for several minutes.

"What was that all about?" asked Bethany. "I've never experienced anything like that before."

Ramona stood stiffly, turning on the lights and replacing the book that had fallen off the end table. "Someone is up to no good. But the Black Madonna —she is stronger than these piddling fools."

"Black Madonna? Is that Mere Noir?"

Ramona smiled mysteriously. "Of course. You've already met her, so I was sure that she would aid you in this spell."

"I have?" asked Bethany, not willing even now to share her dream with Ramona.

Ramona leaned over, her jasmine perfume filling Bethany's nostrils. "Sometimes she comes as an old woman—a hag—but on other occasions you are permitted to see her true self—a glorious black woman holding a babe in her arms. She's been trying to give a message to you, but you've been ignoring her. Ramona knows." The housekeeper tapped her temple.

Bethany's mouth went dry. "How do you know?"

The housekeeper shrugged and opened her arms expansively. "Ramona knows all!"

"Yeah. Right," replied Bethany. "You're a goddess unto yourself."

"Maybe so . . ." said Ramona sweetly. "Maybe so."

Chapter 22

Nine of Hearts reversed: Obstacles

lack Madonna? What is that?" asked Nam, pulling a pail and spade out of the back of her lime-green Geo Tracker.

"Not a what, a who," said Bethany. The sky above was as flat and gray as an old cookie pan.

"Is she the woman in your dream? If she's black, I'm all for her," said Tillie, getting out of the back seat.

"Very funny," replied Nam. "Okay. So who is she?"

Bethany slammed the car door. "Ramona says she's a goddess." She stuffed her long hair up under a turquoise-and-white knit cap. November by the Delaware wasn't like a picnic in the Bahamas. "According to Ramona, in Roman times the worship of the Egyptian goddess Isis was widespread throughout Europe. At the start of Christianity, many of the temples dedicated to Isis became Christian churches." She dug for her gloves in the pockets of her coat. She liked the way the purple and white stripes of the gloves ringed her fingers. "The representations of Isis holding Horus, her son, began to be associated with the Virgin Mary carrying Jesus. Because Isis was dark skinned, these statues were called Black Virgins or Black Madonnas. Ramona calls her Mere Noir, or Black Mother. What is really interesting is that they've found statues like these in France, Germany, Italy, Poland, Spain, Mexico, Africa, and Asia." She slipped her hands into the gloves, her fingers wiggling like purple and white worms. "A friend of Ramona's recently went to France and a caretaker of one of the old churches told the woman all about it. He even had a manuscript he was working on to show that the worship of the Black Madonna continued through the Middle Ages, and then in secret up until about fifty years ago. Her friend is trying to translate it. If she can prove it, the information would be an exciting find."

"That goddess sure got around!" exclaimed Tillie. "My kind of gal!"

"Let's go," said Nam, her boots crunching on the gravel parking lot.

"What are we here for?" asked Tillie, hurrying to catch up. "Nobody comes to Bowmansdale Creek in November." They were about a half-mile from the river, overlooking a small tributary.

Bethany buttoned the top of her jacket. It sure was getting cold.

Nam's cheeks had already turned apple-red. "You said you guys would help me rebuild my project."

"I was thinking more of sitting around your kitchen table with glue, scissors, markers, and a posterboard or two. What are we doing here?" asked Bethany, repeating Tillie's question.

They neared the creek. About a yard away from the drop-off, Nam hunkered down and handed Tillie a spade. "Okay. Dig."

"For what?" asked Tillie, staring at the metal tool.

"Worms," replied Nam.

"Yuck!" said Tillie, dropping the spade. "I'm not digging for any worms! I agreed to help you, but this is the limit! Why can't you get them at a bait and tackle store? Better yet, couldn't we make fake ones?"

Nam sighed impatiently. "No, and the closest bait shop is closed up for the holidays. The guy takes off for Thanksgiving. This year he decided to leave for an extra week. He's in the Bahamas or something."

"A pet store?" Bethany asked hopefully.

"Dig!" commanded Nam. "Part of the project is finding the worms myself."

"It's like concrete," complained Tillie.

While they dug, Bethany told them about the spell she and Ramona cast the night before. She ended by sitting back on her haunches and saying, "There are no worms in this ground." She stabbed the dirt with the spade. "And if they are hiding down there, they'll be below the frost line. We'll get to China before we find them."

Nam looked up from her small pile of dirt. The thin, watery light spilling from a break in the clouds highlighted her tiny form. Bethany drew in her breath. Nam looked ghastly—all skin and bones. What was wrong with her?

Tillie clapped her hands. "It's cold and the worms are hiding. Are you sure we can't buy them somewhere? Bettcr yet, let's go get a burger and fries. I'm starving!"

Nam continued to stab at the ground. It was like she was beating someone rather than digging.

"You keep digging like that," said Bethany, "and you'll cut those worms in half before you ever get them out of the ground."

"Ouuu! Gross!" complained Tillie. A brisk wind picked up the bottom of her red coat and sent the tails flapping. "So, the Black Madonna—she's a strong goddess?"

Bethany hacked at particularly hard crust of ground. "Evidently."

Tillie continued, "So, by Ramona's comment about fools . . . does she think someone is working black magick?"

Nam cast a furtive glance at Bethany. Was there a meaning in that look? "I don't think so. Ramona says that all people are capable of putting thoughts into form, meaning that your thoughts create energy, and energy is the basis of all existence. A person doesn't have to be magickal to cause chaos if their emotions are strong or their desire is great."

"No bad mojo?"

Bethany shook her head. "Just downright meanness."

Tillie stood up and brushed her hands on her jacket. "I wonder if everyone in the world believed that, would they try to think better thoughts?"

"I got one!" cried Nam, pulling a wiggling worm from her hole.

"Excuse me," said Tillie. "I think I'm going to puke."

"That was more than gross," complained Tillie as they scrambled back into the car an hour later. "Remind me not to offer to help you do anything ever again!"

Nam laughed. It was a good sound. She hardly ever smiled anymore.

Tillie said, "What do you think that gray fog was while you were doing the spell?"

Bethany shook her head. "Whatever it was, when Ramona and I finally concentrated on the Black Madonna, it broke up. Exploded. It couldn't have been a good thing."

Nam sobered and started the car, slowly circling the parking lot.

It was Bethany's turn to sit in the back seat so she hunched forward. She didn't want to miss any of the conversation, but no one was saying anything.

Nam finally broke the silence. "Some strange things have been going on. I mean, my project and some other stuff."

"Like?" asked Tillie.

"You guys aren't going to believe this, but that Gillian girl? She's into some pretty weird stuff. I was going to tell you before, but I felt so stupid for running out of your house last week." She eased the Tracker onto the road.

"She lives in that trailer park off the highway," continued Nam. "Range something . . . anyway, that night I stormed out of your place, we drove to her house. I don't know why I went, except maybe because Sidney said that Gillian really wanted to be friends. Anyway, her dad wasn't there when we went in. He does all the landscaping for the people at Cedar Crest Estates . . . that's how she knows Sidney. She helps her dad in the summertime. She's been going over to Sidney's house for several years."

Tillie said, "So far, nothing sounds weird to me."

Nam piloted the Tracker slowly through town. "She wanted to come to Witches' Night Out because she thinks we conjure demons."

"What!" blasted the collective exclamation from Bethany and Tillie. "You owe me a soda!" declared Bethany, laughing and tapping Tillie on the back of the head. "Whatever gave her that idea?"

Tillie snorted. "Movies, books, propaganda. The usual, I'm sure. What did she want the demon for?"

"Not that we go there," remarked Bethany.

"I guess that's what was so strange. I thought it was to get her mom's killer, but—"

Tillie interrupted, "That's a logical explanation. Did you tell her that Witches don't do the demon thing?"

Nam slowed the car and pulled in Bethany's driveway. "Yeah, but I don't think she believed me. I tried to explain to her that demons are a fabrication of the medieval Christian belief system, but she got all mad about it. She asked me to leave."

"You're kidding!" exclaimed Tillie.

Nam gripped the steering wheel, her knuckles white. "Actually, she didn't ask me to leave, she threw me out."

"What did Sidney do?" asked Bethany.

"He picked me up off the sidewalk, apologized until I thought his tongue would drop off, and then went back inside."

"What a scum," said Tillie.

"Don't be mad at Sidney," replied Nam. "She was breaking things in the house. He went back inside to stop her. I'm the one that didn't hang around."

"I heard they go everywhere with each other," remarked Tillie. "I was talking to Vanessa Peters the other night? She says they're almost inseparable. In fact, Sidney took Gillian to the Halloween party."

"You mean they're dating?" asked Nam. "They didn't act like that when I was around them."

Red flags again waved in Bethany's brain. She wasn't sure if it was Tillie's information about Sidney and Gillian or if she was uncomfortable because Tillie had been talking with Vanessa and seemed to be on a gossiping basis with her. "I didn't see Gillian when Sidney came into the gas station."

"Oh, gross," remarked Nam. "Maybe she was in the car. How awful! What if she would have gotten out and seen—?"

Bethany shuddered. "I'm sure she wasn't there. I would have remembered. I'm positive Sidney was alone."

"Maybe he'd already dropped her off," offered Nam.

Tillie shook her head. "No, Vanessa said she left with someone else."

"Who?" asked Nam.

"She doesn't know. She was busy getting more sodas. The only thing she can remember is that someone told her it was a guy, but not Sidney, because Sidney was helping her get the sodas. There's a rumor that someone stole some liquor out of Vanessa's parents' cabinet, but she isn't 'fessing up on that point. Seems Vanessa discovered it and that's why nobody saw Gillian leave. One of the other cheerleaders told me that."

No one said anything for a moment.

Bethany couldn't stand it any longer. "When did you talk to Vanessa Peters?"

"When I picked up my cheer uniform."

Of course.

Tillie shrugged her shoulders. "Winter ball starts soon, they need two squads, one for the wrestling team and one for the basketball team. It doesn't interfere with my swim schedule. I don't think I'll be on Vanessa's squad. She's varsity and they usually do wrestling since we're always the state champs. I think I'm doing J.V."

"I thought you said there was only one spot?"

Tillie smiled sarcastically. "That's what Vanessa told me, but I found out different. We had tryouts yesterday. There were quite a few spots open. Some of the girls only do fall ball so they can be involved in other stuff, like the operetta. Several of the girls left the varsity squad because they can't stand Vanessa. She isn't the easiest person to get along with."

Nam turned the heater up in the car. "Thanks for helping me, you guys, but I've got to go."

"I was going to ask you both in for supper. Ramona is making chicken pot pie," said Bethany.

"Oh man," said Tillie, "I love that stuff. But I have to meet the squad at the gym at seven o'clock."

"I've got to work on my project," said Nam. "Michael is coming over to help me. Thanks anyway."

"Have you told Michael yet?" asked Bethany. She was sorry she asked as soon as the words were out of her mouth. Nam's hands froze on the steering wheel and all the life that seemed to be coming back drained out of her face.

"Like I said, I don't want to be late," said Nam quietly, staring straight ahead. She pulled into Bethany's driveway. "Tell Ramona I said hi and thanks for the spell."

Chapter 23

Ace of Hearts: Love

Nam had a boyfriend, Tillie had the cheer squad, and hockey season was over. Bethany tilted back in her chair and played with the track ball on her computer mouse. Annabelle Arneau's file popped up. Her father and his partner interviewed over sixty people from the park, Linnex's apartment building, Annabelle's school, employees of the Witches' Attic, Linnex's former employer . . . the list was almost endless. With each day that passed, the hope of finding Annabelle's killer deteriorated and the time her father had to work on the case stretched to the minimum. Soon his boss would force him to concentrate on more recent homicides. She could still see Linnex's drawn face and hear the words, "I need closure. I need to know what happened to my little girl."

Bethany swallowed hard, determination narrowing her eyes. She scrolled back and re-read the files. At first, they'd hoped that Annabelle simply wandered away from her mother. Then, they found her yellow jacket covered in blood and one of her little red sneakers. A rookie police officer discovered the

204

sock close by. Bethany continued the tedious process of reading through the police interviews. Her eyes lit on Matthew Starr, aged 22. Starr . . . wasn't that the name of Laslow's boyfriend? This guy was awfully young. She read down through the report. Electrician—subcontracted. He belonged to a union. Manhattan address. Pretty pricey apartment for an electrician, but hey, the most unlikely people made good money, especially if they were union, and he might live in rent control that existed since the fifties. That often happened. Look at the building her father owned. However, this must be the guy Laslow was dating, unless he had an older brother that was also an electrician—possible, but highly unlikely.

She scanned several more lines. The report mentioned that Starr was, indeed, Sergeant Laslow's boyfriend at the time. Sergeant Laslow's close association with Linnex Arneau was annotated, but there was no information regarding Laslow's interest in Wicca. She continued to read. Boring. What did she care about this guy, anyway? He wasn't a suspect, and the only reason he was in this file was because her dad interviewed anybody and everybody he could get his hands on. Maybe he was interested in Laslow then, and thought he'd see just how attached she was to this guy. Wouldn't be the first time a cop did that—in fact, that's how he'd met her own mother. It worked for him once, maybe he figured it would work for him again.

She tapped her fingers on the edge of the keyboard. Laslow gave her the impression that she would do anything to find Annabelle's killer. Bethany wondered if that "anything" included dating her father. She hoped not. He had such lousy luck with women! She read a few more lines, found nothing of interest, and went on to the next one.

"Gotta get me some," said Ramona from the doorway of her bedroom.

"Fifty-nine stars!" exclaimed Bethany, almost falling off her chair.

"Girl, you're going to give Ramona a heart attack shouting like that," said Ramona, pulling on her coat. "What are you talking about?"

But the moment she grasped the thought, she lost it. The dream. Her mother said it was time for Annabelle to go home, and something about fifty-nine stars, but Ramona was talking, interrupting her thought process. She tried to hold onto it, but the dream tendrils melted away.

Ramona finished by saying, "I'm going out to pick up some milk, do you want anything?"

"No, thanks. I've got to make a phone call."

"I have got to talk to you," said Sidney, desperation pitching his voice into a whine.

Bethany brushed past him. "Can't now. I have to get home. Maybe some other time."

Sidney grabbed her arm and she almost slid into a locker, his grip surprisingly strong. "Get your hands off of me," she said softly, letting the menace she felt curl the syllables of her speech.

He didn't let go. "I've got to see you. Alone."

Bethany twisted her lip. "If you don't take your hand off of me, I'm going to scream, and that will bring the whole school running." Her voice echoed in the empty corridor and she realized how stupid that sounded. An alien could materialize and rip her to shreds and no one would pay attention. School let out over forty minutes ago. She shouldn't have been screwing around in the library.

He let go reluctantly but moved in, his body almost touching hers. She realized that she'd never really looked at Sidney before. He had the most intense blue-green eyes, like the color of the Mediterranean Sea in picture books. How come she never noticed that before? His eyes were rimmed by long, dark lashes. Actually, he wasn't that dorky looking. Maybe it was the boring clothes or the way he moved that led her to the assumption that he was too ordinary. Maybe it was because he was so quiet. He never spoke to anyone. Well . . . he talked to the air, but that didn't count.

She could feel the flush crawl up her neck and she backed away. "I'm late," she mumbled, unable to call up the imperious tone she normally used for the likes of Sidney.

"I know you're angry with me," said Sidney, "but I don't have anyone to talk to. Please, can you spare some time?"

Caught. Their eyes locked. Bethany rarely looked at another person straight in the eye, not because she was untruthful or trying to hide something, but because she could access their emotions. Go way deep. Private places and feelings that she felt she had no right to approach. She'd gotten into the habit of scanning someone's face when she talked to them so she wouldn't appear rude by not paying attention, but at the same time not penetrate that inner space. In fact, she made such a habit of ignoring the emotions of others that she forgot she could scan at all. Not this time. Her breath caught in her throat and she tore her gaze away.

"It's not for me," he said. "It's about Nam."

"I told you before," said Bethany firmly. "I don't interfere in the lives of my friends. If she wants to tell me something, she can."

"She won't tell you this."

"Ramona thinks that you stopped off at the fast food place and gorged yourself," said the housekeeper, hands on white-clad hips, stew spoon waving in the air. "You have not touched a single thing on your plate. Food is expensive. If you will not eat, Ramona will not buy."

Bethany pushed her plate away and stared glumly at the blue and white checkered tablecloth. "I'm not hungry, but I didn't have anything after school. Word of honor."

"A Witch is as good as her word," remarked Ramona. She scooped another ladle of stew on her own plate, then drew a banishing pentagram in the air over the bowl.

"Why do you do that?" asked Bethany. "Why do you make that sign over your food?"

"All things should be blessed before they enter the body."

"All things?" asked Bethany, giggling. "Do you bless your toothpaste, too?"

"Don't go there," chided Ramona.

"I called Linnex," said Bethany. "She said it was okay to undo what I did. I'm not sure how to do that."

"You'll think of something," said Ramona. "But that's not really what's bothering you."

Silence weighed heavily between them.

Ramona hunched over and peered at her reflection in the stainless steel stew pot. "Why thank you, Ramona, for cooking such a lovely stew. It is very good. Where would my stomach be without you?" She sat up and answered herself, "How kind of you to notice that I spent all afternoon making this stew, dear Ramona. It was very good if I do say so myself!"

Bethany cocked her eyebrows, judging the sanity of the housekeeper.

"And what is wrong with the little one?" asked Ramona, peering again at the cooking pot. "I don't know," she answered herself as she sat upright again.

"Perhaps she has boy troubles?" Her liquid dark eyes seemed to penetrate Bethany's brain, going past the bone of her skull and into dangerous territory. A drill couldn't have done a better job.

The hair on Bethany's arms stood up. How could she have known? That was, however, only part of the problem.

Ramona bent and spoke to the pot. "But that is not all. No. There is more."

"Stop it!" screeched Bethany.

Ramona looked slightly insulted. "You do not want Ramona to divine by pot?"

Bethany slapped her hands over her eyes, laughter and frustration battling in her brain. "You are driving me crazy!"

Ramona shrugged. "Ramona is eating. You are driving crazy because you are not eating."

"I've got a problem," announced Bethany.

"So it would seem."

"I guess now is when I'm supposed to spill my guts."

"Just don't get them near the stew. Health hazard."

Bethany pulled her hair. "Ugh!"

Ramona leaned back in her chair. "So what is the difficulty?"

Bethany looked at the ceiling. "What do you do if you find out something terrible about a friend? If you say something to her, you know she is going to deny it. If you go behind her back and tell someone else, then you're a rat, and she'll probably hate you and never talk to you again, but if you don't say something, then she could be in serious trouble, and something bad will happen," blurted Bethany. Her throat constricted. "She might die," she finished.

"This sounds very serious," said Ramona, leaning her elbows on the table. "Are you planning to tell Ramona the fine points, or do I have to use the pot?"

Bethany shook her head. Part of her wanted to mouth off and tell Ramona where she could stick her pot, but she knew her reaction was because of her own frustration. She wished she'd never talked to Sidney this afternoon. "If I tell you," she said slowly, "then you won't let me handle it myself. You'll blab."

"Ah," said Ramona, getting up from the table and rinsing her bowl in the sink.

The silence in the kitchen was broken only by Ramona's motions of putting the bowl in the dishwasher. Finally, the housekeeper turned, and said, "And you want time to decide what to do?"

Bethany chewed on her lower lip. "Yes."

Ramona nodded. "Can your friend afford the time you think you need?"

Blinking, Bethany replied, "I'm not sure."

Ramona sat back down at the table. "Have you talked to your friend?"

"No. I'm afraid to."

"Afraid because she will be angry, or afraid because what you have heard may be the truth?"

Bethany thought about that for a moment. "Both. What do real Witches do about things like this?"

Ramona smoothed her creamy-brown hands over the tablecloth. "In the old days, the information was given to the High Priestess of the coven or the matriarch of the Clan by the Waylander."

"What's that?"

"Sometimes he was called the man in black. It was his job to carry messages from the High Priestess to the other members of the coven, and vice versa. He was also responsible for keeping an eye on everyone and accessing their needs. Even today, there isn't much that a High Priestess of a coven does not know about her members. Someone always talks."

"Then a Waylander was like an information pipeline?"

Ramona smiled and nodded her head. "Yes, only one person was used in an effort to keep the gossip at a minimum. Once the High Priestess obtained the information she would then go to her altar, or take a walk in the woods to a sacred place, and she would ask the Mother and the Ancestors to help her see clearly. She would ask for guidance and wisdom . . . and most of all . . . the strength to do the right thing."

"Are you telling me you are the High Priestess?"

Ramona chuckled. "A teacher . . . perhaps. The High Priestess of your group? No—that's your job, and welcome to it. I don't want the responsibility. Been there. Done that. You are the leader of your group. You are stuck with it. It's time you learned that having a group, even a small one, isn't all fun and games and magick." She yawned. "Ramona is tired now, and she is reading a very good book. Ramona likes Mary Roberts Reinhart. Her famous line is, 'If only I had known.'"

"Meaning?"

Ramona got up from the table. "I wouldn't wait too long, if I were you."

Chapter 24

Ace of Spades: Beware!

Bethany stood at the back door, pulling on her purple Cedar Crest letter coat. The back yard was black as pitch and she wondered about the wisdom of walking out there alone when just last week someone tried to get in her bedroom window. The last time she'd been out there she found Sidney lurking in the darkness. Sidney . . . she hated to admit it, but there was something alluring about him. She started when Ramona appeared behind her, wrapped in a white woolen coat and carrying an intricately carved staff.

"I wish you would stop sneaking up on me like that!" Bethany snapped. "What do you think you're doing?"

Ramona silently handed her the staff.

"What is this?" asked Bethany, running her hands over the smooth wood, the beautiful carvings of vines and animals a sensory pleasure to her finger-tips.

"Is yours," said Ramona. "If you journey for wisdom, you take the staff."

For a moment she was overcome. "I can't take this," she stated firmly, trying to hand it back. A silver bell attached with a leather thong at the top of the staff tinkled merrily.

"Refusing a gift of magick from one older than you is not only unseemly, but in poor taste. One never insults an elder." Her eyes were unreadable.

Bethany gripped the staff, the wood singing beneath her fingers. She liked that pulse of power. "Will it help me see the truth?"

"Actually, it is good to beat over the heads of burglars. I will not interfere, but I have promised your father to care for you. We will walk together."

Bethany carried the incense around the family room, censing each corner with the gentle aroma of sandalwood and sage. A single candle sputtered on the hearth, and a merry fire burned in the fireplace. She'd chosen the nine sacred woods of the Witch, building the fire with a piece of each. A chunk of elder wood, sacred to the Black Madonna, sat beside the candle. She double-checked everything. Yes, she was ready. The emergency Saturday-night meeting of Witches' Night Out was less than thirty minutes away. She'd had to cancel Thursday because Tillie had a game and Nam claimed she couldn't spare the time—the project was all important. Or so she said. Sidney would have come on Thursday, but she didn't want to be alone with him. She didn't trust herself. Suddenly, she liked Sidney too much.

They filtered slowly into the den. Tillie was first, chewing on a piece of licorice. Nam showed up a few minutes later, looking pale and drawn. Sidney stumbled over the coffee table, but quickly recovered. Gillian was the last to arrive. They sat in a circle by the fireplace, each in their own way questioning why an emergency meeting was called. Tillie, her hair twisted in an intricate French knot at the back of her neck, looked very confused when she saw Gillian.

Bethany took a deep breath. "I called you all here this evening because we need to talk. Each of us, in our own way, is an outcast." She threw a handful of pumpkin spice on the fire. A kaleidoscope of colors now edged the flames.

They all nodded their heads. Tillie was seated on Bethany's right, Nam on the left, Gillian sat opposite, knees touching Sidney. Bethany tried to ignore their intimacy, stifling a pang of jealousy.

Bethany cleared her throat. "I took a long walk the other night, and I realized that the bond of the original Witches' Night Out group was broken when Joe died. The group mind changed. Then, we talked about letting new people in the group, and we, those of us left," she looked at Tillie and Nam, "have been worried that new people would mess up our friendship."

"That's true," said Tillie softly. "And it almost did." She looked sternly at Sidney, who focused on the carpet.

"In the meantime," continued Bethany, "We all got lost in our own fears. So, tonight, we are going to have a Fear Night."

"I don't want to do this," said Gillian, beginning to rise. She looked at Sidney, her face flushed with anger. "You told me that we would do something about my mother. That we would conjure a demon! You didn't say anything about playing a psychodrama game. None of you are qualified to do anything like that. This is bull!" She clutched her purse defiantly. "I bet you couldn't conjure a demon if you tried."

Tillie rolled her eyes. "Girl, you are so full of it. You know there are no such things as demons, only people who walk around and act like them. That's the real evil. Sit down and shut up!"

Sidney laid a hand gently on her shoulder. "You need this, Gillian, and so do the rest of us."

Bethany watched an unspoken exchange between them. Ever since she talked to Sidney she couldn't stop thinking about him. This was just crazy! Two days ago he was a troublesome pest. Now she watched his every move. He really wasn't all that great looking . . . or was he? She didn't like these confused feelings.

Gillian finally sat down, but none too happily.

"The rules are simple," said Bethany, looking at each of them. "What we talk about cannot go beyond this room. And," she raked her eyes from one to another. "You must be absolutely honest."

"Can you conjure a demon?" asked Gillian.

"No!" replied Bethany.

"Uh-huh," muttered Tillie, stretching a long piece of licorice out from her mouth. "Who starts?"

"You do," said Bethany, throwing more pumpkin spice on the fire to add to the atmosphere. "Starting now."

Tillie unloaded. School. Grades. Being black in a virtually all-white area. It was heavy, and most of them did what they were supposed to do—they supported her. Only Gillian remained silent, her legs tucked underneath her, shoulders hunched as if to avoid physical attack. Every now and then she would look into the deep shadows of the room and shiver.

Sidney went next. Many of his fears were the same as Tillie's. They discovered that living with the richest father in town wasn't all that great. Bethany felt that he was holding back. That there was more, but she didn't press. After all, he'd never sat with them before, never done ritual with them, never shared energy. He probably didn't feel comfortable. Gillian picked at the carpet. Bethany threw more spice on the fire to keep from staring at Sidney.

"I'm also afraid all of you won't like me once you know me better," continued Sidney. "Coming here and finding the Craft is like coming home. I don't know how else to explain it. I really admire Bethany. She's strong and caring. I've been watching. She tries to do the right thing for the group and doesn't let her personal feelings override what she thinks might be best for the whole. That's really hard to do."

"Suck up," said Tillie, laughter trailing the edge of her voice.

Bethany explained that she was afraid of her friends leaving her, probably because of the death of her mother five years before. She talked about being selfish, and how much she hated herself for being a little overweight. Her fear of her father selling the house out from under her and sending her to a private school. "If I get into any more trouble," she said, hugging herself, "he'll send me away. And on top of it all, we're supposed to be picking what we want to do with the rest of our lives, and I have no clue!"

"I hear that!" said Tillie. "My dad is pushing me to go into computers, he says that's where the money is, but I want to be in emergency medicine. I want to save people when it counts, and scoop dead bodies up off the road when I can't."

"That's morbid!" exclaimed Nam, her eyes wide.

Tillie shrugged. "It's what I really want to do."

"But you don't like worms," said Nam. "How are you going to deal with a dead body? The bugs often tell the forensic pathologist how a person died."

"I don't want to be a forensic whatever. I want to drive the EMT vehicle!" replied Tillie.

Sidney nodded. "Most kids change majors after they get to college. It's like . . . you grow up thinking you want to do one thing, and then you're there . . . and you don't want to do it anymore. It isn't fair that they force us to choose so soon. Between school and my dad pressuring me, I just don't know what I want to do."

"I live in a trailer park," said Gillian, staring at the carpet. "People make fun of me because I live there. They call me trailer trash. I'm not. Really, I'm not!" She buried her head on her knees. Slowly, she lifted her head, eyes glittering in the soft light. "I'm big boned and people make fun of me because I'm not pretty. I've been mean to a lot of kids because they've been mean to me! They deserve it."

No one said anything.

"My mother used to say," continued Gillian softly, "that you should do what you have a passion for. It's not how much money you make or what kind of fame you get, but what makes you feel good inside. What makes you feel whole." She laced her fingers together and then opened her palms. "At night?" she continued. "I think that the person who killed my mother is going to come and kill me. They'll kill me because I have been so cruel. Because I hate."

"I think all of us try to work out the things we hate," said Nam, ending with a sigh. "And we don't always manage those feelings in a productive way. It's human to be angry."

Gillian bit her lip. "I'm really sorry I was so nasty to you the other day."

"It's okay," replied Nam.

They sat silently. The fire crackled. The candle burned steady. Bethany thought Gillian was through, and was eager to get to Nam. She knew it wasn't right to push away from Gillian's troubles. Part of her felt guilty, and it wasn't that she didn't sympathize, but Nam was one of her closest friends. And it was true. Gillian's behavior lately had been less than kind. She'd only invited her to Witches' Night Out because Sidney had pushed so hard. The girl made a conscious effort to make herself an outsider. In school she never socialized with anyone, at least nobody that Bethany knew about. Besides, she didn't like the attention that Sidney always gave her. It was weird ... unless he had a thing for her.

Gillian, however, was not done. Looking at Sidney, she blurted, "We have a secret," and began to cry. "A terrible, terrible secret."

Sidney paled. "Don't ..." he whispered. "Please don't say anything."

Bethany's heart fluttered. *Oh, great,* she thought. *She's pregnant.* She mentally kicked herself for being attracted to Sidney. *Here we go again.*

Gillian buried her head in her hands, tears dribbling out from underneath her palms. Sidney drew back, as if waiting for a terrible blow. Tillie leaned forward, her dark eyes fastened on Gillian as if to yank the information out of the girl's bobbing head. Nam sucked on her lips, the rest of her small body perfectly still.

"Sidney is my half-brother," said Gillian.

Bethany's jaw dropped.

Tillie coughed on her licorice.

Nam breathed, "Oh, my stars!" while pounding Tillie on the back.

Sidney groaned, looking right above Bethany's shoulder. "Keep out of this!" he hissed.

"Too late now," said Tillie.

Sidney sighed. "I didn't mean . . . oh, never mind."

A log in the fire popped, cracked, split and half of it fell through the grate. Bethany fingered the truth stone in her pocket. The smooth surface was so hot it almost burned her fingers.

Chapter 25

King of Clubs: Danger

Stunned. There wasn't another word for it. Bethany looked at Gillian, then swung her gaze to Sidney. There was a resemblance. A faint one.

"I don't get it," said Nam flatly.

Sidney looked guiltily at Gillian. "My dad. Gillian's mom worked for my father. They had an affair. Gillian was born. Gillian's dad doesn't know. He thinks Gillian is his."

Tillie let out a guttural, animal sound.

"And Gillian isn't the only one. There are others, or at least I think there are. My dad was a busy man. He thought money meant he could do anything. He paid off a couple of women—except Gillian's mom, she wouldn't hear of it, instead she had Gillian and married the father Gillian has now."

"When my dad was out of work," said Gillian, "Sidney's father . . ." her lips curled in disdain, "offered to put my dad in the landscaping business. Mr. Hecklesdorf thought it was a big joke. My mother tried to keep my dad from doing it, but she couldn't give him a good reason why."

"But how did you two find out?" asked Nam.

"My fault," said Sidney. "We have a big house. There's a room we call the junk hole. It's got all sorts of stuff in it. I was looking for my baseball glove and found Gillian's birth certificate in one of the boxes. I figured that my mom must know about it, or else it wouldn't be in there. So I asked her. It was not a good day."

Nam frowned. "Your mother didn't know?"

"Oh, she knew all right!"

"Why would your mother have Gillian's birth certificate?" asked Nam.

"Mom was going to adopt Gillian. She's used to my dad messing around. She wanted a little girl because she couldn't have any more children. Daughters are a big deal to Native American women. I mean, all children are important, but she wanted to teach her daughter the old ways. My mom really pressured Mrs. Merriday, I mean she wasn't Mrs. Merriday then . . . but you get the idea. Gillian's mom agreed that if anything happened to her, that my mother would be her guardian, but that was before Gillian's mom married the Merriday guy."

Nam's eyes grew wide. "But something did happen to your mother! What will you do now?"

Gillian laughed ruefully. "I'm too old. Sidney's mom doesn't want anything to do with me. I'm big. I'm fat. I'm not attractive at all."

"That's not it," said Sidney. "I've been trying to tell you, but you won't listen. My mom is planning to divorce my dad. She doesn't want to mess up your life more than it already is."

Gillian sighed. "It's just as well. I don't want my father ever to know. It does hurt, though, especially when I see everyone paying so much attention to Sidney because he's rich. If I was living with Sidney's parents, people wouldn't treat me so badly. I love my dad, though." Bethany watched Gillian's horribly twisted face and silently thanked the Goddess that she didn't have this kind of mess in her own life.

"Money isn't important," said Nam.

"Easy for you to say!" snapped Gillian. "You all have nice things, live in nice houses . . . you drive an expensive car . . . you don't know what it is like to sit outside in your beat-up jalopy and watch other people who have . . . and you don't!"

Tillie teased a piece of licorice with her teeth. "You don't know us very well," she said. "My father's a minister. There's no money in that, at least, not the way my father runs the church. He doesn't cheat people. We live right in town. I drive an old Toyota. Anybody can see we're not rich."

"My parents aren't rich either," said Nam. "They spent all their savings to bring my brothers and sisters over from China. We eat hot dogs and macaroni and cheese for dinner a lot. My car was a gift from my uncle, but I can't keep up the insurance payments on it. If I don't come up with some cash soon, I won't be able to drive it. The house is too crowded now that the rest of my family is here, and they've changed. I have to share my room with my two older sisters. They're having trouble adjusting to the way people live in America. My oldest sister left two weeks ago and moved to New York City because she doesn't like the new ways of my parents in this country." Her lower lip trembled. "Then my parents left. Business in Japan and I'm stuck under the iron thumb of one of my older sisters. She's so bossy! The whole family says I'm too sensitive," her voice gathered speed, "and they call me fat and so I don't eat . . ."

Tillie sat up straight. "Who calls you fat?"

Nam's eyes turned to liquid green. "My boyfriend. Michael. He says I'm too fat, and that I'll never amount to anything."

Bethany felt anger curling in her stomach. "Michael Raines? That kid that started here this year? He's been telling you that?"

"He's been trying to force me to have sex with him, but I'm not ready yet . . ." Tears slid down her hollow cheeks. "He says that I'm supposed to."

Gillian's face grew pale. "Your boyfriend is Michael Raines?"

Nam nodded.

"Since when?" Her face contorted, anger shaking her voice.

Nam shrugged timidly. "Not long . . . He came to my house. We spent the day together, and . . ."

"I've had enough of this crap," screamed Gillian, jumping up. "This was all a set-up. You people are horrid!" She turned on Sidney. "How could you! You're just like them! Evil! You're all evil!"

They watched in stunned silence as Gillian kicked Sidney, spun and ran out of the house.

"I don't understand," said Nam tearfully. "What did I do?"

"You didn't do anything," replied Sidney, leaning his head in one hand. "It's my fault."

Tillie threw another log on the fire. The light belched from the fireplace, illuminating Sidney's shaken expression. Bethany turned on him. "What aren't you telling us?"

"Michael Raines has been sneaking over to Gillian's house late at night. I thought that if Gillian and Nam got to talking . . . well, they would find out."

"Did anyone tell you that stupid should be your middle name?" asked Tillie. "Why didn't you just tell Gillian, or Nam?"

Sidney looked miserable. "Because I didn't want them to be mad at each other. Michael is playing them both, and he wants them to find out."

"Why?" asked Bethany, trying desperately to control her anger.

"Because then they'll fight over him."

"That's the most ridiculous thing I ever heard!" exclaimed Bethany. "Just downright dumb! Who is this yo-yo, anyway?" She looked at the quivering Nam.

Nam sniffled. "He moved here from the city in August. He's smart."

"I could think of a few other words to describe him other than smart," said Tillie nastily.

"It's just that I never had a boyfriend before. I guess I didn't realize that in a good relationship, people don't say mean things to you or make you feel bad about yourself. I just wanted someone to pay some attention to me. The family is too busy right now. Before my brother and sisters came, my parents went to everything I was involved in. Lately it's like I don't seem to exist. I know it's terrible, but I wish they'd never brought everyone else here!" She burst into tears.

"So you were starving yourself because you thought that Michael would pay attention to you?"

Nam nodded miserably. "He's smart. You should see his project. All sorts of gizmos and stuff."

"I want to break his neck," growled Tillie. "He's using you. Trying to control others is a sickness!" She slapped her fist into her palm. "Just wait until I get my hands on him! What do you like about this guy?"

Nam's eyes roved. "I don't know. He seems to know a lot. About life. People . . ."

"Enough to be an abuser," said Bethany.

Sidney stood up. "I guess I really made a mess of things. I'm sorry, Nam."

"It isn't your fault," she said. "I was just so desperate . . . how did you know that he was seeing Gillian?" She turned to look at Sidney.

"I saw him climbing out of her window the other night," he answered. "Don't ask me why I went over there. I just did. So, I waited and knocked on the door. Obviously, her dad doesn't know she's seeing him. Michael brought pot into the house when he first started to date her and Gillian's dad threw him out. I thought she wasn't seeing him anymore. I confronted her about it, and she admitted that she'd been seeing him all along."

Bethany sat very still. Looking at Nam, she said, "Where did you say Michael came from?"

"New York City."

"Where . . . exactly."

Nam fidgeted.

"You were in the city last weekend, weren't you?" said Bethany with an accusing tone.

"We went to see one of his friends, then I went on into Chinatown. My sister . . ." Nam laughed weakly, "is very protective. She . . . doesn't approve of Michael. She moved there—to Chinatown—recently. Michael wasn't happy about it . . . about her insisting on tagging along." She ground her fingers together in her lap. "He thought we'd be spending the whole weekend together . . . but my sister . . . Michael wanted me to tell my parents that I was in the city with you . . . like I said, there's no privacy in my house. I share my room with my sisters, and one of them overheard me on the phone. That's why I eventually ended up in Chinatown. We took the Acel into Penn Station. I didn't know it, but my sister and some of her friends were there. They followed us! It was so humiliating!"

"So I did see you!" exclaimed Tillie. "What were you doing in Manhattan in front of the precinct building?"

"Michael has a friend that works there, if you can believe that."

"Who is it?" asked Bethany.

She shrugged. "He made me stay in the lobby. I didn't see. When I got outside, Bethany's dad was gone, but my sister and her friends were there, waiting for me on the steps. I didn't know she'd been at the train station. She was furious with me! While she was yelling, Michael just . . . slipped away. So, I ended up in Chinatown for the weekend. After I got over my embarrassment, I actually had a good time."

Bethany threw another log on the fire. The flames danced merrily. "He hit you, didn't he, Nam?"

Tillie made a grumbling noise. Sidney said nothing.

"I did see a bruise on your face last week, didn't I?"

A single tear drifted down Nam's cheek. That was answer enough.

Bethany looked at Sidney. "How great of a whiz are you on that computer of yours?"

He coughed. "Not bad. Why?"

"I want you to find out where Michael Raines came from. Exactly."

"How's he going to do that? The school's system isn't online," said Nam.

"Then we'll have to get it from the school."

Tillie rubbed her temples. "Oh man, that's illegal. You could get Sidney into a lot of trouble. Besides, how is he going to get to an unattended terminal?"

"There's one in the guidance office," said Nam. "When one of the counselors talks to people in the inner office, nobody's watching the computer. I know because I've helped out down there putting DARE packages together for the middle-school kids. I'm in the big buddy program. If one of us keeps him busy long enough, Sidney could get in, I know he could."

"Which one of us is going to make an appointment after school with the guidance counselor?" asked Bethany.

"Not me, that's for sure," said Tillie. "I hate that guy. I mean, he means well . . . but . . ."

"Sidney can't do it," said Bethany. "He has to hack into the system. You do it, Nam."

"Why me?" asked Nam fearfully.

"Because you need to talk to them anyway. I bet your grades are slipping," said Bethany.

Nam didn't answer.

Bethany continued, "You've been through a traumatic experience with your family moving in and you got caught up with an abusive boyfriend. Besides, if you talk about Michael's behavior, they might enter it into his school records."

"I don't know . . ." said Nam. "This is private. I don't want the teachers to know I've been stupid."

Sidney spoke up. "You can't risk not getting help because you're afraid of what people will think of you," he said firmly. "Yes, sometimes adults handle things badly. They're not perfect either, but even so, you can't quit before you start. That's just rationalizing the problem to meet your own psychodrama. Most school counselors really care about the kids."

"And if it blows up in her face?" asked Tillie.

"Then there are other options," replied Bethany. "And we'll find them. Look, the counselor for our class isn't such a bad guy," said Bethany, throwing Tillie a dirty look. "He's not the brightest, but really, Nam, the fact that you've been starving yourself is not healthy. If you don't want to talk to him, you could ask him to refer you to another counselor. A lady if it makes you feel more comfortable. Just keep him talking!"

Nam rubbed her eyes. "Why can't you do it, Bethany?"

"Because I'm not involved in an abusive situation," replied Bethany bluntly. "You'd be the most credible in there. Even if the counselor doesn't do anything about Michael, it will give Sidney all the time he needs to hack into the system. There's something really strange going on here."

Nam trembled. "This isn't going to be easy."

Tillie picked up the phone.

"What are you doing?" asked Bethany.

"Ordering pizza."

"Nam?" said Bethany. "I have to ask you a serious question."

Nam didn't answer. She just blinked.

"With all you've read, and the training Ramona is giving you, why didn't you do any magick or a ritual to help yourself?"

Nam rubbed her temples. "I forgot, at first. Things were in chaos around the house, my sisters made fun of my altar, so I put most of my things away. Then Michael told me I was living in a fantasy world—that magick wasn't real and that WitchCraft was a joke. I wanted his approval so badly, I just didn't try. I was afraid that he was right, and that anything I did would bomb."

"But you've worked magick before with a lot of success," said Tillie. "Why would you believe him?"

Nam bowed her head. "Because I wanted to believe in him, and if he was wrong, then I guess I thought that the other things he said were wrong, too. I just wanted to be loved."

Tillie smiled sadly. "We love you, Nam."

Nam ran her hands over her face. "There's something else. Someone's been sending me threatening notes. I have at least five of them."

"Probably from Michael Raines," muttered Tillie. "Sounds like he'd be just the type. Try to keep you in line. Make you think someone's after you."

Sidney looked perplexed. "The Red sent them."

Bethany sat up straight. "The who?"

"Do you know something about the letters?" asked Tillie, a suspicious frown creasing her caramel brow.

He laughed weakly. "I don't know what made me say that. Just . . . tip of the tongue thing."

"Amanda Nevins has red hair," said Bethany. "Maybe it was her."

"I'm telling you," said Nam, "I don't know Amanda Nevins. I talked to her that one time—in the rest room, the day you broke the mirror. What would she have to do with the letters?"

Tillie opened her mouth, looked at Bethany, and then snapped it shut. "Nothing. Probably nothing at all."

Things couldn't possibly get any worse.

Chapter 26

Five of Spades: Prepare for change

What are you going to do if you get caught?" asked Nam fearfully as they walked down the hall.

"We'll talk our way out of it," said Bethany, piloting Nam in front of her. Tillie and Sidney walked behind. They passed the main office. It was close to 3:45. The secretaries were still here, but clock watching. The guidance office was the last one on the left. "Keep him talking," said Bethany as they neared the door. "Give us at least twenty minutes."

"I can be in and out before that," said Sidney.

Nam looked up hopefully. "Then I wouldn't have to go into detail."

"At least twenty minutes," said Bethany firmly.

Nam's color scheme for the day was purple with lilac accents. She wavered at the door of the outer office, then went in—purple shoes and all.

Bethany looked at Sidney. "Give her five minutes to get Mr. McGovern into the inner office. Then you go in, Sidney, and do your thing. Tillie and I will wait. If someone tries to go in, you'll hear us talking."

Bethany leaned against the wall, close to the door so she could hear the inner office door open and close. After what seemed like forever she nodded to Sidney. He looked over his shoulder, nodded, and slipped into the outer office.

Tillie stood on the other side of the hall, leaning against the smooth beige tile of the wall. One or two students hurried by, anxious to either catch a bus or get to an after-school activity. The minutes ticked by. No Sidney.

Michael Raines rounded the corner. Tillie stood up, dropping her red backpack by her feet. Bethany continued to lounge by the door. She shook her head slightly at Tillie. Her eyes tried to send the message, "Wait until we see what he wants." Evidently she understood, relaxing slightly.

Michael wore baggie tan pants and a yellow polo shirt. His expensive sneakers squeaked on the linoleum. "What are you two beautiful ladies doing here?" he asked, sidling up to Bethany. She thought she could smell alcohol on his breath.

"Funny, you never bothered to talk to us before," said Bethany. "Why now?"

"Just trying to be friendly," he said, glancing at Tillie. "So, why are you guys still here?"

"None of your business," said Tillie.

Just then the guidance door opened and Sidney stepped out. His hands were empty. Michael squared his shoulders. "Needed a little counseling?" sneered Michael, "or has your friendship with that crazy

Gillian brought you the need for some old-fashioned psychoanalysis? You know, you're just the guy I want to see. I hear you're poking into my business," he said casually, moving closer to Sidney.

"Who told you that?" asked Sidney.

"I'll bet a little bird by the name of Gillian," said Tillie.

Bethany stepped forward. Tillie tensed. Michael's eyes swept the three of them, then focused on Sidney. "You and I have some business to discuss," he said. "I don't like people butting into my affairs." He looked pointedly at Bethany. Gillian must have gushed like a waterfall.

"In my experience," replied Sidney, "only cowards hit little girls."

Michael's jaw worked.

"And if you stay here," said Tillie, her voice low and menacing, "we're going to pay you back. You got that? Another little bird's been singing, if you get my drift. There seems to be a whole darned chorus these days." She poked a finger in his chest, the gold bangles on her wrist tinkling in the pregnant silence.

Michael reached out to snatch Tillie's hand, but Sidney was too quick for him, stepping forward and pushing Michael's back into the lockers. "You stay away from my friends—creep," snarled Sidney.

Bethany blinked. This was a side of Sidney she'd never seen.

The guidance office door opened for the second time. Nam stepped out, her face pale and drawn, her green eyes widening when she saw Sidney pressing Michael against the lockers.

"Were you talking about me, bitch?" seethed Michael, arching his neck to see over Sidney's shoulder.

Nam backed away. "Of course not!" she lied. "I'm trying to catch up on my science project. I need more time. The instructor won't give it to me." She threw a hateful glance at Bethany.

Michael shrugged off Sidney, straightening his shirt. "You've been saying things about me behind my back!" he accused her.

Nam shook her head furiously. "That's not true!"

Michael looked around at the others, then back to Nam. "It's okay, babe, you won't always have your friends around to protect you. I'll get my pound of flesh." He turned and stalked off.

"Nice going, Sidney," said Bethany, trying to keep the admiration out of her voice. He was getting more appealing to her by the minute.

"I'll say," said Tillie. "Good moves."

"Which one of you told!" Nam asked hotly. She looked at Bethany. "You promised everything we said the other night was in confidence! You lied!"

Bethany shook head in protest. "I didn't . . ."

"It was my fault," said Tillie. "I'm sorry. My temper sort of got in the way."

Nam's thin jaw jutted. "I gotta go," she said, buttoning her coat.

"No way," said Tillie. "You heard him. He threatened you! We're going to stick close."

"That isn't necessary," replied Nam. "I'm not afraid of him. He's just a bully, after all."

Bethany didn't like the way Nam was holding herself. "How did it go?" she jerked her thumb at the door.

"Fine." She took a deep breath. "Did you get what you wanted, Sidney?"

He nodded. "And then some. Boy, I almost had heart failure in there for a moment. McGovern opened the inner door a bit and I heard Nam saying she wasn't finished, so he shut it again. I thought for sure I was toast!"

Bethany wasn't satisfied. Something wasn't right. "So what did he say? The guidance counselor?"

Nam looked in the direction Michael had gone, but the hall was empty. "Oh, the same old stuff. Basically what you said. Look, I gotta go."

"We'll walk you to your car," said Tillie.

Nam's face flushed. "I said I would be fine. I'm not a baby."

The guidance door opened and Mr. McGovern stepped out. "Good luck on your science project," he said to Nam as he turned and locked the door.

But she was already gone.

Ryan's Pool Hall was located in an old mini-mall near the edge of town. Most of the adjacent stores were gone, replaced by tax consultants, physical therapists, and a sleazy loan company. The sub shop was still there, so you could buy a gyro and a soda, then take it over to the hall, if you wanted. The Hall, as Bethany's friends called it, was a hangout for kids under twenty-one. No booze, but bets were made and the occasional drug deal went down. Not too much, though, because old man Ryan was a stickler about keeping a clean place.

Ryan usually got his biggest crowd on the weekends and after dinner, and tonight was no exception. The pool tables were filled. Bethany and Tillie grabbed a few chairs and sat down out front, the juke box blaring first a country and western tune, then switching to rap, and onto hard rock. Cedar Crest was a community of many tastes.

"Classic," said Bethany, sipping her soda. "Abuse victims think they've done something wrong, or that they deserve being abused. According to my dad, it's programming. Over a period of time the abuser uses physical and mental violence to radically change the behavior of another person. When it's time to make the break from that behavior, the victim often drifts back because the negative programming hasn't been removed."

Tillie shook her head. "But Nam's only been with him, what, a few weeks?"

"That we know of," replied Bethany. "He's been here since the beginning of school. She could have been seeing him for almost four months. That's still short, but enough time for him to get his claws into her. I'm sure she didn't talk to the counselor about any of this. I think she only asked him for an extension on her science project."

"That doesn't surprise me. It may take her a while." Tillie strained her neck, looking for a free table. None was to be had, and they didn't feel like putting their quarters up to play anyone at the moment. "You think she ran after him, don't you?" asked Tillie, a nervous edge to her voice.

"I'd bet on it," said Bethany, dumping her quarters down on scarred wooden table.

Tillie munched from a bag of potato chips. "You're right. I bet she didn't tell the guidance counselor diddly. I'm really afraid for her. I called her house—her sister said she left with some guy after dinner. The place was so noisy, I could hardly hear her. I bet she went somewhere with Michael."

"You're going to be more afraid when I tell you what I got," said Sidney, brushing close to Bethany and grabbing a chair from another table so he could sit with them.

He was so close she trembled. *Stop that!* she commanded herself. *This is about Nam and Michael, not about you!*

Tillie leaned forward. "Okay, shoot."

Amanda Nevins walked up to their table before Sidney could say anything. "Where's that Nam friend of yours?" she asked.

Bethany looked at her coldly. "You know, there's something wrong with you. You're sick. She never got your present. She doesn't even know you exist."

Amanda cracked her gum. Her red hair was totally frizzed and down to her lower back. "Yeah. Right." She looked uncertain. "What present?"

"The dog shit in the box," said Tillie. "We watched you put it in front of her house. We took it."

Amanda tossed her red-gold hair. "I didn't put no—"

Tillie held up her palm, her gold bracelets jingling. "Save it. I don't know why everyone's got the hots for this Raines guy—he's nothing but trouble. Bug off while you can. He's going to be in deep by the time we get done with him."

"What do you mean?" asked Amanda. She worked her gum as if her jaw would pop off.

"Michael Raines isn't even a high-school student," said Sidney.

Amanda's eyes widened, her jaw finally stone still. Tillie gasped. Bethany opened her mouth, then closed it. Finally, she said, "Come again?"

Sidney reached into his jacket pocket and unfolded some papers. "Cedar Crest High is hiding him. Some sort of protection program. Looks like he ratted out on a gang he was in. He dropped out of school when he was in the eighth grade. He's eighteen, so they stuck him here until the trial, at least that's what the report indicates."

Tillie squashed her chip bag. "You know, he seems older than that. Maybe it's his time on the street. I can't believe that they'd put someone like that in our school!"

Sidney tapped the papers. "It's all here. The aunt he's staying with? She's seeing some guy on the school board. I got that out of my dad this evening at dinner. He thinks it's funny. The boyfriend got Michael in Cedar Crest. Everybody is turning their heads on whatever he does, hoping that he'll be out of here soon, but some teachers have been complaining."

"Which means if Nam said anything about Michael, nobody would pay any attention to her," said Bethany.

Amanda drummed her fingers on the table. Her pink nails had little rhinestones on them that glittered in the stained-glass ceiling lights that hung low over the tables. "Why would Nam say anything about Michael?"

They'd forgotten Amanda was there.

Sidney slapped the papers with his hand and ignored her, answering Bethany instead. "That's about right. Oh, McGovern would have put it in the file— Gillian's father already complained about the drugs, but they're not doing anything about it. They don't want the rest of the parents to know that they put a delinquent in with the normal kids. Bad press."

"This is terrible!" said Bethany. "What are we going to do? I think Nam ran right back to him."

"And if Gillian finds out," said Sidney, "she'll tear Nam apart."

"If Michael doesn't hurt her first," remarked Tillie.

Amanda pounded the table. "Gillian who? Merriday? Why would she care?"

Again, they ignored her.

"What's the name of that aunt he's living with?" asked Bethany.

"Violet Starr."

Bethany jerked forward, grabbing the papers out of Sidney's hands. "Let me see that!" Hands shaking, she read the printed report. "Matthew Michael Starr alias Michael Raines. Oh my God!" she said, jumping up from the table. "My father interviewed him for one of the cases he's working on. Michael Raines is not a teenager! He's in his early twenties. We've got to find Nam!"

Amanda cracked her gum. "You've got magickal powers," she sneered, "why don't you do some of your Hoodoo, Witch-girl?"

"You're not finding anyone," said Gillian, stepping from the back of the pool room. "I'll teach you to mess in my life!" she exclaimed, and promptly hit Bethany over the head with a pool cue.

Chapter 27

Seven of Clubs: Loss or theft

That was more than brilliant!" yelled Sidney, grabbing the pool cue from Gillian while Bethany desperately tried to blink away the thousand points of light dancing before her eyes. So this is what they meant by seeing stars. Thank you, but she could do without the experience. She wobbled and collapsed, but not before Tillie caught her and shoved a chair beneath her.

"She's got no right to mess in my life!" wailed Gillian, her eyes widening in fear as Sidney roughly pushed her away.

"That's all you ever think about," said Sidney. "Yourself! I'm sick of dealing with your poor-me attitude. You could make something of yourself if you wanted to, but all you ever want to do is bully people and wallow in your own crap. You disgust me!"

Gillian trembled between rage and despair, taking another step toward Bethany.

"What do you care about Michael Raines?" asked Amanda Nevins.

"He's my boyfriend, stupid!" screamed Gillian, moving toward Bethany, her fists raised.

Sidney stood in her way. "You've done enough damage. Your boyfriend?" He snorted. "Michael Raines? He's a druggie and he ratted out his friends. The criminal justice system stuck him here to hide him till the trial comes up. He's been using you, Gillian, just like he's been using Nam, and you both are too stupid to see it."

"You're just saying that to protect her!" said Gillian, her face red and tear streaked. Her limp hair stuck like plaster to her forehead.

"Have I ever lied to you before?" asked Sidney, his eyes fierce.

Gillian faltered. She choked.

"He's got a record, Gillian." He waved the computerized report in front of her. "Breaking and entering, assault . . . they picked him up on a drug bust and he squealed on his buddies. It's all here." He smacked the paper with his hand. "He's not even a teenager. He's an adult!"

Bethany blinked repeatedly. The stars were gone but her vision wasn't quite right and her head hurt like crazy. A rivulet of blood trickled down over her right eye. Tillie used an oil-sodden napkin from her gyro to try and wipe it away.

The owner of the pool hall busted through the gathering crowd. "See here, none of this in my place," he said. "All of ya, get out!"

The fresh air slowly helped to clear Bethany's head. "We've got to find Nam," said Bethany. "I just know he's going to hurt her."

Sidney held his arm protectively around Bethany, and looked at Gillian. "Yeah, thanks to your big mouth. I bet you talked to him this afternoon, didn't you? Did you spill all of it? Everything we said the other night? Haven't you got any sense?"

"I . . . I wanted him to like me b-best," spluttered Gillian. "I didn't know . . . I mean . . . I thought . . ."

"But you did know," said Sidney, clutching Bethany tightly. "You knew he was into drugs. You're far from stupid, Gillian."

"I just wanted someone to like me," she said quietly.

Tillie stepped forward. "If you want people to like you, then you treat them with respect. You're nice to them. Being a good person is how you get people to want to be around you. Not money. Not clothes. Not religion. Not bragging or telling lies. Not covering up for someone who commits crimes and does drugs, or offering booze. How you act—that's what's important! Do you have any idea where he might have taken Nam?"

Gillian chewed on the inside of her cheek. "Lookout Point. He would have taken her there."

"What happened to Amanda Nevins?" mumbled Bethany.

"She's probably still in there," said Tillie. "Good riddance to bad rubbish."

Sidney drove Bethany's car, with Tillie and Gillian piled in the back. Bethany sat in the passenger seat, her head throbbing. She pawed in her purse for her cell phone. First she called Nam, but the automated voice said her receiver wasn't turned on. Then she called Sergeant Laslow's apartment. After all, if Michael Raines and this Starr guy were one in the same, surely Laslow could help them. Maybe she could shed some light on this mystery. No answer. Great.

"Why do you think he took her to Lookout Point?" Tillie asked Gillian.

"Because that's where he goes sometimes, when he wants to be . . . private. Nobody goes up there anymore. Too dangerous with the excavation down below. He knows that if he hurts you, no one can hear you scream."

Bethany's blood ran cold. She turned around in her seat too fast, and her head started to reel. She grit her teeth. "Did Michael ever hit you, Gillian?"

"Yeah, but he stopped when I belted him back. Then I didn't see him for awhile."

"That must be when he started seeing Nam. You wouldn't be a victim, so he had to find one to satisfy his craving for power. Creep." Bethany slowly rested her head against the seat. It was weird to be the passenger in her own car.

"We should call the police," said Tillie.

"And tell them what?" snapped Bethany. "They won't believe us. We're just kids!"

"Your father would believe us," said Tillie.

"After what I did the other night? Forget it. Our best bet is to get out there and find them ourselves," said Bethany.

"I'm sorry I hit you," floated Gillian's rough voice over the seat. "I knew he had other girlfriends, even before I found out about Nam. He'd come and spend the night, you know, when my parents were out, or went to bed early. Before my mother died, he'd sneak in through the window. Anyway, he would cry out in his sleep. Girl's names. I hoped they were old girlfriends, you know?"

Sidney guided the car off the interstate and onto the secondary road leading to Lookout Point.

"Whose name did he call out?" asked Tillie. "Inquiring minds want to know."

"Can you hurry, Sidney?" asked Bethany, holding her head. "I've got a really bad feeling."

"I'm not sure," said Gillian. "There was more than one, and he slurred. He drank a lot, or was high . . ."

Sidney slued the car onto a dirt road. The sky above was foreboding, as if someone spray-painted the stars black. No moon, not even a hint of radiance. The further they moved away from the city lights, the darker it got, and the more nervous Bethany became. They passed a vacant sedan parked alongside the road. Her head hurt terribly. Maybe if she just closed her eyes . . .

"I understand," said Sidney quietly.

Bethany turned her head slightly. "What did you say?"

"You have to stay awake," said Sidney, staring intently ahead. "You may have a concussion. We should really be driving you to the hospital."

"We're not going anywhere until we get Nam," said Bethany firmly, wincing because raising her voice hurt her head.

"We're coming up on the Point," said Tillie, leaning between the two front seats. "Look up there. Close to the edge. Isn't that Nam's car?"

"The windows are steamed," said Gillian. "Maybe she's okay . . . I mean, maybe she was able to . . . never mind."

They scrambled out of the car, calling Nam's name. The lime-green interior of the Geo Tracker remained dark . . . and silent.

Bethany tried to run to the car, but every step made her head pound. Tillie and Sidney quickly outdistanced her. Gillian hung behind. "If they're doing it," she said to Bethany, "I don't want to see it."

Bethany stumbled and Gillian caught her. "I'm real sorry," she mumbled, dragging Bethany forward.

"She's not in the car," called Tillie, standing by the open door. "No one's in here."

"Where could they be?" asked Sidney, looking along the barren stretch. Over the cliff the city lights winked.

"Oh man . . ." said Tillie, leaning into the car. "There's blood on the steering wheel."

Bethany's head spun. She knew she was in no condition to help find her friend. "Oh, Black Madonna," she whispered, "give me strength. Clear my head. Please help us find Nam before it's too late."

She didn't know if it was the cold air, the prayer, or the terror that began pumping adrenaline into her system. And really, she didn't care. She blinked and raised her head. The fog in her brain began to clear. "There's a flashlight in the trunk of my car. Sidney? Go get it. You have the keys. Tillie, take the tire iron out of the back of Nam's Tracker. I know it's in there because I had to move it the other week when we were collecting the worms. Take it and Gillian and go east along the Point. If Michael jumps you, whap him one. Gillian? Does Michael have a gun?"

Gillian shook her head. "He never talked about one and I've never seen him carry a weapon. He does have a knife. Switchblade."

"Thank the Goddess for small favors, but we can't risk that he doesn't have a gun."

"A knife is bad enough," muttered Tillie.

"Be careful, both of you," Bethany said. "When Sidney gets back, we'll go west. Keep shouting to us. The Point's not that long, but we won't be able to see you in the dark. Nam's also got a flashlight under the seat. Gillian, you get that." A loon screamed somewhere in the darkness. The temperature dipped around sundown, and it seemed to fall relentlessly every second. They all shivered and stamped their feet on the ground.

"This is more than creepy," pronounced Tillie, rummaging in the back of the Tracker and producing the tire iron.

Sidney returned with the flashlight and Bethany's tire iron. The five of them stood around the Tracker, flashlights and tire irons in hand. Bethany could feel the group mind pulsing. Their thoughts coming together. "Concentrate on Nam," she whispered. "Put her in a white, protective light." She could feel their combined breathing settle as one. When she thought they were ready, she said, "Okay. Let's find them."

In less than five minutes they separated, looking for Michael and Nam.

Tillie grabbed the front of Gillian's coat. "Come on, sister, let's go find us a monster."

Chapter 28

Four of Hearts: Unusual friend

Tillie or Gillian called out every few minutes, their voices growing fainter.

Sidney swept the sparse foliage on the edge of the cliff with the flashlight, then swerved back to the black, raw-limbed trees behind them. Bethany shivered and drew her coat closer. Her head didn't hurt quite as much. She took a deep breath and closed her eyes, concentrating on Nam's face, trying to touch her friend with her mind. She thought she felt a spark just ahead. She almost tripped over the motorcycle in the dark. "Hey! Whose cycle is this?"

Sidney shrugged. "Obviously, we're not alone out here."

"But we haven't seen anyone."

"Strange, someone leaving such an expensive bike out here. Maybe it's broken. Keep going," said Bethany, pointing with the tire iron. "Over there, where the edge of the cliff is out the farthest. Right by that big boulder."

Sidney played the light along the short scrub. The face of the boulder came to life, the cliff dropping off behind it. Something on the surface glistened. "Hey, it looks like its been trampled over there." He rushed forward, playing the light along the rock and the cliff edge. "There's blood on that rock!" he exclaimed as they moved closer. The loon screamed again, this time much nearer than before.

"Dear Goddess," prayed Bethany, "please let Nam be okay." She hurried over, but Nam was nowhere to be seen. There was, however, blood on the rock. Bethany gently touched the spot with her finger. "It's still wet." She rubbed her finger on her pants. Her palms sweated profusely. "Play the light on the other side of the boulder."

"Caught ya!" screamed Amanda Nevins, popping up from behind the rock like some maniacal jack-in-the-box. She must have been teetering on the cliff edge, waiting for them to come closer. Amanda pointed a gun at Sidney's chest. "Take another step, and the boyfriend dies," she said, laughing gaily. "I always wanted to say that!" she giggled.

Bethany shifted her weight, hiding the tire iron behind her back. "What are you doing here?"

"Catching that cheating rat-face Michael. Forget about your friend. He beat her to a pulp. I watched. It was quite entertaining."

"You're lying," said Sidney.

"You'll never know," said Amanda, raising the muzzle of the gun and cocking the hammer.

Keep her talking, thought Bethany. *You don't know if what she says is true or not, but you do know she's standing here with a gun, and Nam isn't in any imme-diate danger. She's either already dead, or somewhere safe.* She remembered what Sidney said about the Nevins girl, about how she threatened her brother with a knife. This girl was definitely bad news and not wrapped too tight.

"I didn't know you were dating Michael," said Bethany. "Looks like he's a popular guy."

Amanda's hand faltered slightly. "Dating? No. No."

Bethany shook her head in confusion. "I don't understand."

"He said I was his best friend, and that you can't date a best friend. Yeah, like I believe that."

Sidney leaned forward. "So basically you let him know you loved him and he blew you off with the friend speech."

Amanda's face turned mean. "Insightful guess. Yeah, that's about right."

"Where's Michael?" asked Bethany.

"Oh . . . I'm not sure . . ." mumbled Amanda. She swayed a little. It was hard to see her face in the dark. Sidney's light shook on the boulder. "Michael's my boyfriend, you know. Nam shouldn't have been messing around with my guy."

"But he wasn't your guy. He was dating Nam," said Bethany slowly. "He never told her about any-one."

"Shut up!" screamed Amanda. "He's weak, you know. So weak. He calls me Big Red." She giggled again, then sobered. "But he likes the small ones. The ones that look like little girls. I can look like a little girl."

Bethany felt her breath hitch in her chest.

"He belongs to me!" said Amanda.

"I certainly don't want him," said Bethany. "Why don't you just put the gun away and go home."

The pistol wavered. "I . . . I don't know where Michael is. I can't leave without him. You did something with him, didn't you? I lost him. I can't find him," her voice took on a quavering, little-girl tone. "He likes me best!" she said petulantly.

"Of course he does," said Sidney. "He loves you just like I love Bethany."

Bethany's heart skipped a beat. *Love?* He was just playing with Amanda's head.

Amanda spat on the ground. "Who do you think you're kidding? He doesn't love me."

"Where'd you get that gun?" asked Sidney.

"In a minute, you won't care," spat Amanda.

Bethany considered throwing the tire iron at her head, but she was afraid that she'd miss or that Amanda might shoot Sidney if she didn't hit her just right. *Keep her talking,* said a little, desperate voice inside her head. "You can't kill us, Amanda. The cops will find out. They're on their way. I called them on the cell phone."

Amanda laughed. "No, you didn't. Besides, they're so stupid. By the time I've cleaned up here, they'll think you did some cult thing. I've watched people die before, you know. They didn't catch the killer. They're running around in circles. I can get away with it. It's not so hard." In the dim light her frizzed hair made her head look twice as large as a normal person's. A real monster. Bethany wished she could see the girl's eyes better, but right now they just looked like black holes in a pasty-white face.

"You watched a murder?" asked Bethany. The bushes behind her rustled, but she didn't turn. If Tillie and Gillian were out there, she didn't want Amanda to know and try to shoot them.

"Michael is all mine," said Amanda, "because I know what a sicko he is. Gillian's mother found out about his record, then she caught him stealing at the convenience store. She threatened to tell everyone. He had to get rid of her. I told him afterward that it was a stupid thing to do."

"Where is Michael?" asked Bethany again. The bushes rustled to the right, but she dared not turn her head in that direction, instead she looked to the left, at Sidney.

"Michael was mad that I saw the whole thing. He didn't know I'd followed him. I've been following him all over the place. Even when he went into the city. I told him tonight that I would tell about Gillian's mother unless he got rid of Nam, too. He told me I was nothing but a selfish, conniving bitch!"

Bethany prodded. "You tried to blackmail him? And Michael is where right now?"

The gun shook and Bethany feared it would go off.

"He, he was standing by the cliff. And . . . and he said all those terrible, terrible things . . . but, he's here now. And he's all mine. Forever." She giggled.

The scream was unearthly, a cross between an animal howl and human rage, but Bethany could hear the timbre of Tillie's voice and the edge that it wasn't real, only meant to frighten Amanda. Tillie must be hiding in the woods, listening. What a major actress. Amanda jerked to her left, the gun firing several shots in succession. Silence. A scream from the right, a different voice. The girl fired in that direction, her hand shaking. "Who's out there?" she cried fearfully.

"The dead," said Sidney in a soft voice. "You didn't think that the dead let murderers and their accomplices get away, did you? Michael may have killed Gillian's mom, but you were out there, standing guard behind the dumpster. You could have stopped it at any time, but you didn't. You just watched the whole thing go down. Mesmerized. Then, you crept away before anyone could see you." He cocked his head. "Michael didn't know you were watching until tonight. Am I right?"

"Yeah. So?"

"But you didn't count on Witches getting involved, did you? We can talk to the dead, you know. And now Gillian's mother is out there. Waiting for you. Watching you. You'll never, ever sleep again."

Bethany thought Amanda's eyes would pop out of her head from fear. As if on cue, Tillie and Gillian moaned again, louder this time. Amanda screamed and fired another shot. How many was that? Five? Six? Bethany couldn't be sure.

A whoosh, and Sidney's flashlight caught the gleam of black steel as a tire iron flew out of the blackness and clanged on the boulder by Amanda's feet. Gillian must have thrown the one she carried from Nam's car.

"See?" said Sidney. "Gillian's mother is coming to get you."

Amanda backed up a step.

More howls out of the darkness.

Another step.

"Don't!" screamed Bethany, but it was too late. Amanda backed up right over the edge of the cliff. She shrieked as she fell into the cold darkness of the valley below.

Sidney rushed forward, the flashlight bobbing. Gillian appeared behind him, holding a bleeding shoulder. "Shit," she said.

"I didn't mean for her to fall!" cried Sidney, fear and horror mixing in his voice.

Bethany knelt, peering over the cliff, but she could see nothing. She tried to swallow, but her heart was in the way. She turned to look at the other two. When she found her voice, she said, "Gillian! Are you shot?"

"She missed," exclaimed Gillian, "the stupid twit missed! I scraped my arm on a blasted tree."

Bethany rose slowly.

"Good thinking about that dead thing," said Gillian, looking at Sidney. "I never would never have thought of that. Personally, I would have preferred to bash her brains in."

They heard a terrible crash in the brush. Sidney swung his light around, catching Tillie pulling a bedraggled Nam by the hand.

Bethany rushed up to her small friend. "You're not shot? You're not mauled?"

Nam wearily shook her head. "I slipped down over the side. They thought I fell off the cliff, but it was dark and I managed to pull myself up on a shelf where they couldn't see me."

"What happened?" asked Bethany, putting her arms around Nam. It was so good to feel her bony shoulders!

Nam plopped down on the ground. "You wouldn't believe it. Michael didn't know that Amanda Nevins saw him murder Gillian's mother. She followed us here tonight. You were right, Bethany, he was bad . . . very bad." Her voice cracked. "When I demanded an explanation, he popped me in the nose."

"The blood on the steering wheel and windshield," said Sidney.

Nam nodded. "I think my nose is broken." She touched the swollen appendage delicately. "Anyway, I bled everywhere and managed to stumble out of the car. He came tearing after me, but Amanda grabbed his arm and demanded that he finish me off like Gillian's mother. That she would tell everything unless I was out of the picture. It was so strange, she started declaring her undying love for him. He laughed at her. Told her she was nuts." Nam's thin figure shook.

"Then she pulled out that gun. Said it was from her father's collection, or something."

Nam continued. "The whole time I was asking the Black Madonna to help me, you know . . . in my head? Over and over again, like a mantra. When Michael didn't make a move toward me, Amanda came at me with the gun. He just stood there, as if nothing mattered. I'll never forget his eyes—cold, bottomless. Like nobody was home. He just didn't care. Not about her, and definitely not about me. I ran as best I could, but there was blood in my eyes and so much pain that I ran the wrong way, tripped and slipped on the edge of the cliff. I fell off but luckily I hit the hidden ledge underneath."

Sidney whistled.

"And you guys thought I was a nutcase," said Gillian.

"They both thought I was dead," said Nam. "Michael just laughed."

"What happened to him?" asked Gillian, her voice soft and trembling.

Nam gulped. "I managed to crawl up to the edge and peek over. You wouldn't have believed it. Michael told Amanda to get lost. He pushed her away, at least, that's what it sounded like, and grabbed the gun from her at the same time. I think

he hit her with it and he threatened to shoot her."
Nam shook her head in disbelief. "Then Gillian
screamed something horrible and ran into the
woods. I heard a motorcycle. A woman's voice. She
accused Michael of killing a little girl!" Nam almost
wailed the last part. "Something about Annabelle
Arneau."

Nam started to shake, and Gillian hugged her.
"And then . . . then Amanda snuck up behind the
woman and brained her with a rock. Michael started
screaming. The next thing I knew, Amanda had a
gun in her hands and she shot him! Just like that!
His gun flew out over my head and hit the rocks
below. All I can think of is that he must have had it
raised to shoot Amanda. I was afraid to move."

"You think he shot in self-defense?" asked Tillie.

Nam shrugged.

"Where's his body?" asked Tillie. "We didn't come
across it looking for you."

Nam's voice trembled. "I heard Amanda dragging
it. Then another shot. And then, after a while . . . I
didn't hear anything at all. I tried to climb back out
by myself, but I wasn't strong enough."

Gillian hiccuped and shivered. "That's the name I
heard him calling in his sleep! And I thought his
other girlfriend was Annabelle."

"Annabelle was a little girl. She was murdered."
Bethany sat on the boulder. "Wait a minute. What
woman?"

Sidney played the light to Bethany's right. "That one."

All eyes riveted to the light and the bloody boot jutting out from behind the boulder.

"Oh, my Goddess!" exclaimed Bethany. "It's Sergeant Laslow!"

Tillie checked to see if she was still breathing. "Dead," she said. "Amanda must have been getting ready to pitch her off the cliff when we surprised her."

"But where did Amanda get the gun? If she hit Laslow with a rock, where did the gun come from?"

Tillie checked Sergeant Laslow's body, her fingers running over the empty shoulder holster. "From her."

The loon screamed.

Chapter 29

Three of Diamonds: Change for the better

The members of Witches' Night Out officially dedicated Sidney Bluefeather the following week. The group mind now encompassed four souls including Nam Chu, Tillie Alexander, and Bethany Salem. Three guests were also present at the ceremony—Gillian Merriday, Ramona, and Linnex Arneau. At the end of the ritual they did a crossing ceremony for Annabelle Arneau, Mrs. Merriday, and Sergeant Laslow. Hecate remained close to the feast table, hoping to rescue some of the ham from its cellophane covering. Thankfully, Linnex left her bird in the shop. Hecate would have tried to add the big black bird to their Esbat feast.

Tonight they all wore black robes with tiny red pentacles ringing the sleeves—gifts from Linnex to all the members of Witches' Night Out. Gillian, not a member, wore black pants and a long-sleeved black shirt. At Ramona's request, Linnex brought Gillian a gorgeous black shawl. Bethany stood in the center of the circle, holding Sidney's hand, his fingers warmly entwined with hers, her other hand clasped firmly around the staff Ramona had given her. Tillie stepped forward and placed the Witches' Night Out necklace around Sidney's neck. "Welcome to our clan," she said, smiling gaily, then kissed him on the cheek.

Hecate darted out from under the feast table and tugged on the bottom of Sidney's robe.

"Guess he's telling you that you are part of the group now," laughed Nam.

Bethany held up Sidney's hand and said, "Great Mother and Glorious Father, Sidney comes seeking entrance into Witches' Night Out. We ask that you bless him as he places his foot upon the path of enlightenment. Give him your special gifts. Be gentle with him as he learns the secrets of the Wise. So mote it be."

The group responded, "So mote it be."

Sidney looked at Linnex. "Did you bring them?"

Linnex smiled, withdrawing a small blue box from under the altar. "As is tradition," said Linnex, "Sidney brought gifts to the other members of your group."

Sidney smiled and opened the box. He handed each person in the circle a silver charm bracelet. "I had Linnex get them for me," he said, among the oohs and ahhs. "The WNO members' bracelets have little pentacles. Gillian's has a silver paintbrush." To Ramona, he handed a little golden statue of the goddess Oshun. Ramona giggled and thanked him in French.

The girls followed ritual procedure to release the circle, repeating as a group, "Merry meet, merry part, until we merry meet again. For we are the people, we are the power, and we are the change!"

The group sat around the fire, laughing and packing away as much food as possible. Hecate planted himself in Linnex's lap, begging for a kitty treat. He wasn't disappointed. Bethany rested against Sidney's knees while he stroked her hair. They hadn't said much since the disaster, but the feelings were definitely there.

"They searched his apartment," said Linnex, "and found Annabelle's other shoe."

The upbeat atmosphere dissipated.

"You don't have to talk about this, if you don't want to," said Tillie, folding her robe and putting it in her ritual bag.

"It's okay," said Linnex. "Tonight is a night of closure as well as beginnings. It needs to be said."

Silence.

"We think that he didn't really mean to kill her," she continued. "He may have lured her away as a joke, or maybe as revenge. We just don't know. The lab found Annabelle's blood and some of her hair on his old jacket hidden between the mattress and box spring."

"Dumb," said Tillie. "Why didn't he just get rid of it?"

Linnex shrugged. "It was so bizarre. About a month before he killed Annabelle, the police picked him up on an unrelated drug charge. He rolled over. His aunt has some pull here with the Cedar Crest police and the school board. She convinced the justice system to place him here, under her care, until the trial."

Tillie helped herself to a hefty bowl of chicken soup and two biscuits. "Which is how he got to Cedar Crest," she said. "How did Sergeant Laslow get involved with such a creep?"

"He was a runaway several years ago. Laslow was a sort of mentor to him, and I guess things just escalated, and before she knew it, she was deep in this bizarre relationship. He was nothing but a common thug, if you ask me. She and I talked about it often. She made sure he got into a decent trade, encouraged him to get his GED. In July, when he landed in all that trouble, she didn't break up with him. Instead, she helped to arrange his stay at Cedar Crest. He commuted often to see her during the end of July and the beginning of August. Finally, she couldn't take it anymore, and she broke up with him the morning before Annabelle disappeared. Michael must have snatched Annabelle then. He knew that Laslow and I were close, and that I didn't like him. He probably assumed that I'm the one that pushed her to dump him. He was right. He disappeared from the city for a while, evidently right after he killed Annabelle. Carl Salem called him in and interviewed him the day Laslow escorted you girls around the city. She didn't see him, though."

"So that's why he had to go to the precinct," said Nam, as she hung her new robe on a hanger and placed it by her ritual bag. This evening she was dressed in various shades of vibrant blues.

"The whole time you waited in the lobby, he was upstairs with Bethany's father, giving a statement," said Linnex.

"But who attacked Bethany?" asked Sidney.

"I can answer that one," said Tillie, her mouth full of biscuit, "compliments of Vanessa Peters, who, by the way, was kicked off the cheer squad this week. She knew all about Amanda terrorizing Nam. Amanda wrote the notes, she destroyed Nam's project, and she tried to grab Bethany through the window. She might have thought Bethany saw her at the convenience store. She was hiding behind the dumpster in the parking lot. When Bethany didn't come forward with any information, Amanda decided to back off."

Linnex leaned forward. "How do you know she was behind the dumpster?"

Tillie finished the biscuit, then leaned forward. "She told Vanessa, except she said that she didn't know who killed Mrs. Merriday and just happened to be walking by when the cops finally got there. She told Vanessa it was no use to get involved because she didn't see anything."

Bethany curled a strand of dark hair around her finger. "But Sidney knew about Amanda hiding behind the dumpster. How did you know that?"

Sidney smiled. "Simple process of deduction."

Tillie did not look convinced. "Yeah, right."

"What was it," mused Bethany, "with Michael Raines, er . . . Starr?"

"Evil," said Ramona.

"Charisma," said Tillie.

"Raw energy," said Gillian.

"Attention," replied Nam.

Hecate growled.

Bethany just shook her head. "Amazing," she said. "How's the counseling going?"

Nam and Gillian spoke at once, then giggled together.

"The counselor at school is helping. I'm learning about family dynamics," said Nam. "Pretty interesting. I've even started to gain back the weight I lost . . . and I got an 'A' on my science project, thanks to all of you!"

Everyone clapped.

Gillian handed Bethany a wrapped package. "I'm sorry I hit you with the pool cue."

Bethany tore the paper off to reveal a painting of the Black Madonna. "It's beautiful!" she breathed. "Where did you get it?"

"I painted it," replied Gillian quietly.

"Gillian has some good news," said Sidney, helping Bethany set the painting in a safe place until she could hang it.

Gillian looked a lot better. Nam took her shopping and to a local hair dresser for a total makeover.

The new highlights in her hair did a lot to soften her features. "My father and Mrs. Merriday had a long talk. I'll be leaving for a special art school in New York City next week. It's something I've always wanted."

"I'll hang your painting in my bedroom," said Bethany proudly, "and when you become rich and famous, I'll brag to everyone that I know you!"

Gillian smiled shyly.

"Speaking of the city," said Tillie, turning to Bethany. "How's your father doing?"

Bethany twirled a piece of hair on the end of her finger. "Okay, I guess. He wasn't happy about my involvement, and he was furious that I snooped in his files. I might be grounded for that one—the parental jury is still out, so to speak." She sighed. "But even he said that if I hadn't started to investigate, something horrible could have happened to Nam, so I guess everything will be all right. At least he's not sending me away to a private school or anything. He's upset about Laslow. All the cops at the precinct are."

Linnex nodded sadly.

"Bethany had to promise her father that she'll call the proper authorities next time instead of winding up in the hospital, saved by the grace of the Goddess and a major bump on her head," said Ramona sternly.

Tillie munched on a carrot stick. "What about that guy that came into the convenience store? You called him Ranger Rick?"

"The police found traces of paint from his truck on Amanda's car. They think she ran him off the road to protect Michael," replied Bethany.

They were silent for a moment.

"You know," said Bethany. "My mother tried to tell me in a dream about Michael." She looked carefully at Linnex. "She was holding Annabelle."

The woman's eyes filled with tears, but she didn't cry.

"She was happy . . . Annabelle. My mother said that I should remember the fifty-seven stars. I didn't understand. I should have caught it when Sergeant Laslow explained about the ceiling in Grand Central Station. There are fifty-seven stars in the ceiling and Michael's last name was Starr. I just didn't put it together. I can't understand why she wasn't clearer in her message."

"I can answer that, I think," said Sidney.

All eyes turned in his direction. Ramona smiled.

"The dead . . . well, they sometimes talk to me, but . . . it's hard to get through. And, they're human after all, so they get things mixed up, or we translate it wrong. To the dead, thought is different . . . streamlined. Language is an inconvenience. They forget about all our social and religious blocks."

Tillie opened her mouth, shut it, then opened it again. "So, you mean, you talk to the dead?"

"Well, they sort of talk to me. Sometimes. But it's not like picking up a phone and carrying on a long conversation. It's hard to explain . . ." his voice drifted. "I'm not a medium or anything. I just pick stuff up now and then. I thought you guys could do it, too," he said sheepishly, "but then I realized that you didn't hear it. They put people away that hear voices, you know. Pump them full of drugs. I've never told anyone because I was afraid that my father would send me to expensive psychiatrists and change me. I don't want to go there. I'm not nuts, I just can do something most people can't."

"You talk to the dead?" asked Nam, her eyes round.

"Like I said," explained Sidney, "you can't turn it on and off like a light bulb. I was hoping to work with Ramona so that I can control it better. I don't understand how it works, and I can't call specific people—they just sort of show up, and I don't always know who they are."

Ramona looked at him severely. "Such a skill is a gift and a burden, but Ramona must have your father's permission before she can work with you."

"He's just getting over the fact that I joined Witches' Night Out. That will take time. He and my mother are trying to save their marriage, but I think it's too far gone. He has his mind on that."

"Ramona can wait."

The group began picking up cups, plates, and other trash. Hecate stole a significant slice of ham and scurried behind the sofa before Ramona could catch him. The older women carried the leftover food out to the kitchen.

The kids gathered around Bethany.

"So, what do we do next?" asked Tillie, her eyes gleaming.

Carl Salem knocked on the den door, then entered with long, lanky strides. "Actually," he said to Tillie. "I've been talking to Ramona."

"Dad!" exclaimed Bethany, jumping up and giving him a hug.

Mr. Salem smiled. "If you all study very hard, I'll let you help me with some of my cases. But," he held up his hands, "only from a distance. You can use your divination skills and magick, however, you have to clear it with Ramona first, and only when she says that you are ready."

"How cool!" exclaimed Tillie, clapping her hands. The gold bracelets on her arms jingled.

"Is that okay with you, Bethany?" asked Mr. Salem.

Bethany grinned. "You bet!"

"Gotta get me some . . ." whispered through the room.

"Did any of you guys say anything?" asked Bethany.

Everyone shook their heads. Bethany looked pointedly at Sidney, but he shrugged his shoulders.

"I think we better light a candle for Ranger Rick," said Bethany.

"What for?" asked Nam.

"Love," replied Bethany. "I think he's gotta get him some."

Sidney and Bethany watched the sun rise over Locust Point, the morning crisp—the light dazzling. A flock of Canadian geese flew overhead, honking and heading south. The birds were a little late. Bethany wondered where they'd been, and where they were going.

"I still don't understand Michael's motive for murder," mused Sidney.

Bethany's thoughts clouded. "My father thinks he was a serial killer in the making. I know that sounds drastic, but they all start somewhere. Annabelle may not have been his first victim. We'll just never know."

"I guess murder is never simple."

"Not in real life," Bethany replied. "Which is why my father's case load is backed up and there's never enough money or people to track down all the details. Murders go unsolved every day. It's just that we live in such a big country that we often forget about that."

"Something else is bothering me," said Sidney, a sigh dovetailing the remark.

Sidney sighed. "How did Laslow get here, if she was in New York City?"

"After my father spoke to Michael in that interview, he talked to Laslow about it. Something must have made her suspicious. She's the one that went to his apartment and found the jacket. She knew he was in Cedar Crest because she helped to make the arrangements to send him here. She hopped on her motorcycle and came here searching for him. Linnex told me that he brought her to Locust Point once or twice, that's how she knew about this place. It was a fluke that she arrived when she did."

Sidney put his arms around her.

Bethany looked out at the bright sky over the cliff as she leaned her back against his chest, and said, "Rest in peace, my sister. Merry meet and merry part, until we merry meet again. For we are the people, we are the power, and we are the change."

"So mote it be," whispered Sidney, holding her tightly.

Bethany smiled and wiped a lone tear from her cheek.

Behind them, a loon screamed.

"She says," said Sidney, "that you are to take good care of yourself and your father."

Bethany stiffened. "You can see her?"

Sidney nuzzled her ear. "Not exactly. More like hear her. It's as if there is a lot of distance between us." He cocked his head. "She also says: Remember perfect love and perfect trust, whatever that means."

"You'll understand soon enough," said Bethany. "Is she still here?"

He shook his head, his long hair loose around his face. "She's gone," he said, and sighed.

Bethany turned around, her fingers reaching to touch the soft strands of his hair. He turned his head, brushing her fingers with his lips. They walked to her car, arms encircling each other's waists. She scooted into the front seat and adjusted the rearview as Sidney walked around to the other side, sliding in beside her. The trees behind her sprung to life in the mirror. Bethany looked up to check her reflection and stopped short.

For the briefest second, the face of the Black Madonna smiled back at her.

Epilogue

Playing Card Divination Deck

Although this story about Bethany and her friends is a work of fiction, magick and the religion of Wicca is very real. Today, Witchcraft is the fastest growing religion in the United States. The religion's earth-centered appeal and its premise that all are equal regardless of race, religion, income bracket, or sexual preference, combined with its teachings that everyone has personal power and the ability to achieve whatever he or she desires in a positive way, has rocketed the Old Religion to new heights. With domestic and overseas sales of my books hitting all-time highs, I realize the importance of how I present the information of the Craft to you.

To make your own divination deck you need not practice the Wiccan faith. Every individual has the ability to learn how to use a divination tool, and can use this tool within the framework of their chosen religion. All you need is a regular deck of playing cards and a black pen. Following the key below, write the words that correspond to each card on that card. If you have an old typewriter around, you can type the definitions right on the card rather than writing them.

The Clubs: Business, Communication

Ace: Letter, term papers, written homework. Much prosperity.

Ace reversed: Great success but you must work for it.

2: An agreement.

2 reversed: Go slow. Question in two months will be a success.

3: Project with others.

3 reversed: Study the situation.

4: Short journey.

4 reversed: Popularity will not last.

5: Good news and a change.

5 reversed: Look out for the law. Follow the rules.

6: Peace of mind.

6 reversed: Confusion.

7: Loss or theft.

7 reversed: Movement of a situation; deep talk.

8: Someone makes you unhappy.

8 reversed: A group of people are involved.

9: After-school activities or fun with friends.

9 reversed: Investigate before you decide.

10: Long-distance journey or work pays off.

10 reversed: Success.

Jack: Study and you will pass the test. (no reverse)

Queen: Good advice, but watch for mischief. (no reverse)

King: Danger. (no reverse)

The Diamonds: Money, Success

Ace: An opportunity to make money.

Ace reversed: Success in money if you work.

2: Favorable union.

2 reversed: Kisses.

3: Change for the better.

3 reversed: Surprise!

4: Good news.

4 reversed: A gift.

5: Bright future. A change in money matters.

5 reversed: Good chance, make the most of it.

6: Clear path ahead.

6 reversed: Favorable loans.

7: Don't overspend.

7 reversed: Repairs needed.

8: Money. Learning something new.

8 reversed: Travel over water.

9: Don't lend money.

9 reversed: A good chance. Take it.

10: Lots of money coming.

10 reversed: A very successful year ahead.

Jack: Make a talisman for money. (no reverse)

Queen: Burn a candle for prosperity. (no reverse)

King: True friend. (no reverse)

The Spades: Challenges

Ace: Follow the rules to find success.

Ace reversed: Beware of smiling faces.

2: Lies, gossip.

2 reversed: An unfaithful person.

3: Work to overcome challenges.

3 reversed: A mean person.

4: Journey possible.

4 reversed: Boredom.

5: Prepare for change.

5 reversed: Don't pass notes; watch out for trouble.

6: Internet chats or messages.

6 reversed: Positive turn to unpleasant situation.

7: Birth.

7 reversed: Change in job.

8: A warning.

8 reversed: Bad advice.

9: Disappointment.

9 reversed: Self-deceit.

10: Transformation.

10 reversed: Earned rewards.

Jack: Don't flirt with darkness; beware of two-faced person. (No reverse)

Queen: Jealous woman. (No reverse)

King: Beware, stern critic. (No reverse)

The Hearts: Love, Passion, Emotions

Ace: Love.

Ace reversed: Happiness and success.

2: Partnership or friendship.

2 reversed: Small gift.

3: Someone new.

3 reversed: Quarrel.

4: Unusual friend.

4 reversed: Parties.

5: A change for the better.

5 reversed: A pleasant surprise.

6: Friendship.

6 reversed: Social success.

7: Laughter.

7 reversed: Reunion.

8: New clothes.

8 reversed: Possible pregnancy.

9: Wishes come true.

9 reversed: Obstacles. You must meditate.

10: Wedding or joy.

10 reversed: To win.

Jack: Use magick. (No reverse)

Queen: Burn a candle for success. (No reverse)

King: Success in love or friendship. (No reverse)

When you have written all the definitions on the cards, sprinkle them with holy water or your chosen magickal oil. Leave them under a full moon for at least one hour. If you use the cards often, cleanse them by sprinkling them with a bit of holy water, or leave them in direct sunlight or moonlight. Some magickal people choose to wrap the deck in a black cloth when not using them to keep negative vibrations away from the cards.

As a reminder, the definitions are not meant to scare people, but to give them a tool to enhance their lives. These definitions are specifically designed for the teen seeker. To enhance the divination, place a half-full, clear glass of water on the table and pray for divine assistance before you begin. Remember, if you have a real problem, seek the assistance of your parents, guardian, or qualified counselor—do not rely on the cards. They are, after all, only a tool.

National Hotlines

The following numbers were collected by a Pennsylvania sheriff (a friend of mine) in case you ever need them. Don't be shy. If you need help, please call. If you have to do a report in school on any of the issues listed below, the people at these numbers will be happy to supply you with information.

Alcohol and Drug Abuse

Al-Anon & Alateen: 1-800-356-9996

National Clearinghouse for Alcohol & Drug Information: 1-800-SAY-NOTO

National Cocaine Hotline: 1-800-262-2463

Alcohol & Drug Dependency Hopeline: 1-800-622-2255

National Institute on Drug Abuse Hotline: 1-800-622-HELP

Mothers Against Drunk Driving: 1-800-438-MADD

Abuse

Bureau of Indian Affairs Child Abuse Hotline: 1-800-633-5133

Boy's Town: 1-800-448-3000

Child Help USA: 1-800-422-4453

National Respite Locaters Service: 1-800-773-5433

National Domestic Violence Hotline:
1-800-799-7233

National Clearinghouse of Child Abuse and
Neglect: 1-800-394-3366

National Resource Center on Domestic Violence:
1-800-553-2508

Rape, Abuse & Incest National Network:
1-800-656-4673

Resource Center on Domestic Violence, Child
Protection and Custody: 1-800-527-3223

Runaways Hotlines

Covenant House Nineline: 1-800-999-9999

National Runaway Switchboard: 1-800-621-4000

National Child Welfare

Child Find of America: 1-800-I-AM-LOST

Child Quest International Sighting Line:
1-800-248-8020

National Referral Network for Kids in Crisis:
1-800-KID-SAVE

Health & AIDS/HIV

AIDS Helpline: 1-800-548-4659

Ask A Nurse Connection: 1-800-535-1111

National AIDS Hotline: 1-800-342-AIDS

STD National Hotline: 1-800-227-8922

About Silver

Silver RavenWolf is the author of over fifteen how-to and fictional books relating to the application of the magickal sciences. She resides in south-central Pennsylvania with her husband of twenty-one years, four children, sheltie, and pet rat. Her primary interests are divinatory tools, astrology, hypnotherapy, reading, swimming, and getting through life in a positive and productive way. To read about Silver, her touring schedule, upcoming events, and books, visit Silver's website at:

http://www.silverravenwolf.com

To Write to Silver

If you wish to contact the author or would like more information about this book, please write to:

Silver RavenWolf
℅ Llewellyn Worldwide
P.O. Box 64383, Dept. 1-56718-718-8
St. Paul, MN 55164-0383, U.S.A.

Please enclose a self-addressed stamped envelope for reply, or $1.00 to cover costs. If outside U.S.A., enclose international postal reply coupon.

About the Series

In September of 1998 my book titled *Teen Witch* was published, shocking myself and the publishing world with phenomenal sales. I wrote the book because I cared about kids and I wanted them to have legitimate information on how to work real magick. I hung the rave reviews and the advertising poster given to me by Llewellyn above my desk. For me, it was a dream come true. I'd written a book that would make a difference in people's lives. While working on other projects, I would stare at that poster, thinking about the thousands of teens reading my book.

One afternoon, my sixteen-year-old daughter, Falcon, caught me at my desk once again mesmerized by that poster. "Too bad those kids on the cover of your book aren't real," she said. "I mean, they look like real people, don't they?"

The hairs on the back of my neck stood up as I continued to look at the poster. "Yeah," I breathed. "I've stared at this picture so long, they *do* seem like they are more than just a book cover. It's like . . . I don't know . . . as if I've known them all along. That one's Bethany," I said, pointing to the dark-haired girl in the center of the picture. "And I think the

African-American girl looks just like a Tillie. What do you think?"

Falcon surveyed the poster, then turned to me with a sly smile. "You know, Echo is always complaining that you never wrote fiction for us." Echo is Falcon's older sister. "Why don't you write a story about the kids on the poster?"

And that's how the Witches' Night Out series was born. Although the story is entirely fictional, I set about to devise a world where the teens use real magick, not the fairy-tale stuff. It wasn't easy. In the world of fiction, anything can happen. It would have been so easy to give Bethany and her friends superpowers, but I know that real magick doesn't work that way. Conjuring magick is a skill that one acquires after hard work and practice. It takes longer than a snap of your fingers, and it almost never happens with the bells and whistles of a Hollywood film—but it does happen. Bethany and her friends are students of magick, which in a way makes it all the more fun! They will make mistakes as they wrestle with school, family problems, and relationships with peers—not to mention the pain of dealing with a job at the same time, an already rocky road for any kid. Throw in the desire to solve crimes, and the characters become people like you are me. That's why their world is such an interesting one!

Because . . . it *could* be real.

☽ REACH FOR THE MOON

Llewellyn publishes hundreds of books on your favorite subjects! To get these exciting books, including the ones on the following pages, check your local bookstore or order them directly from Llewellyn.

ORDER BY PHONE
- Call toll-free within the U.S. and Canada, 1-800-THE MOON
- In Minnesota, call (651) 291-1970
- We accept VISA, MasterCard, and American Express

ORDER BY MAIL
- Send the full price of your order (MN residents add 7% sales tax) in U.S. funds, plus postage & handling to:

  Llewellyn Worldwide
  P.O. Box 64383, Dept. 1-56718-718-8
  St. Paul, MN 55164-0383, U.S.A.

POSTAGE & HANDLING
- $4.00 for orders $15.00 and under; $5.00 for orders over $15.00
- No charge for orders over $100.00 (For the U.S., Canada, and Mexico)

We ship UPS in the continental United States. We ship standard mail to P.O. boxes. Orders shipped to Alaska, Hawaii, the Virgin Islands, and Puerto Rico are sent first-class mail. Orders shipped to Canada and Mexico are sent surface mail.

International orders: Airmail—add freight equal to price of each book to the total price of order, plus $5.00 for each non-book item (audio tapes, etc.). **Surface mail**—Add $1.00 per item. *Allow 2 weeks for delivery on all orders. Postage and handling rates subject to change.*

DISCOUNTS

We offer a 20% discount to group leaders or agents. You must order a minimum of 5 copies of the same book to get our special quantity price.

FREE CATALOG

Get a free copy of our color catalog, *New Worlds of Mind and Spirit*. Subscribe for just $10.00 in the United States and Canada ($30.00 overseas, airmail). Many bookstores carry *New Worlds*—ask for it!

Visit our website at www.llewellyn.com for more information.

Teen Witch Kit: Everything You Need to Make Magick!

Silver RavenWolf

Here is everything the novice spell-caster needs to practice the Craft of the Wise—and be a force for good. Step into the sacred space and discover the secrets of one of the world's oldest mysteries: the art and science of white magick, a gentle, loving practice. The kit contains a beautifully illustrated book of instruction, plus six magickal talismans, salt, and a spell bag. The kit box converts into your own personal altar.

Silver RavenWolf, one of today's most famous Witches and author of the best-selling *Teen Witch*, provides the quick-reading guidebook, complete with instructions on how to prepare yourself for magick, create a sacred space, call up the spirit, and draw down the Moon.

All the spells are tailored to 13- to 18-year olds, and can be cast using the items in the kit and common objects found around the house. It's easy to follow the step-by-step instructions and clear magickal symbols. There is even a section on how to write your own spells. The book also reveals the white magick code of honor, and includes a glossary of terms, a suggested reading list, and a guide to the top magickal Internet sites.

1-56718-554-1 $24.95

7½ x 7½ boxed kit contains:
128-pp. illus. book • spell bag • spell salt • golden coin • silver wish cord • silver bell • natural quartz crystal • silver pentacle pendant • yes/no coin

To order, call 1-800-THE MOON

Prices subject to change without notice

Teen Witch: Wicca for a New Generation

Silver RavenWolf

Teenagers and young adults comprise a growing market for books on Witchcraft and magick, yet there has never been a book written specifically for the teen seeker. Now, Silver RavenWolf, one of the most well-known Wiccans today and the mother of four young Witches, gives teens their own handbook on what it takes and what it means to be a Witch. Humorous and compassionate, *Teen Witch* gives practical advice for dealing with everyday life in a magickal way. From homework and crabby teachers to parents and dating, this book guides teens through the ups and downs of life as they move into adulthood. Spells are provided that address their specific concerns, such as the "Call Me Spell" and "The Exam Spell."

Parents will also find this book informative and useful as a discussion tool with their children. Discover the beliefs of Witchcraft, Wiccan traditions, symbols, holidays, rituals, and more.

1-56718-725-0
288 pp., 7 x 10   **$12.95**

To order, call 1-800-THE MOON
Prices subject to change without notice

Witches' Night Out
Silver RavenWolf

Now, from the author of *Teen Witch*—the wildly popular guide to Witchcraft—comes the first in a new series of spellbinders written specifically for teens. Featuring the five characters on the cover of *Teen Witch*, these fictional books will focus on the strength, courage, and willpower of the teens to overcome seemingly insurmountable obstacles, with enough authentic magickal practice thrown in to keep you on the edge of your seat. Every book features a spell that readers can do themselves.

Main character Bethany Salem, 16, is on her own most of the time. Five years ago her mother died, leaving her in the care of her father, a New York City cop, who has deposited her in the suburbs with their Santerían housekeeper.

The adventure begins when enterprising Bethany starts a coven with her friends. In *Witches' Night Out*, the teens find themselves sleuthing to determine who caused the fatal automobile wreck of their friend Joe.

1-56718-728-5
240 pp., 4⅛ x 6¾ $4.99

To order, call 1-800-THE MOON
Prices subject to change without notice

Silver's Spells for Love
Silver RavenWolf

Does your current relationship need a spicy boost? Have you been browsing for love in all the wrong places? Maybe you want to conceive a magickal baby? From finding a new lover to handling that couch potato partner, *Silver's Spells for Love* has more than 100 ideas, potions, and incantations to bring titillating passion into your waiting arms. Whether you want affection, commitment, or a hot time on the town tonight, this book will teach you the nuances of spellcasting for love!

- Prepare incenses, oils, and powders for love
- Learn how to wisely draw a lover toward you
- Boost the passion in your current relationship
- Make the right moves when good love goes bad

... and learn dozens of ways to tap into that universal energy called love!

1-56718-552-5
312 pp., 5³⁄₁₆ x 6, illus. $7.95

To order, call 1-800-THE MOON
Prices subject to change without notice

Angels: Companions in Magick

Silver RavenWolf

Angels do exist. Here, in this complete text, you will find practical information on how to invite these angelic beings into your life. Build an angelic altar . . . meet the archangels in meditation . . . contact your guardian angel . . . create angel sigils and talismans . . . work magick with the Angelic Rosary . . . talk to the deceased. You will learn to work with angels to gain personal insights and assist in the healing of the planet as well as yourself.

Angels do not belong to any particular religious structure—they are universal and open their arms to humans of all faiths, bringing love and power into people's lives.

1-56718-724-2
288 pp., 7 x 10, illus.   **$14.95**

To order, call 1-800-THE MOON
Prices subject to change without notice

To Ride a Silver Broomstick: New Generation Witchcraft

Silver RavenWolf

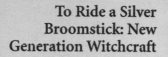

.Full of the author's warmth, humor, and personal anecdotes, *To Ride a Silver Broomstick* leads you step-by-step through the various lessons with exercises and journal writing assignments. This is the complete Witchcraft 101, teaching you to celebrate the Sabbats, deal with coming out of the broom closet, choose a magickal name, visualize the Goddess and God, meditate, design a sacred space, acquire magickal tools, design and perform rituals, network, spell cast, perform color and candle magick, divination, healing, telepathy, psychometry, astral projection, and much, much more.

0-87542-791-X
320 pp., 7 x 10, illus. $14.95

To order, call 1-800-THE MOON
Prices subject to change without notice